THE DEADLIES

Twice As Deadly

A. C. MILLER

iUniverse, Inc.
Bloomington

Twice As Deadly
The Deadlies

iUniverse books may be ordered through booksellers or by contacting:

iUniverse
1663 Liberty Drive
Bloomington, IN 47403
www.iuniverse.com
1-800-Authors (1-800-288-4677)

ISBN: 978-1-4759-3811-1 (sc)
ISBN: 978-1-4759-3812-8 (hc)
ISBN: 978-1-4759-3813-5 (e)

Library of Congress Control Number: 2012912381

Printed in the United States of America

iUniverse rev. date: 7/23/2012

ACKNOWLEDGMENTS

As always, I would like to extend special thank yous to some very special people...

To my husband, Jim, who found a way to fund the second, third and fourth books even if it means living in a cardboard box hereafter, there is no one with whom I would rather share my cardboard box. Love you.

To Cady, who enthusiastically tells everyone she meets about her mom's books, someday I will do the same for you. Keep writing, kiddo!

To Lexie, who looked at the first book when I proudly displayed it to her and then looked at me before turning back to her computer game, I am sure I saw the excitement in your eyes, honey. I am sure of it.

To Sally Brooks, my proofreader, editor, friend and sometimes "victim," thanks for all your hard work and for taking the teasing so well. Anyone else would have mugged me for those last four chapters and even though I know you thought about it, you managed to restrain yourself. Thank you.

To Susan Finch, my publicist and friend, thank you for your help during the first signing when I spent the first hour looking like a deer caught in the headlights as well as during the other signings when I was already an "old pro." Two books down and two to go!

To the Roadies who bought the first book (even when they admitted that it wasn't their kind of book), and then came back and demanded the second one—you always know how to boost my self-esteem just when I need it most!

To my parents, you have encouraged me since I was a child. Thank you for your support.

My in-laws, Bob, Ruth Ann Miller, Jody and Jim Brethet, and my three beautiful nieces—love you!

To everyone who bought the first book and encouraged me by loudly demanding the second—thank you and here it is...

CHAPTER ONE

U NDER THE THREAT OF never driving again, I had to promise my brother that I would drive slowly and that I would stay at least six car lengths behind his motorcycle. I know the motorcycle was a mass of dents but I swear Demon drove twenty kilometres an hour just to piss me off.

I was grumbling much to the amusement of the other Deadly riding with me as we followed Demon down the long, narrow gravel driveway. A large wooded area obscures the view of the house from the road. As we came into the clearing just beyond the woods, my brother came to a stop in front of the house and shut off the bike. I parked behind him and got out of the van, slamming the door as my brother swung his leg over his motorcycle. "Hey, Demon, I think you got passed by a tortoise back there!" I yelled at him.

"And you managed to stay on the road," he retorted, applauding lightly. "I guess the farmer's cornfields are safe for another day, Bane." Demon held his hand out for the keys to the van.

I dropped them into his upturned palm. "If it is any consolation, you blew the doors off that snail we passed on Bridgeton Road."

"You managed to miss the three cruisers but the two officers you nearly flattened when you swerved will never be the same," Demon responded.

"At least *I* do not drive like someone's dead granny."

"Tell that to the officer who was curled up in a ball weeping on top of one of the cruisers. Daedalus will probably make you pay for his therapy."

Demon gazed at me coolly waiting as I struggled for a comeback. Finally, I gave up, scowling. "I hate it when you do that."

"You are losing your touch, brother," Demon said with a wicked smile.

I heard Riot Hellcurse snickering behind me. "Burned," he remarked.

"*You* are going to get burned if you make one more smartass remark," I said, pointing my finger at him.

"I'm terrified," Riot said cheerfully.

"Asshole."

The front door banged open and Dev Xander raced out of the house. Alarmed, our hands automatically went to our weapons.

Dev stopped short, gaping at us. No, he was gaping at Demon. "Holy shit!"

I looked at my brother. While my hand was on my blade, it was still in its sheath. Not Demon's. His blade was in his hand, ready to use. Flames leapt in his blue eyes. The air around him shimmered like heat rising from the earth, still charged with his energy and the excitement from the chase and execution.

Aw, crud.

"What is the matter?" Demon's voice had dropped to a low Wrath growl. It made the hair on the back of my neck stand up. Wrath was edgy and an edgy Wrath is a dangerous one.

"Shit, would you look at that?" Riot hissed as the air around Demon swirled visibly. "Shouldn't that have drained away by now?"

Riot was right. Demon should not have been stirring the air like that. I had hoped that the ride home would calm him some. I was really hoping to avoid having to toss my brother into the basement to work some of that off. Demon and I are identical twins but even on his off-days, he can clean my clock.

"Nothing is the matter," Dev said shooting an anxious look at me. "But, I thought you were going to talk to Scummer."

"We are," Demon told him. We all heaved sighs of relief when he replaced his blade. "However, we cannot drive through Blackridge like that." He pointed at the roofless black van. "We have only come back to trade vehicles." He started walking toward the garage.

I studied my brother. His eyes glittered with intensity, his face flushed. He was so tense that I was afraid he would snap and that really would scare the hell out of Scummer, so much so that he would probably shut down and we would get nothing useful from him.

"Demon, wait," I called after him. "I will go."

Demon turned back frowning.

"It will not take all of us to interview an informant. Riot and Dev can go with me," I told him. "Besides, if *I* was Scummer and I ran into you right now, I would sooner throw myself under the nearest bus than face you."

Demon winced. "Is it that obvious?" He sighed. "Very well then, I will remain here. I would not want Scummer to commit hari-kari with public transportation."

I led the way into the apartment building where our informant lived. Riot walked beside me up the front stairs. We decided that it was better to stay out of the elevators and stick to the stairwells where people would be less likely to see us. We were at this particular building earlier in the evening and…well…there were a few complications. We did not want anyone recognizing us and calling the cops.

Behind us, Dev was whistling softly, hands stuffed in his pockets. Though a few hours ago he had hit a tree at 150 kilometers an hour, his arm had completely healed now and he had removed the bandage. You could still see the scar, but it would be gone by daybreak. "Could you knock off the whistling?" I asked, scowling at him. "We are supposed to be sneaking here."

Dev met my eyes with a big grin on his face. "Sneaking? Is that official Enforcer lingo? Anyway, we only hunt and execute the bad guys. I thought Scummer was on our side. So why are we sneaking up on him?"

"We're *Enforcers*," I said. "Do you think he is going to open his front door and offer us a beer?"

"And he's going to be happier if we sneak up on tippy-toes instead?" Dev asked sarcastically.

"Now I'm sure that term is in the Enforcers' official handbook," Riot remarked.

"We are highly trained assassins. We do *not* tippy-toe," I said haughtily. "Anyway, have you got a better plan?"

"Nope," Dev began to hum softly. I rolled my eyes.

"How much further is it?" Riot complained. I glanced at my friend. He had pulled his long white blond hair back in a tail. His brilliant golden eyes glared up the stairs. I sincerely hoped that we would not run into any prostitutes and their johns in the stairwell. I was afraid that if we did happen upon such a couple, the lady would quickly forget her client and start offering Riot a free sample. Then we would have a pissed off john on our hands as well. Brawls in the stairwell are not conducive to sneakiness either. I had a real reason to fear this particular scenario. Riot is Lust and this had happened before.

"Oh, come on," Dev spoke up. "Four flights of stairs would be nothing to Fechín. He wouldn't bother with stealth. He'd fly up the stairs."

Demon and I learned long ago that humans consider our first names unsuitable for polite society, especially with a surname like Hellblazer, so we chose names more acceptable for human males. I chose Brandon and my brother chose the name Fechín. Why he thought that was a more normal human name is beyond me.

I shook my head. "In the state Fechín was in when we left him, he would also punch in Scummer's door with his fist, grab him by the throat, and make the man piss himself."

My brother is not renowned for his subtlety.

Dev's brown eyes lit up and he opened his mouth to speak.

"No," I interrupted him hastily. "We *can't*."

"Party pooper," Dev frowned.

"Yeah, it's too bad. It's always fun watching Fechín go to work," Riot agreed. He looked at me and raised an eyebrow. "So?"

I sighed. "It is apartment A on the fifth floor. We are almost there."

We reached the fifth floor and, much to my relief, without running into any ladies of the evening or their surly customers. We moved silently down the hallway to apartment 5A and listened at the door. All was silent. I knocked. There was no response. There wasn't even a whisper of movement from inside.

Suddenly the door of the apartment across the hall flew open and banged against the wall with enough force to shake the floor beneath our feet. We jumped and whirled around. *"Yikes!"* Dev exclaimed at the apparition that confronted us.

An elderly human glared out at us. I wasn't certain at first, but I thought it was a female. She wore a pink and red flowered housedress that was far too large for her thin, bony body. She looked to be about ninety with a few curlers wrapped optimistically around the remaining strands of gray hair on her head. She was about four feet tall.

I thought at first that the old woman was a displaced dryad because her small brown face had the appearance and texture of tree bark. However, the voice that came out of that tiny woman was definitely not the wind-rustling-in-the-leaves voice of a dryad. "Who the hell are you?" she demanded in a deep, raspy voice.

"Electric Company," Dev told her.

She glared at us for a minute longer and then ducked back into the apartment, slamming the door. Riot groaned. "She's calling the cops. I know it."

I glanced sideways at Dev. "Electric Company?" I repeated incredulously. "At 2 a.m.?"

He shrugged.

"Let's get a move on before the human police show up," Riot urged. He glared at Dev too. "Of course, if you want to be the one to call Fechín when we get hauled off to jail, I have no objection."

"I'll pass," Dev remarked.

We turned back to the door. I tried the knob gently. The door didn't budge. "Maybe the door sticks," Dev suggested in a whisper. "It usually does in places like this."

I turned it a little more forcefully but it still didn't move. "I should have known it could not be that easy," I sighed.

"Now what are we supposed to do?" Dev whispered.

"We could take it down," Riot suggested.

"And what do we tell the scary little dryad in the next apartment then?" Dev wanted to know in an uncharacteristic display of practicality. "She really *will* call the cops."

Riot glared at the door. "Fechín would just take it down," he muttered.

"He can hypnotize people into forgetting that he was ever here," I reminded him. "We cannot."

"So how are we getting inside then?" Riot demanded.

I had to think about that. Then I noticed a small flowerpot sitting next to the door. Call me prejudiced, but I was betting that Scummer was not a flowerpot kind of guy. Following my hunch, I turned it over.

"Voila." I brandished a key. "We walk in."

"What an idiot," Riot muttered. I trusted he was directing that term at Scummer.

"Lucky for us he *is* an idiot," Dev shot back obviously taking Riot's comment the same way. "Or we would be climbing in through the windows. I hate getting stuck with my ass hanging out of a window."

5

Having wings is a definite disadvantage to sneaking into places.

I unlocked the door and opened it. Immediately, the smell of death overwhelmed me. "Shit," I muttered.

"Or something very close to it," Riot held his hand over his face in an attempt to defend his nose from the smell.

The three of us slipped inside the apartment. I closed and re-locked the door behind us. We did not want any more curious neighbours coming over to find out who we were. I doubted any of them would buy the Electric Company story either.

We found the body curled up in a ball on the living room floor. The mouth was wide open in a silent scream. A pair of dull brown eyes gazed up at us, frozen in horror. There was no life in them. Our informant was dead and whatever had killed him had not been delicate about it. It had shredded him. His jeans were in tatters and there wasn't much left of the denim jacket that he was wearing. He was wearing one green and white running shoe. The other was missing. A pool of blood spread around him, soaking into his shaggy brown hair and what was left of his clothing.

"Someone obviously didn't want him talking to us," Dev commented.

I fumbled for my cell phone and attempted to flip it open the way I had seen Demon do it. It opened and immediately snapped closed again. I cursed. Demon had insisted that I get one if I was going to lead executions. I had had it for a while now but was nowhere near being as adept with it as my brother was. It was obvious that I needed practice.

"Who are you calling?" Riot asked curiously, as I carefully opened the phone avoiding the wrist snap that Demon used to open his.

"When you got a body, lying in your home..." Dev sang. "Who you gonna call?"

Riot groaned. "Not the Boogeys!"

"You like the Boogeys," I reminded him.

"Yeah, but this is a damned small space to invite them into! There is no ventilation and I doubt Fechín would appreciate it if we threw back the curtains and opened the windows!"

"They couldn't make it smell any worse in here than it already does," Dev pointed out.

"Want to make a bet?"

"Relax, Riot," I told him. "I'm just calling Fechín to find out what he wants us to do."

He answered the phone after the second ring and I spoke to my brother, briefly, explaining the situation. I hung up and turned to Riot. He wasn't going to like this.

"He wants us to call the Satana CSI-Team," I said.

"Okay," Riot said, relieved.

"Then he wants us to call the Boogeys to come and get rid of the body afterward."

Riot groaned.

I knew he wasn't going to like this.

CHAPTER TWO

THE HUMAN COPS SHOWED up about fifteen minutes after the Satana and, as the only shapeshifter present, I had to pretend to be Scummer in order to convince them to leave. When I opened the door, the old woman from across the hall was with them so I knew immediately who had called them. She was hiding behind them and kept peeking around the taller cop to glare at me.

"Yes?" I asked glaring back at her.

"Is this the gentleman who lives here, ma'am?" one of the officers asked the dryad.

She sniffed at me but nodded reluctantly. "It *looks* like him."

Thank goodness. I did not really know what Scummer looked like. I had only the corpse to go by and there was not much left of it.

"Excuse me, sir." The other officer touched the brim of his hat in an old-fashioned gesture that nearly made me grin. "But your neighbour here said she saw some men lurking outside your door. She didn't know who they were and was afraid that they were up to no good."

"No, officer," I pretended to yawn as though they had gotten me out of bed. "I know the young men. Everything is fine."

It didn't take much to convince the cops that the neighbour had made a mistake. After the cops left, the old woman remained standing in the hallway, still glaring at me suspiciously.

"Was there something more, ma'am?' I asked her.

"What's wrong with your voice?" the old dryad asked.

"I beg your pardon?" I said surprised.

She shook her head. "You may look like Mr. Scummer, but you sure don't sound like him," she said. "You're too genteel."

Oops. It is one of the pitfalls of being as old as I am. Demon and I have a hard time with the casual dialogue of modern times. We were born when words meant something and carried weight. You spoke carefully because whatever you said could make things happen, bad or good. Now, anyone can say anything. They threaten to kill people when they are angry. Curses have become part of everyday vocabulary. It does not have the same power as it once did. It is such a shame because it makes people less careful and considerate.

"So who was the kid who told me that he was with the Electric Company?" she demanded.

I went with the story we had devised before the police arrived. "He was my nephew," I explained, trying to sound less polite without being outright rude. A mischievous thought sparked in my head, so I rolled with it. "He can be a bit of an ass when he has been drinking."

"Hey, stick to the script!" I heard Dev hiss, obviously irritated by my ad-lib. He was hiding behind the door in case I had to produce my "nephew" for questioning.

"And why are you wearing a coat at this time of night?" she demanded.

Shit. She should have been a cop. The police officers had not even blinked at the coat. "I am coming down with a cold," I told her.

"Humph." The old dryad gave me one last glare before she shuffled back into her apartment and closed the door.

"You are *so* clever, Bane," Dev said sarcastically as I closed the door. "I am coming down with a cold," he mimicked.

I glared at him. "You started it with your lame-ass excuse."

"I didn't hear *you* coming up with a better one!"

"Excuse me." Chief Daedalus Hellcurse stood in the doorway between the living room and the front hallway with his arms folded across his broad chest, staring at us pointedly. Daedalus is Riot's uncle. He is shorter than Riot is, and has dark hair. His eyes are emerald green and his skin is daemon red. He looks, as most daemons do, about twenty-five years of age physically. However, Daedalus is closer to my age chronologically.

"If we could continue with our investigation, then perhaps we could all get the hell out of here sometime before noon," Daedalus went on.

He was exaggerating. It was nearly three now and I was sure that the investigation would not take nine hours, but Dev and I meekly followed the chief back into the living room.

Riot was lounging against the arm of the sofa watching the Satana's M.E. as he examined the body. Scummer's appearance and smell had not improved in the last five minutes. The M.E. glanced up at us; the thick glasses he wore magnified his pure black eyes. He looked like a cockroach. His skin was redder than Daedalus' skin and that was rather dark red as it was. He blinked. "Someone ate him," he announced as his glasses slid down his long, pointed nose. "Partially."

"Ew!" Dev exclaimed wrinkling his nose.

The M.E. known as Maggot pushed his glasses back up. I am certain that, once upon a time, we had all known what his real name was, but I was damned if I could remember it. We had always called him Maggot.

"He's been dead at least five hours but it could be as much as eight," Maggot told us. "There's something else. He is a werewolf, but not a shifter."

"How can you tell?" Dev demanded.

"Top secret scientific hocus pocus. I'd explain it but I'm afraid your head would explode," Maggot grinned.

Dev snorted. "I'd survive it but it wouldn't be pretty. So, why didn't he shift and protect himself?"

Maggot shrugged. "It beats the hell out of me. Maybe he didn't have time."

"Perhaps he didn't see his killer as a threat," I suggested.

"Right up until it started chewing on him," Dev added. Maggot grinned again. For some reason, he loves Dev's humour. Go figure.

"What else?" Daedalus prompted.

Maggot sighed. "I'm going to need a few more minutes to get a toxicology done, chief."

"Then do it," Daedalus told him shortly. He turned to us. "Where is Fechín?"

"He opted to remain behind."

Since Demon rarely opts to stay behind, Daedalus was stunned. "He didn't come with you to question an informant?" he asked, incredulously.

"He was not quite up to it," I explained.

Daedalus eyed me. "He was wound rather tightly when you guys left the scene of the execution. Is he still having trouble?"

"I felt that in Demon's present condition Scummer might be discouraged from talking if he accompanied us."

"That means "hell, yes," Riot translated.

"For some reason people seem to be speechless with terror around Wrath," Dev quipped. "It must have something to do with his tendency to take their heads off when they're naughty."

Behind us, Maggot gave a snort of laughter.

"I suppose I can understand that," Daedalus replied with a slight smile. "Perhaps you would be so good as to give your statements now while we finish up in here, and then you can go."

He turned to three officers standing nearby. "Jezebel, you can interview Dev. Jordis, you can talk to Bane."

Daedalus wisely assigned a male to interview Riot. Jezebel sighed in disappointment. Jezebel's eyes had not left Riot since she walked into the apartment and she continued to stare at him as he followed the male officer into another room. Riot must have sensed it because he turned around at the last second and gave her wink and a smile before closing the door. Jezebel blushed and giggled, then caught Jordis glaring at her. She quickly led Dev to another part of the room away from Jordis' disapproving gaze.

Jordis sighed and turned to me. "We'll go into the kitchen, Bane," she said tiredly.

I pitied Jezebel. She got the short end of the stick in trying to get anything serious out of Dev. As Jordis and I entered the kitchen, we heard Maggot give a shout of laughter. Jordis looked at me. I shrugged. "Just be glad that you were not obliged to interview him."

Jordis rolled her eyes and gestured to a chair at the kitchen table. We sat down. Jordis took a notepad and pen out of her pocket. "Okay, Bane. Tell me what happened here."

I explained to her why we were there and how we had found the body. "And when did you talk to Scummer last?" she asked, jotting down the information in her notebook.

"We did not get the chance to speak to him. We were here earlier but as you know we had to abandon that plan to go after Scarletti."

Jordis nodded. She was one of the officers at the scene after Dev had executed the rogue vampire. "Then what happened?"

There was another burst of laughter from Maggot in the living room, temporarily distracting us from the subject. I grimaced. "Daedalus is going to throttle them both and then I am going to have to explain the fingermarks on Dev's neck to Demon. Do you know how nerve-racking that is going to be? I shall be traumatized."

"*Shall* you?" Jordis grinned. I glared at her. "I doubt that Daedalus will react so violently," she told me. "He enjoys Dev's sense of humour almost as much as Maggot does. The chief just pretends to frown on it. Now, you were saying?"

I was exhausted and wanted to relax in the chair, but it was impossible to do with the wings. Instead, I had carefully arranged them to fall over the sides of the seat. "We went home to exchange our van for one less conspicuous then, we came right back here to interview Scummer."

"About how much time elapsed since you left here execution and when you returned?" she asked.

"It must have been an hour at least."

"What was the hurry?"

"I do not understand," I said frowning. "He had information—"

"Yes, but why not just wait until later this morning? Did you have reason to believe that Scummer might be in danger?"

I hesitated. "We are in the middle of a hunt and it is possible that Scummer knew who the rogue sovereign is. He was afraid to talk to us. We were trying to reach him but he wasn't answering his phone."

Jordis eyed me sharply. She knew that I was holding back but I could not tell her that Tanith and her vampires had disappeared before we lost contact with Scummer. After all, we had no proof that Tanith was involved in this. We were not even certain whether she was the rogue sovereign or not.

"Bane, are you telling me everything?" she asked suspiciously.

"It is all I can tell you right now, Jordis. If we find any evidence that tie to Scummer's death, Demon will certainly let Daedalus know," I told her.

Jordis nodded, accepting the promise of this professional courtesy and closed her notebook. "Okay." She paused as she tucked the notebook away. Then she looked at me. "Bane, can I ask you something personal?"

I must have looked surprised because she blushed. "Well, not about you. It is about Riot."

Of course it was.

She did not ask her question right away. She paused again, waiting for the laughter from the living room to die down. It sounded as though other people besides Maggot found Dev amusing.

"I just wanted to ask you a question," Jordis went on.

"Okay, but if you want to know something personal about Riot, you should be asking him," I said warily.

"I don't think I could do that," she said hastily. "Riot and I—" She broke off in confusion and I waited for her to continue, but she didn't. Now this was interesting. I had not been aware that Jordis had any connection with Riot. I had never noticed any interest in her on his part, though I had certainly seen her send a few longing looks his way. However, that is normal with him.

"Yes? What about you and Riot?" I asked.

Before she could ask her question however, another officer burst into the kitchen looking extremely green and sickly. He raced for the window, threw it open, and began sucking in air like there was a shortage.

"Let me guess," Jordis said to him. "The Boogeys are here."

The officer turned toward us still looking sick. "They're here, all right. How the chief can stand there and not gag I don't know."

Rookie.

I got up and walked past him. "It takes practice," I told him.

"Oh." He eyed me with interest. "So, you're an Enforcer."

"Yes. My name is Bane." I stopped at the doorway, waiting for the inevitable, "oh I've always wanted to be an Enforcer," but he didn't say it. Instead, he frowned, apparently puzzled by my first name. I sighed. "I am Vanity."

Now he understood. He nodded. "Oh. So, you're not Wrath?"

"No."

"Oh." He looked relieved and disappointed at the same time. Demon's reputation preceded him it seemed.

"You must be new to the force if you have not yet met my brother," I said.

He nodded. "I've been here for a year but I just got on the S.I.T a few months ago," he admitted, sheepishly. "This is my first murder case though."

"Has Maggot declared it a murder then?" I asked surprised.

"Well, no. Not yet, but it's pretty obvious, isn't it?"

I shook my head. "Nothing is written in stone until Maggot says it is."

"But if something killed him and ate him…" He trailed off and stuck his head out of the window again, breathing deeply in an attempt to stave off the nausea.

"What did you say your name was?"

He drew his head back in and turned to me. "Officer Caleb Fireskull," he said.

"Well, Caleb, allow me to give you some advice. Never eat before you come out to a suspicious death or any death actually," I told him. "It usually ends in a call to the Crew. And never assume anything about a crime scene without hard evidence to back it up."

He brightened up. Apparently, he was feeling much better. "Okay, thanks!"

I stepped into the living room and it was all I could do not to gag too. I glanced at Dev who was turning blue with the effort to hold his breath. I hoped he would not pass out. Demon would be most displeased if we did anything to diminish our cold-blooded assassins' reputation. Nightscare was standing in the middle of the room, hunched almost double because his ten-foot body did not quite fit comfortably in an apartment with a seven-foot ceiling. He glanced at me with bright yellow eyes as I entered the room.

"We're eating well this week thanks to you guys," he remarked.

I held up my hands. "Do not look at us. He was like this when we got here."

Nightscare looked at Daedalus. "This was not an execution?" he asked.

Daedalus shook his head. "Hmm," Nightscare leaned down and sniffed the body. "Smells like werewolf." His nose wrinkled as though he smelled something bad.

Riot, Dev, and I stifled our laughter. I have seen Nightscare happily carry off some rather nasty things, like bodies that had lain about for a few weeks. He often travelled to murder sites by way of the sewers and through closets filled with dirty clothes and rotten gym shoes. Every Boogey we knew had the same exceptionally rancid odour, but the smell of a werewolf put Nightscare off his food.

"He *is* a werewolf," Daedalus told him. "Maggot says he isn't a shifter though."

"What's the difference?" Caleb asked in the strangled voice of one trying to talk without breathing in.

"The difference is that those werewolves who start out as humans and then are turned are considered hybrids. The werewolves who are born that way are the purebred werewolves. They are the true shifters because they can control whether or not they turn into a werewolf. Hybrids can't do that usually." I explained.

"Of course," Dev added cheerfully. "It doesn't matter which kind bites you. You'll still end up a werewolf."

"Purebred or hybrid, they all taste the same to me," Nightscare observed shrugging his shoulders. Something truly disgusting fell out of the long, shaggy fur under his arm. Caleb was looking a bit peaked again.

"You dislike the taste?" I asked, curiously.

"They aren't the tastiest kind of body, but I'm not picky." Nightscare heaved the body up onto his shoulders. As he did, some of Blacktooth's insides slid out onto the floor with a plop. It was too much for Caleb. He raced out of the room, gagging. I heard him throw up in the hallway.

"Damn it!" Daedalus roared as he stalked into the hallway after the officer. "You're going to clean that up before we leave!"

"Aw, hell," Nightscare said, staring down at the body innards in consternation. "Those are the best parts."

"Would you like me to get you a doggie bag?" Dev asked with an almost straight face while Riot and I bit our lips to keep from laughing.

"Yeah," Nightscare said earnestly. "That'd be great."

Dev went into the kitchen and returned a minute later with a plastic bag and a pair of tongs. He picked up the innards that had fallen out and placed them in the bag along with the tongs. He tied it up and solemnly handed it to Nightscare. Riot snorted and turned away quickly, both of his hands covering his mouth in an effort to stifle his laughter.

"Thanks, Dev," Nightscare said gratefully.

"No problem."

Nightscare glanced at the clock on the wall. "It's getting close to dawn so I'm out of here. You sure you're all done with him?" he asked Maggot.

Maggot nodded, holding his breath. Nightscare stepped back into the closet and closed the door behind him. Daedalus came back into the room, scowling. "If you've finished with your statements, you can head out," he said. "We'll finish cleaning up."

"We're done," I told him. Daedalus nodded and turned away, dismissing us.

As we walked out the front door of the apartment, Dev glanced back. "I wonder," he commented. "What kind of bodies *are* the tastiest?"

CHAPTER THREE

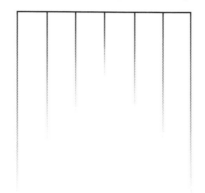

WE LIVE ON THE outskirts of Blackridge—*way* on the outskirts. It takes more than half hour to drive from mid-Blackridge to our three-storey farmhouse. It was quite late by the time we left Scummer's and drove home. I figured that most everyone would be in bed by this time, but I knew better than to believe my brother would do so. Therefore, I was not surprised to see the gleam of a single light emanating through the front window in the library as we drove up to the house.

We entered the house through the garage door and into the large kitchen. Hex had left a light on for us before she went to bed. She had also left a tea tray for us on the table. The teapot was full of cold tea and there was a plate of cookies.

"I'm not drinking that," Dev announced. "My night has been traumatic enough."

I had to agree. Hex's tea is *brutal.* I dumped the tea down the sink while Dev found colas in the fridge for us. We were looking over our shoulders guiltily the whole time. We cleared the plate of cookies however. Hex may not be much with tea but her chocolate chip cookies are amazing.

With our hands full of cookies, we wandered out into the long hallway. Before we made it halfway down the hall, the library door opened and Demon stepped out. "There you are. I thought I heard the car come in." He glanced at the cookies in our hands and smirked. "What? No tea?"

"Shut up," Dev told him cheerfully through a mouth full of cookie. Demon stepped back and held the door for us.

When we entered the library, I saw to my surprise that the other Deadlies had waited up with Demon. Dev stepped into the library behind me and frowned at Maia who was sitting on the sofa looking anxious. He joined her on the sofa, pulling her into his arms. "What are you doing up? I thought you were asleep when I left."

"Nightmares," Maia whispered hoarsely. "I keep seeing Scarletti over and over, that blade through his head..." Suddenly, she burst out. "How do you do this? How do you execute people every day and not go completely *insane?*"

Dev winced. Scarletti was Maia's ex-boyfriend and he had had himself turned into a vampire in a desperate bid to win her back. When that bid failed, he kidnapped Maia in front of Scummer's apartment building. The problem was that Scarletti had not fed for several days and that is a dangerous thing for any vampire let alone a brand-new one. They become like feral dogs, hunting and killing anything that crosses their path. Dev had ended up executing him in front of Maia.

I handed Demon the report that Maggot had given us. He sat behind the desk and read it while I explained to everyone else what we had found at Scummer's apartment. By the time I finished, Maia was sobbing in Dev's arms. Scummer was her informant and she had a hard time convincing him to speak to us. He had finally agreed and then reneged. Now he was dead. I knew Maia well enough to know that she was going over all the what-ifs in her mind. The list could be endless and the result, pointless.

When Demon finished reading the report, he sat staring thoughtfully out of the window. "So Maggot declared it a homicide," Demon said.

"Yes, but he cannot confirm whether or not it was a vampire attack due to the damage to the body," I replied.

"Oh no," Maia exclaimed. "Was it—was it that bad?"

I nodded. "I am afraid so. The body was partially eaten just like the human bodies they discovered in the cages at the zoo."

"However, Scummer's body was in his apartment, not at the zoo," Demon said quietly. "So what ate him?"

"Maggot didn't know, but—" Dev began and then he glanced down at Maia, cuddled against his chest, her face pale and tears streaming down her cheeks. "Never mind," he finished softly.

Demon continued. "What I am getting at is if a vampire killed him, he or she would drain the body of blood, and it seems unlikely that the vampire would bring something along with him to hide the evidence."

"So you think that something came in after the vampire left and—" I glanced at Maia too before I finished. "Er—"

"Or it was already in the apartment." Demon held up the report that I had given him. "According to Maggot, he found rodent saliva on the tissues."

"Do you mean rats?" Riot asked, wrinkling his nose.

"Not necessarily," Demon said. "There are certain supernatural creatures whose saliva can be mistaken for rodent saliva."

He tossed the report onto the desk and got up to pace. "I think that we can safely assume Scummer's murder had something to do with the rogue sovereign that we have been hunting. Whoever it is, he must have found out that he was going to talk to us. But how could the sovereign have found out so quickly?"

"He could have had a human servant watching Scummer," Dev suggested.

"And why should he? Who was Scummer to the rogues? What is the connection between a werewolf and a rogue vampire?" Demon demanded. No one had an answer. He looked at me. "Was there anything in the apartment that might give us a lead?"

"You mean did he write out his killer's name on the floor in his own blood?" I shook my head. "Sorry. There was nothing dramatic. In fact, there was no cryptic messages written on a scrap of paper, no key to a locker at the train depot, no tickets for the Orient Express—"

"Smartass."

I grinned at him.

Demon smiled back briefly and then turned to Maia. "Did Scummer have any friends or a girlfriend? Perhaps he talked to someone or someone might know what he was involved in."

She shook her head. "As far as I know, Scummer kept to himself. He didn't even associate with other werewolves."

"What about an ex-wife, children, a mother?" Demon pressed.

Maia frowned. "I really don't know, Demon, but I can find out."

Demon nodded. "Do that. See who you can find for us."

Maia sat up, her face calm now, determined. Leave it to Demon to give someone a mission to pull her out of her grief. "Will do."

"So where do we start looking for the rogues now?" Dev asked. "The bars were a bust. Our only lead has fizzled. We don't know where Tanith and her entourage disappeared to." He threw his hands up. "We've got nothing!"

"We start over," Demon told him. "We go back to the bars. We talk to Hadrian again. We interview as many of our informants as possible. We start interviewing every supernatural we can find. Someone must know something or has heard something."

Everyone groaned. "So far, the bars and informants haven't gotten us anywhere," Riot pointed out.

"It will if we keep at it. People will eventually get tired of seeing us and they will give us whatever information they can to get rid of us. We need every scrap of information no matter how insignificant it may seem. Every piece eventually makes the puzzle."

Demon rose from behind the desk. "Get some sleep. We will start looking for the rogue vampires again tomorrow."

CHAPTER FOUR

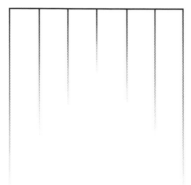

IT WAS AFTER ONE o'clock in the afternoon when I finally staggered down the stairs. I went directly into the library, guessing that my brother would already be there. I was right. He was sitting behind the desk, his feet up and reading some papers. The low back of the chair kept him from falling backward but how he could be comfortable with his feet up like that, I don't know. I would have fallen on my head. However, his long black hair was loose, cascading over his shoulders like a river of darkness. Demon rarely wears his hair out of a braid even when we aren't going on an execution. Me, I take my hair out of the braid as soon as I get in the van. I was surprised to see him actually relaxing for a change.

I stood in the doorway, watching him for a minute before he spoke. "If you're coming in, close the door and sit down," he said without looking up from his papers. "Don't hover, Bane."

It was pointless to argue that I was *not* hovering because we both knew that I was. "How long did you actually sleep?" I asked, moving into the room.

"I have only been up for an hour," he replied setting aside a sheet of paper and going onto the next. He appeared to be very intent on his papers. Demon rarely lies, but it always makes me suspicious when my brother will not or cannot meet my eyes.

"So you have had a full eight hours sleep?" I asked, raising my eyebrows. "Why don't I believe that?"

Finally, he glanced up and his feet dropped onto the floor. "Because you are naturally suspicious and cynical?" he suggested.

I grinned and perched on the edge of the desk. "What are you reading?" I jerked my chin at the papers in his hand.

"It is Maggot's report." He set it aside. "It says that the body was not completely drained of blood."

"Still, he *was* bitten."

"Yes. It would be hard to tell after the rats got to him, or whatever it was that ate him."

"Well, there is an unpleasant image just before breakfast."

"It is past lunchtime," Demon corrected and then shrugged. "We have certainly seen worse."

"We have *done* worse. We are the Enforcers," I reminded him.

He looked up. "The humans had another name for us, remember?" he said bitterly.

I studied him closely. Demon does not often give way to bitter reflections. "There have been so many over the years," I told him carefully.

"Monsters," Demon said softly.

"We have been called nastier names," I pointed out.

"Some of them are unrepeatable," Demon agreed, tapping his fingers on the desk. "Of all the names we have been called, that is the one that sticks with me the most."

"It does for me too," I admitted. "I am not certain why that name hurts more than any of the others."

He shrugged. "Perhaps that is because we had never seen ourselves as monsters before. Up until then, almost everyone we met liked us."

"I think the women liked us a little more than the men did." I smiled, fondly remembering a few women who had liked me.

Demon's thoughts were not so warm. He looked away. "Not enough," he replied.

I winced. "Demon..."

"I know how to pick them, don't I?" he asked with a smile meant to be cheerful. Instead, it looked painful. "First Tanith, then Elizabeth——"

"None of that was your fault. All you did was trust the wrong person."

"I do that a lot." Demon shook his head and sat up, picking up the report again and straightening the pages. "I do not want to talk about it." He tossed the report onto the desk and, miraculously, the pages all stayed together instead of scattering.

"Very well, we will not talk about that. Let's talk about Kit instead," I suggested cheerfully, shifting gears. "Now there is a woman who is far better suited to you than Tanith or Elizabeth."

If only you would stop acting like a jackass.

"I do not wish to talk about Kit either," Demon said.

I sighed in annoyance. "Then, what do you want to talk about?"

Demon growled. "How about we talk about Carys?"

"Point taken," I glared at him and then lifted my chin.

I was in love with or thought I was in love with Carys Grace, also known as Love. I was never sure if the feelings were real or not. When she was around me, the feelings that she inspired in me were so intense I could hardly bear it. After she had gone, I always wondered what it was I saw in her. I tried to avoid her as much as possible. When I had no other choice, I ignored her as much as possible. I am certain that she knew how I felt about her and that my behaviour puzzled her, but I figured that there was no other way to keep my sanity to be perfectly honest. I had never discussed this with anyone, not even my brother.

I changed the subject to one less uncomfortable. "So did you find anything else of interest in the report?"

"No."

I sighed. "We have never had this much trouble finding an execution. Hell, we have never had this much trouble identifying an execution!"

"Whoever killed Scummer is not yet our problem," Demon reminded me. "This is the Satana's investigation until they solve it and give an execution order to us. Our current responsibility is finding the rogue sovereign."

"We could turn that over to the Satana as well," I pointed out.

He shook his head as he rose from his chair. "We do not need an order from Daedalus since I have already put the rogue on the list."

"But we do not know who it is."

He gave me a look. "You know what I mean."

It meant that he was going to execute whoever the rogue was with or without Daedalus' approval. That was our job and Demon made those kinds of calls weekly. However, one of the sovereigns that we were investigating was the woman who had turned Demon into a vampire. She claimed that her only purpose in Blackridge was to reunite with him, but I didn't trust Tanith and I did not want her anywhere near my brother. My greatest fear was that he was not entirely over her.

"Demon..." I began.

"What?" Demon asked, stretching.

I started to speak and then, I thought the better of it. I shook my head. "Let's see if Hex has lunch ready."

I followed my brother into the kitchen. Hex was there, making sandwiches. She turned as we came in and her lips thinned in displeasure. "You could have told me that you weren't going to be up for breakfast," she said pointedly.

Oops. Demon and I exchanged guilty looks. "My apologies, Hex," he said. "Is there a lot of food wasted?"

She waved her little hand. "Nothing is ever wasted here. I simply cooked everything and put it in the fridge. I figured you would be down here looking for food at some point." She paused and then, as if she felt she might have forgiven us too soon, she scolded, "But, that doesn't excuse your thoughtlessness."

Demon and I were sitting at the table eating egg and bacon sandwiches when Dev shuffled in. He is not a morning person, being Sloth. If we would let him, he would probably sleep all day. However, this is not an option when you are a Deadly.

He muttered incoherently in response to our greetings as he staggered toward the coffeepot. He poured himself a cup of coffee and then joined us at the table, clutching the mug protectively with both hands as if it was full of liquid gold. At this point, it was probably worth more than gold to Dev. Hex set a plate with a sandwich on it in front of him. Dev stared at it blankly as if he didn't know what it was or what to do with it. It took a whole cup of coffee before his brain made the connection that there was food in front of him. Once he recognized the substance was edible, it didn't take him long to devour it.

We ate in silence for a few minutes and then Riot and Kaz Shade came in. They sat down and Hex served them. No one said anything until after Morgana and Onyx had joined us and Hex left the kitchen to dust the library.

Onyx Hellcurse is Riot's younger brother. He does not look much like Riot. His hair is not as pale and it is short and curly. His skin is daemon red and his eyes, when his Deadly is not overwhelming him, are blue. We feed on the sins of humanity, consuming as much as we can to prevent an outright explosion of evil among humans. Unfortunately, for some of us this can be devastating.

We do not consume the humans' sins consciously. It is like a constant light rain—drip, drip, drip—you don't notice it. However, for someone like Onyx or Demon, it is more like a downpour and there is no way to turn it off. For the last few months, Onyx had struggled, overpowered by an excess of jealousy. Like wrath, it is one of the more potent emotions. A little goes a long way. However, we were all trying to help Onyx and he was doing better. In fact, I was pleased to see that he was smiling as he slipped into a seat beside his brother.

Morgana Bloodvine is the second youngest of the Deadlies and she is desperately in love with my brother. Unfortunately, he does not feel the same way about her. This annoys Morgana. She glanced at Demon who was intent on his meal. She swept her long black hair over one shoulder and pretended that she was completely indifferent to him. "Did you sleep well, Demon?" she asked in a stiff, polite tone.

He looked up coolly. "Yes, thank you."

I winced. It was a painful scene to witness. It is not natural in Demon to be so cold with the other Deadlies, and it is certainly not natural in Morgana. This had come about just in the last week after they had a big blow up over Demon leaving her behind on a couple of hunts. Since then she had made a few remarks about Demon's leadership—at least that is the way he saw it—and they had been very aloof with each other ever since. It was hard for the rest of us to watch because we loved them both.

We looked from Demon to Morgana, nervously, waiting for the explosion. None came. Instead, Morgana looked at her plate and bit her lip. I wondered if she was about to cry. Looking around the table, I saw the same panicked thought running through the others' eyes. We should have known Morgana better. If she were going to cry over Demon, she certainly would not do it in front of us.

"So," she said taking a deep breath. "Now that Scarletti is taken care of, we're going back to hunting the rogues?"

Demon got up and poured himself another coffee. He sat down again before he answered. "Yes. The rogues are at the top of the list, of course, but we have about four outstanding executions that were put on hold last week."

"Four?" Dev frowned. "I thought there were only two."

"Two more came in while you were at your mother's house with Maia," Demon told him.

"The supernatural criminals have been busy this week." Dev shook his head. "So, who is on the list now?"

"Star Silverdew is our first contestant," Demon began. "She is wanted for the robbery of a jewellery store."

"Robbery does not usually involve an execution," I said.

"It does when you are armed and actually shoot the proprietor of the store," Demon continued.

"Did she kill him?" Dev asked.

"No, but shooting someone still puts her name on the list."

"Who else is slated for termination?" I asked.

"Bael Dagger."

Kaz spoke up. "I know him. He's an ogre and a nasty bastard." He frowned. "Who did he kill?"

"He raped a human. He didn't kill her but he is the type that now he has had a taste of power, he will not stop with one human," Demon replied. He paused. "Humans are fragile. The next one may not survive him."

"Daedalus gave you an order for him?" I asked sceptically.

Demon met my gaze steadily. "*I* put him on the list."

"Does Daedalus know that?" Dev asked.

"He will."

"He really hates it when you execute first and inform him later," Riot pointed out.

"He will get over it," Demon said. "The sooner Dagger is dead, the better."

"I can take the ogre," Kaz said. "Just give me your official go-ahead."

"As soon as you find him, you are cleared to execute. You do not need to call me first."

"Oh, let me go with Kaz. Please," Morgana said with a tight smile that boded ill for Bael Dagger.

"No, Gana," Demon said gently.

She glared at him, her green and yellow cat's eyes sparking dangerously. "Why not?"

"Dagger doesn't like women," Demon said. "As much as I would love to have a woman kick his ass for that very reason, your presence will just enrage him. I know he cannot kill you but he can still hurt you. None of us could live with that."

The sparks died out of her eyes and she stared at Demon. "That's the real reason you don't want me to go with Kaz?"

"That's it," he said quietly.

She glanced around the table at our stern faces. Finally, she gave us a small smile. "I love you guys too," she said.

We all took a deep breath and then we began to laugh. In that instant, the coolness between Demon and Morgana seemed to dissolve.

Demon returned to business. "Kaz, take Riot with you. Dagger will follow the lust that he generates or Riot can track him through the power lust," Demon said. "Morgana, you and Onyx can take Silverdew. You should be able to track her through the greed."

"Who is left?" I asked.

"Vervain Swamp."

"He is a werewolf, isn't he?"

"Yes. We will talk to Conall first. He'll probably know where Swamp is to be found."

"Is he one of Conall's then?" Dev frowned. "Will he willingly give one of his own people up to us to be executed?"

Most humans become werewolves when a werewolf bites them. Conall Wolfsbane was the very first purebred werewolf. Conall is almost as old as Demon and I. He is also a friend.

"Conall frowns on his people killing humans or turning them into werewolves," Demon reminded him.

We all looked up, falling silent as Maia came into the kitchen. One of Conall's grandsons was the werewolf that attacked Maia. She wouldn't let us execute the bastard and while that had pissed us off, it had earned her Conall's eternal gratitude and respect.

Maia smiled sleepily at us and wandered over to give Dev a rather passionate good morning kiss. Dev looked pleased but seemed bewildered as if he did not understand why a woman like Maia would love him. Sometimes, Dev underrates himself.

"What are you all up to today?" Maia asked as she drew back from Dev. She went to the sideboard to pour herself a cup of coffee.

"We have a few executions," Demon told her. "What about you?"

She took a sip of coffee and came back over to the table, snatching the other half of Dev's sandwich. It was his third so I do not think he minded. "I called into work and told my boss what happened. Sachmet said to take a few days off. It looks like I'll be a lady of leisure for a few days. Will you be gone long?" Maia tried to sound casual but the look she gave Dev was wistful.

"I'll be home as soon as I can," he assured her. He rose from the table and kissed her lightly on the mouth.

She gently touched his cheek and held him in the kiss for a few seconds longer, and then she drew back, smiling. "I guess I'll have to get used to this," she told him.

He smiled back still holding her in his arms. "You've got an eternity," he reminded her.

She melted against him, nuzzling her cheek into his chest. "Lucky me," she purred.

"Oh, *please!*" I snorted. "Take the gooey stuff somewhere else, will you?"

Maia giggled and Dev glared at me. "Jealous," he snapped.

"Am not!"

"Are too!"

"He's jealous," Onyx added, licking his lips.

I glared at him. "No fair feeding off the other Deadlies!"

"Then stop sending out such tasty morsels to tempt me with," Onyx teased.

I growled at Onyx who just grinned at me. Demon was trying to hide a smile with his coffee cup but since I could still hear his snickers, he was failing miserably. I shook my head and stood. "Deadlies, it's time to work."

"Hey!" Demon protested mildly. "That's my line."

CHAPTER FIVE

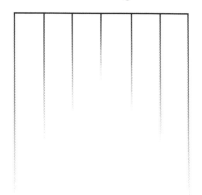

DEMON INSISTED ON DRIVING, of course.

With the van temporarily out of commission, Dev, Demon, and I decided to take the SUV. Demon has other, smaller vehicles but we rarely use them. The smaller cars are mostly for show. They are pretty but impractical. We only took one of them when it was just one or two of us going out. There are six of us male Deadlies and we are all big men. When you factor in the wings, no matter how small and slender Morgana is, you will not squeeze the seven of us into anything smaller than a full-size van or an SUV. Even three would be tight, not to mention just trying to see out of the rear view mirror past all those feathers is next to impossible.

Demon met my suggestion that we call ahead to tell Conall that we were coming with scorn. I tried to convince him that since we were not on our way to execute Conall, a phone call was socially acceptable. He had tossed me his cell phone and growled, "Go ahead and call him then."

I glared at him and then, to make my point and because he had challenged me, I tried to make the call—four times. Finally, I snapped the cell phone closed in frustration and handed it back to Demon. He put it back in his pocket making no comment and without taking his eyes off the road, but he was smirking. I chose to let it slide. Starting a fight with my brother while he was driving was dangerous...fun, but dangerous.

Conall likes his privacy and does not encourage visitors. The Wolfsbane compound is on the outskirts of Blackridge. It is actually a large farm. He had fenced it off with a ten-foot wall of bricks. Barbed wire tops the brick wall in case the wall itself isn't forbidding enough to an intruder. However, if the barbed wire doesn't deter you and if you are determined to get inside, you could scale the wall but once on top of it, you would look down and see two or three real wolves watching you with hungry yellow eyes, waiting for you to topple in. If you came up to the driveway, you were discouraged from entering by a huge gate protected by armed guards. No drug lord is as protected as Conall.

Conall is a gruff kind of man and not easy to deal with in the best of his moods. He seemed to like us, however, and I believe it was because he knew that he could not intimidate us. Conall has no tolerance for weakness, especially physical weakness. He cannot harm the Deadlies and I think it scares the shit out of him and, though he will never admit it, he respects us.

When we arrived at the compound, one of Conall's sons met us at the gate. CJ is the youngest of Conall's sixteen sons as well as one of the least objectionable. He and his twin sister are the children of Conall's most recent wife, Ellen. CJ sauntered over to the driver's side of the vehicle, one hand resting casually on the gun holstered on his hip, and peered in. He recognized us and grinned. "Fechín and company," he exclaimed. "Long time no see, Enforcers! What brings you out here?"

"Need to talk to the Big Bad Wolf," Demon told him.

CJ's smile gave way to a serious expression. "Don't know if it's gonna be possible, Fechín. Big Bad Wolf's in a Big Bad Mood."

"Anything we can do to help?"

CJ thought about that and then shook his head. "Not unless you guys can get a werewolf put on your execution list."

"What did the werewolf do to get on Big Bad's bad side?" Dev asked, leaning forward curiously.

CJ started to open his mouth and then closed it. "Never mind," he said. "We'll handle it."

We all froze and looked at each other. "What do you mean, "handle it?" Demon demanded.

"It's nothing," CJ said trying to backtrack.

It was too late for that. The phrase "we'll handle it" set off alarm bells and

Demon was instantly suspicious. "CJ," Demon warned. "Do not do anything foolish. If this is something the Enforcers should be dealing with…"

"It isn't. Look, Fechín, just forget I said anything."

Demon and I looked at each other. We *could* drop it or… "I could just ask Big Bad," Demon suggested quietly.

CJ looked alarmed. "Good god, are you trying to get me killed? I like my head where it is. I don't need him to hand it to me. Just leave it alone. Please."

Demon eyed him steadily for a moment.

"I promise no one will do anything stupid," CJ insisted.

Finally, Demon shrugged. "Very well, CJ. I will let it go for now. Just make sure that all of your people know I will not tolerate a war in my city."

"Thanks, Fechín."

Demon returned to the reason for our visit. "Listen, have you ever heard of Vervain Swamp?"

"Yeah sure," CJ said. "Why do you want to know?"

"He's on our List."

CJ looked shocked and then gave a low whistle. "You guys are hunting Swamp?"

"Yes. Do you know where we might be able to find him?"

"Sorry, but I don't run with that asshole. He's not one of *us*. Besides, Big Bad would claw my guts out, and then have a witch bring me back to life so he could do it again."

"Graphic. Who knew that you had such a violent imagination, CJ?" Dev remarked.

"Imagination, my ass!"

"Then we really do need to talk to your father," Demon said. "He knows everything that goes on in the werewolf realm."

"He'll probably help you if he has anything to tell. Don't think Big Bad would mind having Swamp eradicated from the planet," CJ admitted. "In fact, he would probably tie him up in a big red bow and leave him on your doorstep if he could get his hands on him. He gives us shifters a bad name."

"He is a shifter?" I asked surprised.

"Hell no," CJ grinned. "Or you guys wouldn't be hunting him. Big Bad would have already taken care of him." He opened the gate to let us pass through.

"Hey," he called out as we drove by. "You be careful! Swamp's a real bad ass!"

"So are we," Demon called back.

Ellen Wolfsbane met us at the door. She was born a human in Britain. Then when she was twenty-six, a werewolf attacked her. She was lucky. She survived the attack. Many werewolf victims do not. That was over thirty years ago. Her aging process had slowed to the point where she still looked twenty-six even though she was over fifty. She could live to be well over 100. Her children, being part daemon, were Eternals like Conall. Knowing that Conall disliked hybrid werewolves made his choice of wife odd.

Ellen is a slender woman, about 5'8, with long soft auburn curls and blue eyes, which both of her children had inherited. She moved toward us gracefully with a warm, welcoming smile. She was a real beauty and as beautiful inside as she was outside. Maybe Conall's attraction to her wasn't so odd after all.

"Why, hello, boys," she said beaming. "What brings you here?"

"We need to speak to Conall." Demon explained why.

Ellen chewed her lower lip thoughtfully. "I'm sure he'll see you. But, he's in a bit of a grump right now."

Behind me, I heard Dev coughing to cover up a laugh. I fought back a smile. Demon's mouth didn't even twitch but his eyes were gleaming. "Grumpy or not," he said with admirable control. "If he could help us in any way, we would appreciate it."

Ellen led the way to Conall's private room and knocked on the door.

"*What is it?*" Conall's rough voice roared from inside.

"If he huffs and puffs and blows that door down, I am *out* of here," Dev whispered to me.

Ellen showed no such inclination to flee. She flung open the door and stalked into the room. She stopped in front of Conall, hands on her hips, glaring at him. "Is that any way to answer the door?" she demanded.

"Damn it, woman, I'm busy!" Conall rose from behind a large wooden desk. He looked like a wolf, even in human form. His skin was bronze. His shaggy black hair curled around his ears, but his goatee and moustache were neat. He turned toward me. His eyes, one blue and one brown, snapped with anger and he flashed his canines as he spoke.

"Don't you flash fang at me, Conall Sean Wolfsbane," Ellen snapped, her fangs flashing back at him. "That may have worked on your first five wives, but you don't scare me!"

31

"Evidently I'm not trying hard enough," he snapped back and then he noticed us. He glared at Ellen. His Irish brogue became perceptible as he spoke. "You didn't tell me we had guests."

"Didn't give me a chance, did you?" she retorted.

Conall scowled. "Hum," he grunted. "Well, order us up some tea and—"

"No tea!" Demon, Dev, and I blurted at once.

Conall blinked in surprise. "Coffee then?" he asked, taken aback by our vehemence.

"That is very kind, thank you," Demon said smoothly.

"Order us up some coffee and sandwiches," Conall said to Ellen.

She crossed her arms over her chest, tapping her foot on the wine red carpet. "At least Fechín remembers his manners!"

Conall glanced sheepishly at us. "Please," he said gruffly.

"That's better, you old fusspot!" Ellen smiled at him and kissed his cheek before she left, closing the door behind her.

Dev nudged me with his elbow and we struggled not to laugh but we didn't fool Conall. He glared at us as Demon took a chair and got down to business. "What can I do for you, Fechín?"

"We are trying to locate Vervain Swamp."

"Is this an execution?" Conall turned his head to look at Demon, distracted from Dev and me. He sat down across from Demon. "What has he done?"

"Does it matter?" my brother asked.

Conall thought about that and then shrugged. "Not really, I guess. However, *I* don't know where he lives," he said haughtily. "I don't associate with riff raff."

"Then what the hell do you call *us*?" Dev demanded.

"Shut up, Dev," Demon and I said at the same time.

Conall grinned. "I stand corrected." His smile faded. "I can tell you where you might find him or someone who might know him."

"Good enough," Demon said.

Conall scribbled something down on a piece of paper and then handed it to Demon. "This is the address of a club that caters only to the Turned. They don't allow shifters inside. They'll probably have more information about Vervain."

"Turned into what—pies?" Dev demanded.

I stepped on his foot but Conall chuckled. "Most likely mincemeat once you guys catch up to them."

While Dev was glaring at me, Demon folded up the paper and pocketed the address. "Thank you. By the way, have you heard anything about the rogue vampires that hit town last week?"

Conall's gaze sharpened. "I did hear that some of Hadrian's people got caught doing something they shouldn't and that there isn't much left of them."

Dev shuddered. He knew all about that. He was the unlucky one who had accompanied Demon that night. Demon doing his Wrath act is not something you soon forget.

"Have you heard anything about who might be the sovereign leading them?" Demon asked.

Conall looked surprised. "It isn't Hadrian?"

"We do not know for certain," Demon told him. "We are still looking for evidence that points conclusively to him or someone else. You have not heard anything?"

Conall shook his head. "No, but I'll be sure to keep my ear to the ground."

Demon rose from his chair. "You have our number. Thank you, Conall." Conall rose too and they shook hands.

As we were leaving the room, Ellen came in with a tray loaded with coffeepot, mugs, and platters of sandwiches and delicate pastries. "You're going already?"

"Places to go, criminals to execute," Dev told her cheerfully.

"At least take a sandwich," she urged. "They're ham and cheese. I made them myself."

Demon took one and then gave Ellen a kiss on the mouth. She licked her lips. "Yum," she purred as Demon smiled down at her. "Tasty."

"Hey!" Conall growled in protest as his wife laughed.

"It could have been worse," Demon said with a wicked grin. "Riot could have been with us."

Conall rolled his eyes and we left.

CHAPTER SIX

THE ADDRESS OF THE private club was not in the better part of Blackridge. Graffiti defaced every building where street gangs had left their tags. Trash littered the streets. There were a few homeless people wandering around. Often the criminals we hunted chose this area to stalk prey because the humans here more vulnerable than say, someone who lived in a nice, clean neighbourhood where the houses had alarm systems and neighbours looking out of their windows every ten seconds. It made me sick to know that this club was probably here because the humans were such easy targets. However, unless we caught the bad guys actually harming someone, we could not do anything about the club being here.

We got out of the SUV and looked around. I caught sight of several pairs of red, glowing eyes watching us from the dark areas. One hovered in the alley, another from a window in the upper floor of the building across the street and even the lid of a garbage can lifted and something inside peered out.

Blackridge is a mixture of modern buildings constructed with convenient materials that crumble like cheese and the two hundred year old, heavy field stone buildings that stand next to them without so much as a chip out of them. The design and the stones used in constructing the buildings was not a coincidence. The gothic style and the ancient stones from the mountain, river, and lake attract the supernaturals that generally live in those environments. Unfortunately, they draw the bad ones as well as the good. These buildings are dark and damp and tend to be the perfect hideouts for some very nasty things, such as the things peeking out of the shadows all around us.

"Demon," I warned softly. "Red Eyes."

"I see them," he replied without looking. He casually removed his long black coat and his wings sprang free. He gave them a little shake and tossed his coat into the backseat of the SUV. Then, he glanced at us. "How are you going to execute Swamp if you can't get at your weapons?"

"But the humans—" I began.

Demon eyed me coolly. "What are they going to do? Call the cops and report three men with big black wings running around? If the cops ever stop laughing, they might come out in an hour or two to look around. However, considering the part of town we are in, I doubt it."

"Good point." I glanced back at the Red Eyes. They had receded back into their dark shelters, apparently having determined that it was better to wait for something smaller and preferably unarmed to come along. I grinned at Demon and removed my coat.

"For a minute there," Dev remarked as he tossed his jacket into the backseat. "I thought we were going to get a warm-up."

Demon shrugged as he locked the car. "I did too."

Dev glanced at the garbage can that contained one of the creatures. "We're not going to just walk away are we? You know that they're up to no good."

"Red Eyes never are. We'll come back later."

"But, what if they kill someone in the meantime?"

"They are shadow creatures," Demon pointed out. "They probably won't attack anyone while it is still light out."

"*Probably?*"

"And they know that we have seen them," Demon went on. "Any attacks in this area will bring us right to their doorstep."

"Besides," I added. "Right now it is Swamp's turn."

"So where is this place anyway?" Dev asked.

Demon glanced around and then pointed. "There it is." He indicated a building across the street, further down. There were no windows and no signs, just a single steel door.

"That's it?" Dev frowned. "How the hell can you tell?"

"*We* aren't supposed to be able to tell. That is the point, I guess." Demon grinned wickedly. "And aren't *they* going to get a hell of a shock?"

Dev laughed. He studied the building again with a critical eye. "Not ones for luxury, are they?"

"We haven't seen the inside yet," I pointed out.

"Then let's have a look, shall we?" Demon said.

We crossed the street and Demon opened the door of the club. We stepped inside. It was immediately clear that Dev was right. Luxury was not high on the list in this club. The owner had painted everything black, the floor, the bar, the chairs and tables, and even the walls. There must have been a sale. There was very little lighting. Several patrons were sitting on hard wooden stools at the bar, hunched over glasses of beer. They glanced up, scowling, as we entered. It only took a second for them to realize who we were and then expressions of horror and disbelief replaced the scowls.

"We ain't done nothin'," the bartender announced shrilly. We turned to look at him. He was a tall, lean man with scraggly brown hair that seemed to grow everywhere. I mean, this guy needed a serious nose hair trimming. I know he is a werewolf but yikes.

"Then you have nothing to worry about," Demon replied, coolly. He glanced around at the patrons. "Vervain Swamp—where is he?"

"He ain't here," the bartender snapped.

Demon turned back to him, slowly. "What is your name?"

The bartender looked alarmed. "I ain't givin' you my name! I ain't done nothin'! I ain't gettin' my name on your list!"

Demon raised his eyebrow at me. I took my cue and shrugged. "I didn't hear you say anything about The List," I said, making sure that I said it in capital letters.

"I just wanted to know the name of the guy with whom we'll be spending the rest of the day," Demon said to me.

"And all night too, if we have to," I agreed.

My brother turned back to the bartender who seemed to be getting paler by the second. "Bane, pick a table," Demon said holding the bartender's gaze steadily.

I sauntered over to a table where anyone walking in would spot us immediately. I unsheathed my blade and laid it out in the open on the table. Then I sat down and propped my feet up next to it. Dev sat down across from me, grinning. "Subtle," he murmured.

"You can't stay here!" the bartender shrieked.

"Watch us," Demon said shortly and ambled over to join us. He drew his weapon and it made an audible "shht" sound as it cleared the sheath. Everyone gave a small gasp. Demon sat down with his back to the bar and set his blade down on the table well within his reach.

"Waitress," I called out to the young woman standing piling beer bottles onto a tray from an empty table.

The bartender hurried into a back room while we ordered beers. The waitress was smiling at me the whole time. "I'll be right back," she purred brushing her breasts across my arm as she bent over to take a full ashtray off the table.

I glanced over to see Demon and Dev grinning at me. "What?" I demanded.

"Every once in a while," Dev murmured. "I forget."

"Forget what?" I fell silent as the waitress returned with our beers and set them down in front of us. Her fingers brushed my hand as she set the bottle and glass in front of me.

Dev waited until she walked away and then looked me right in the eye, grinning broadly. "That hanging out with *you* attracts the ladies just as readily as hanging out with Riot and Demon."

"Do not be ridiculous," I said, turning red and not intentionally.

"Oh, yeah?" Dev said. "What's that under your beer glass?"

Startled, I lifted up the glass and looked at the napkin. I glanced up at Dev. "Looks like a napkin to me."

Dev sighed. "Turn it over, dumbass!"

I did. On the back of the napkin, someone had written the name "Cherie" along with a phone number and a rather suggestive message. I glanced at the waitress. She smiled and winked at me. I folded up the napkin and tucked it, along with its intriguing suggestions into my pocket. Demon laughed softly and I glared at him.

Suddenly the door that the bartender had gone through opened and a heavy-set man in jeans, a short-sleeved dress shirt and leather vest came out. He had a long steel-grey moustache and a tidy grey goatee. He looked like a banker trying to look like a biker, or maybe it was the other way around. He carried it off well anyway.

The bartender was peering over the big man's shoulder, nervously. He pointed us out to his boss who heaved a sigh and then strolled over casually.

"Enforcers," he greeted us. "I'm Linus Burrows."

Dev opened his mouth but all that came out was a yelp of surprise as I rammed the heel of my boot into the top of his foot. He glared at me.

"Let it go, Charlie Brown," I murmured.

Burrows ignored us, keeping his eyes on my brother. Demon nodded at him slightly but did not offer any information or ask for any. Burrows frowned.

"What do I have to do to get rid of you?" Burrows asked bluntly.

"Vervain Swamp," Demon told him. "We need a home address."

Burrows frowned. "Swamp? I don't know if we can help you."

"Now that is a shame." I shook my head and swallowed the last of my beer. I set the bottle down. "We'll have another round," I told Cherie who had drifted over again.

"Look, uh—" Burrows floundered.

I was slightly offended that he didn't know who I was. "Bane Hellblazer," I told him.

"Dev Xander," Dev waggled his fingers at him.

"Right. So, listen, um—" the big man said and looked at Demon expectantly.

"Fechín," my brother added softly.

The big man paled. "Wrath? You're *Wrath*?"

Several of the bar's customers jumped up and headed for the door as soon as they heard that Wrath was there. Demon didn't turn his head. "Sit your asses back down!" he ordered in a firm tone.

They all hesitated at the door. Some of them were debating making a break for it. After all, we couldn't catch them all...could we? They looked at each other and reluctantly straggled back to their seats, apparently having decided not to risk being the werewolf that we did catch.

"Look, Wrath," Burrows began. Then he hesitated.

Demon raised an eyebrow at him. "Yes?"

The man sighed. "Look, we would like to help you but what happens if you don't catch Swamp and he finds out we ratted on him?"

Demon and I looked at each other. He could not seriously be more worried about Swamp than he was about us. Demon raised an eyebrow. "Have you ever heard of the Enforcers *not* catching their prey?"

38

Burrows bit his lip. "Well...no." He thought about that and whatever image came to him, it made him swallow hard. I wondered what he had done to make him afraid of us. If it were something bad, we would find out eventually.

Finally, he nodded. "Okay." He gave us an address.

"Thank you," Demon said politely as we rose to go.

At the door, I turned. "And if Swamp should not be there, say, because someone called to warn him, we *will* be back."

"And we will *not* be happy," Demon added softly.

We stepped outside and Dev closed the door behind us. We sheathed our weapons. "I do love to watch you two go to work," Dev remarked as we started across the street.

Swamp lived in an old shack in the middle of (surprise, surprise) a swamp. It was a few miles out of Blackridge in a heavily wooded area. We parked the SUV on the side of the road and hoofed it back to Swamp's place. It took us a few minutes and a couple of wrong turns to find it. The driveway was so overgrown with weeds that we passed it a few times. By the time we reached the house, we were all feeling more than a bit cranky.

Dev took one look at the tiny grey-board shack and grimaced. He slapped at a mosquito on his arm. "Why can't they ever live in a mansion?"

"What difference does it make?" Demon asked curiously. "It isn't as if you're going to ring the doorbell anyway."

"Yeah, I suppose having the target's butler announce me would defeat the purpose of a surprise attack, huh?"

"Probably," Demon agreed with a smile.

"Look, just peek in a window and see if he is home," I whispered. "May I suggest the one where all the TV sounds are coming from?"

"Smartass." Dev sidled up to the window and peeked in. Then he quickly ducked down and made his way back to us.

"There's a guy sitting on a couch in his underwear," Dev reported. "He's real hairy and has a beer belly. He also looks like he hasn't shaved or showered in ten years and he's scratching his balls."

"That is Swamp," Demon confirmed.

Dev rolled his eyes. "It would have to be. Why do I always get these ones? The guy looks like he has creepy crawlies," he complained.

"Stop griping and get in there," Demon told him.

Dev stuck his tongue out at Demon and stalked around to the front door. I followed to cover him while Demon disappeared to cover the back door. Dev crouched down and stayed low as he moved up the front steps. He stood up and bellowed, "Pizza delivery!" before kicking the door in.

Dev lunged inside and I went after him. We heard a crash and Demon yelled, "He's through the bathroom window! West side!"

Dev raced down the short hallway to the bathroom and dove through the window. The window was tiny. I don't know how he made it through. Hell, I don't know how Swamp made it through.

"He's into the woods, Bane," Dev called over his shoulder and he charged into the woods too. I decided not to risk the bathroom window. I barrelled out of the back door and took off after Dev. I did not see Demon anywhere.

I raced through the woods, ducking under branches and cursing. I lost Dev between the edge of the woods and the small creek running through it. I had forgotten how fast he could move when he wanted to.

Finally, I heard someone crashing around ahead of me. There was the distinct sound of a scuffle. Then, abruptly, all was quiet. I stood silently for a moment, listening carefully and waiting for Dev to return. No one came. I drew my blade and started moving again, careful not to make any noise in case Swamp had gotten away from Dev and was hiding nearby. I heard something stealing through the bushes a few feet away from me. I listened for a second and suddenly Demon appeared by my side from the *other direction*. I nearly jumped out of my skin. I really hate it when he does that.

"Did Dev get him?" Demon asked softly.

"I do not know," I whispered back. "He took off after Swamp and I have not been able to catch up."

"Where did you last see them?"

I explained about the noises ahead and we headed in that direction. A few minutes later, Dev appeared looking irritated and carrying Swamp's head by its greasy ponytail. He hoisted it up to show Demon.

"Execution verified," Demon said. "Where is the rest of him?"

"Back there." Dev jerked his head in that direction. "It's lying in a stream."

"Bane, come with me."

Ten minutes later Demon and I were hauling Swamp's headless body through the woods, trying to keep his insides, inside. "How come you get to carry the lightest part?" I demanded of Dev.

"Bitch, bitch, bitch," Dev said cheerfully. He held up the head and waggled it at me. "Why can't you be happy like Vervain here?" He had the head's tongue sticking out and the eyes were crossed.

I shook my head. "You are *so* weird."

"I prefer to think of myself as slightly skewed," Dev retorted.

When we reached the house, Demon and I stayed hidden in the bushes with the body and head while Dev went out to scout the area and make sure that there were no humans lurking about. A minute or two later, he came back and waved at us. Demon tossed the head to Dev. He held it in one hand and held the door open with other as Demon and I wrestled the body up the stairs. We took it back to the living room and arranged it on the sofa. Dev placed the head in Swamp's lap, its tongue still sticking out. I closed and locked the front door while Demon called the Crew. A few minutes later, we were in the SUV, driving back to Blackridge.

After a few minutes of driving in silence, I looked over at Demon. "How do we do thousands of executions," I asked my brother quietly. "And not go crazy? People are afraid of us. The supernaturals avoid us at all costs and the humans try to kill us."

Dev leaned forward and Demon glanced at me. "Are you worried about losing your mind, Bane?" my brother asked.

"No. Maia asked us last night and I have been thinking about it. How do we do what we do year after year, century after century? Dev tells jokes. You beat up on the concrete blocks in the basement. Riot has an entirely different outlet."

"Lucky bastard," Dev sighed. "Besides, not all humans hate us."

"Name one human who doesn't freak out when they find out who we are!" I argued.

"Maia."

I hesitated for a moment. "She is only half human," I grumbled. "But, what does Onyx do?" I went on. "And Morgana?"

"What do *you* do?" Demon asked.

I frowned, thinking. "The guys we kill are criminals," I said after a minute. "They are not human and that makes them far more dangerous than a human murderer. The police cannot contain them in a jail. I suppose I think of us as being a shield in a way."

Demon smiled. "The humans have the death penalty," he said. "The supernaturals have us."

CHAPTER SEVEN

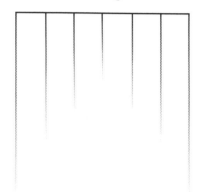

K
AZ CALLED DEMON'S CELL phone before we made it home and asked us to come and confirm the death of Bael Dagger. That was odd since Demon had told him not to bother calling for confirmation. I should have guessed that something was wrong from Demon's expression before he even pulled up in front of the public library. Dev and I gaped up at the building.

"Are you sure you've got the right address?" Dev asked.

"Unfortunately, yes," Demon said grimly as he got out of the van.

"No," I gasped, staring at him. "He must be kidding!"

Riot appeared around the side of the building, quashing that hope. "He's in the basement," he announced as we approached.

We followed Riot around the back of the building and through some hedges. There was a small, windowless door hidden there. Riot opened it and Demon went in first. The basement was in darkness and we could barely see Kaz. His skin is pure black and so is his hair and eyes. He is my height, six foot six, but he blends into the shadows easily, which makes him the perfect assassin. He stepped forward and waved a flashlight at us.

"Turn that off!" Demon ordered, protecting his eyes with his hand.

"Sorry," Kaz said snapping the light off. "I just wanted to make sure you saw me."

Demon looked irritated. "I'm not a kill first and ask questions later kind of guy," he snapped.

"Look," Kaz snapped back. "I've already had two different library workers come down here and they passed within inches of me and the body. So could you save the lecture for later and help me get him the hell out of here before one of them comes back and calls the cops."

Demon's eyes were glowing in the dark now. Kaz was very annoyed and Demon was picking it up. They were the same size and strength, and both skilled as fighters. This could end badly if they lost their tempers and decided to duke it out right then. Someone would get hurt and the other one would feel terribly guilty. I put on my mediator's hat and gently took Kaz's arm. I figured he was the least likely to take a swing at me. I locked eyes with Demon.

"Pull it together," I said quietly. "Try to remember that you are on the same team here and this is no one's fault."

For one tense moment, I wondered if they were going to go at it anyway. Then I felt Kaz relax. Tentatively, I released his arm. The blue flames receded in my brother's eyes. I almost heaved a sigh of relief.

"You are right," Demon said gruffly. Then he put his hand on Kaz's shoulder. "I am sorry for the temper tantrum. You did not deserve that."

Kaz was quiet for a minute and then he said, "Yeah, I'm sorry, too. I didn't really think that you were going to try to attack me. I was angry at Dagger and I—I didn't think about how it might affect you. I guess it's just been that kind of week."

Demon smiled ruefully. "I guess so," he agreed. Then, it was back to business. "So where is the body?"

"I stuffed it in the closet."

"How did you manage to—never mind. Maybe I don't want to know." Demon went over to look. "I need a flashlight." He held out his hand, and both Riot and Kaz moved forward to give him theirs. The three of them looked at each other and grimaced.

"Take mine." Kaz handed his light to Demon.

"Thank you." Demon shone it into the closet briefly and then turned it off. "Yes, that is definitely gross. Execution verified. It is Dagger all right, but why did you execute him down here?"

"This is where we found him," Riot explained. "We think he was lying in wait for one of the librarians to come down."

"Shit."

"At least we found him before he found one of them."

"Did you call the Crew?"

"Yes, but Nightscare wasn't answering."

Demon groaned. "That means that we will have to get the body out of here without being seen and take it to the catacombs back at the house."

"We couldn't just leave him in the closet until the Boogeys can come and get him?" Dev asked.

"And risk a librarian opening this door and finding a dead ogre in her closet?"

Dev wrinkled his nose. "Ah."

Demon turned back to Kaz. "You and Riot came out in the sedan, right?"

Kaz nodded. "But the body should fit in the trunk."

"Someone will have to keep a look out and it will take at least three of us to carry him outside," I said.

Demon nodded. "Okay. Dev, you're on watch." He tossed his cell phone to Dev. "And call Daedalus. Tell him about the execution and ask him to meet us at the house. Riot, you get the car. Bane and Kaz, grab an arm."

We hauled Dagger out of the closet. I realized then what had grossed out Demon. Kaz had folded Dagger's body into thirds to make it fit in the closet. I will spare you the details. It was not pretty. The ogre wasn't too heavy for us but he was well over ten feet tall and it was a small space. It was awkward and took some manoeuvring just to free him of the closet. Once free, the body flopped in five different directions at once. We struggled to keep him together so to speak. Moving Vervain Swamp's body had been a snap compared to this. Finally, we got the body outside and looked at the car.

I looked at Demon. "You must be joking."

Demon shrugged. "Well, here goes."

After five minutes of wrestling, folding and cursing, we stepped back breathing heavily. Even with the ogre being broken in half, we had only managed to get Dagger's head and one arm stuffed into the trunk. "This is *not* going to work," I told Demon. "He is just too damned big."

"I was afraid that you were going to say that," Demon groaned. The hedges hid us well enough, but we could not count on staying inconspicuous with a ten-foot dead ogre. "Okay, I'll bring the SUV around." He dropped Dagger's legs and stalked away.

Kaz and I dragged Dagger's body back out of the trunk so Riot could move the car out of the way. Demon came around in the SUV and backed right up to the hedges so that we didn't have to carry Dagger into view of the sidewalk. We had loaded Dagger into the back and had just shut the doors, when a police car drove up and parked at the curb.

"Damn it," Demon muttered. "This cannot get any worse."

It got worse. Todd Cooper got out of the squad car and started toward the library. Then he saw us and froze.

Dev growled and lunged toward the officer. Demon caught him by the arm. "Dev, get in the car," he ordered. "Riot, take him home. Go!"

It took both Riot and Kaz to shove Dev into the sedan. Riot hopped into the driver's seat. He was holding onto Dev by the strap of his sheath as he tore out of the parking lot. He would probably have to restrain him the whole way home or Dev might just jump out of the car and fly back to kill Cooper.

Cooper barely glanced at the car as it passed him and did not attempt to stop it. He stood staring at us and then he seemed to snap out of his daze. He walked toward us slowly, his brown eyes focused warily on Demon who was looking very irritated with one hand against the back door of the van and the other on his hip. I was willing to bet that Cooper had no trouble remembering what had happened the last time he irritated us. Riot had introduced him to a wall at high speed.

"I got a call about suspicious activity at the back of the library," Cooper began hesitantly. "What are you doing here?"

"Damn all nosy neighbours," Kaz muttered to me.

"It was an execution," Demon told Cooper bluntly.

Kaz and I gaped at him. "*Demon,*" I hissed.

Even Cooper looked stunned. "You are admitting to murdering someone?"

"No. I admitted to executing someone," Demon corrected. He flung open the back door of the SUV and Dagger's foot flopped out. "Have a look."

Cooper backed away. Scarletti's execution had only happened last night and he was front row and centre for the whole show. The image must have been fresh in his mind because he seemed to turn a little green. "Uh, no. That's okay," he said hastily. "I don't need to see whatever it is."

"It's an ogre," Demon told him anyway. "He raped a woman."

Cooper looked startled. "I thought they were fairy tale creatures."

"You would be surprised how many fairy tales are based on truth," Demon said dryly. "Red Riding Hood's granny wasn't eaten by a wolf; she was bitten by a werewolf. The troll under the bridge exists and the fairy godmother in Cinderella was not a fairy, she was a witch, and she did not turn a pumpkin into a coach."

"No?" Cooper asked curiously.

Demon shook his head. "It was a rutabaga."

"What the hell is a rutabaga?"

"It is kind of like a yellow turnip."

Cooper wrinkled his nose. "I think I liked the pumpkin idea better."

"So did Charles Perrault."

"Who?"

"Never mind."

Cooper stared at the back of the van. "So, who did the ogre rape?"

"I told you he raped a woman and beat her up. This is not the first time that this particular ogre has done this, but this time he came very close to killing his victim. An informant, the woman's boyfriend, actually, told us what had happened."

"Was it a human woman?" Cooper asked.

"Does it matter?"

"You murdered—excuse me—executed this ogre because he raped a *human*?" Cooper asked surprised.

"No," Demon answered with disgust. "It had nothing to do with whether or not the victim was supernatural or human. It had to do with Dagger raping and brutalizing another living being. We do not allow that in our world. We are not the monsters you seem to think we are."

"I'm not judging," Cooper told him hastily, holding his hands up as if to prove that he came in peace. "I—I admire that actually. I'm not condoning vigilante justice but after Scarletti—"

"That was not your fault, Todd," Demon said firmly.

"But, it doesn't seem to matter," Cooper told him with a rueful smile. "I see that your friend Dev is still quite upset with me."

"He is very protective of Maia. He loves her."

Cooper nodded. "And she loves him. Mike—" He hesitated over his friend's name. "Mike suspected that Maia's heart wasn't in their relationship anymore. Why she ever moved in with him, I don't understand. Anyway, it didn't last. They were too different. I told him that." He looked embarrassed. "And not in a very polite manner, I'm afraid. I'm sorry for that too."

"What brought on this sudden change of heart?" I demanded suspiciously.

"Go easy," Demon murmured.

Cooper looked at me and then back at my brother. "You could have killed me last night," he said to Demon. "I thought about it all night long and wondered why you didn't. You don't even like me."

"We don't have to like someone to protect him," Demon told him.

"Well," Cooper said with surprise. "Thank you but you didn't have to come to my rescue. I was a jerk. I insulted Maia and everyone in your house. I know your friends think I deserved what I got so...why?"

Demon flipped his cell phone open and dialled. He held the phone up. We could hear the faint ring as Demon's cell called someone.

Suddenly, across the parking lot, we heard a sound. We all looked over at Cooper. He was ringing. Slowly, he put his hand on the cell phone strapped to his belt. He took it out and shut it off. He and Demon stared at each other across the parking lot.

"That is the number of the person who called us to come home the night Kit and Kaz were attacked," Demon said quietly. "That phone call got us home in time to save Kit's life."

Kaz and I gaped at Cooper in amazement. "That was *you?*" I said.

Before he could respond, the radio on Cooper's hip squawked. "Cooper here."

"*Report,*" the radio demanded.

Cooper hesitated and looked at us. "Library's all clear," he answered. "The door is locked," Kaz quickly locked the door. "And there's no sign of any intruders."

Demon grinned at him and waved at the rest of us to climb into the back of the SUV. He got in the driver's door and started the vehicle. Demon nodded at Cooper as we drove away.

"*That* is why I don't go insane," Demon told me quietly. "Sometimes, we get thanked for being who we are and doing what we do."

That was good enough for me.

Daedalus arrived at the house at the same time as we did. He got out of his car and followed us around to the back of the house. We flung open the doors of the SUV as he joined us. He gave the body a passing glance and then focused on my brother.

"Damn it, Fechín," Daedalus roared. "I don't care that you executed Dagger but sometimes I'd like to know about it *before* it happens!"

We left Demon to deal with Daedalus. There were times when I was glad that he was the leader and not me. Riot came out and helped Kaz and I wrestle Dagger's body through the back door and into the catacombs. Dev met us in the basement and had one of the rooms already unlocked. "In here."

We dragged the body into the windowless room. I dropped my end of the body. Kaz and Riot looked at me. "What are you doing?" Kaz asked.

"We cannot put the body in the closet." I gestured toward the small closet. "It will block the portal that Nightscare uses. We'll have to leave it out here on the floor."

Riot looked at Kaz. "That's fine with me. I've wrestled with this damn body enough for one day."

They dropped Dagger onto the floor. Dev propped open the closet door so that the Boogey wouldn't have to struggle to keep the door open while carrying a body as big as he was. Then we went back outside. The SUV was gone and so was Daedalus. However, when we went into the house, we found Daedalus in the library sipping whiskey with Dev's mother curled up on the sofa next to him. Dev sat down in a chair across from them, scowling. Demon was filling out the paperwork that officially put Dagger on our list...a bit late, but better late than never.

Maggie Xander is a drop dead gorgeous woman. She has a lean, spectacular figure that curves in all the right places. She has long blond hair and auburn coloured eyes. Like me, she is able to shapeshift to appear to be what she is not. In Maggie's case, she turns her red daemon skin to pale skin, or dark skin, or whatever the human male wants her to look like. For the moment, however, Maggie looked like herself.

"It must be such hard work to be a Satana chief," Maggie purred in her low sultry voice, her fingers trailing along the back of the sofa.

Dev rolled his eyes, but I had never seen a succubus in action. My parents were very discreet when Demon and I were growing up. Riot doesn't even have to try to seduce anyone. Women just seek him out without any effort on his part. So watching Maggie go to work was intriguing.

"Well, it has its moments," Daedalus was saying. He looked completely bowled over. "You said that you were a succubus?" He was practically drooling.

"Hmm," she purred and let her fingers trail along the back of the sofa just behind his head. "So, are you married, Chief?"

"Uh, n—no," Daedalus stammered. "M—my wife passed many years ago."

Maggie nodded. "So did my husband."

"You're a widow?" Daedalus asked, looking brighter. Then, as if realizing that he sounded far too chipper, his expression became sombre. "I'm sorry."

"That's all right. He passed away some four hundred years ago." She flicked her fingers as if dismissing John Xander. Well, no one expected her to mourn the man after four hundred years. She smiled. "Do you have any children, Chief?"

"Please call me Daedalus. I have one son, Darkfist."

"I have two sons. You already know Dev. Damien is my younger son."

Demon rose and held out the paperwork. "Here is the order."

Daedalus reluctantly got up from the sofa to cross the room and take it. "Thanks, Fechín. Next time, let me know about the execution ahead of time, eh?"

"Sure, Daedalus," Demon agreed easily. Daedalus knew that he was lying through his teeth, but it was easier to pretend that Demon *would* call him next time than try to argue about it.

Daedalus set down his glass as he stood and turned to Maggie. "It was a pleasure to meet you, Mrs. Xander."

"Please call me Maggie." *Or anything else that you like*, her eyes said. She gave him an inviting smile. "It's been a great pleasure to meet you as well, Daedalus. I hope we'll meet again soon."

"Oh. Ah." Daedalus stammered his way out of the library and the front door.

As soon as he was gone, Dev turned to his mother. "If you marry him, can I call him Daddy?" he demanded sarcastically.

She rolled her eyes as she got up. "Really, Dev," she laughed lightly. "It was just a bit of light flirting! There's nothing wrong with keeping a hand in, is there?"

"Depends on where *his* hands end up."

"Sometimes, you act like *I'm* the child!"

"If the shoe fits, Mom. And I suppose you hardly noticed the puddle of drool at your feet."

"I'm delighted that you think your mother is still drool worthy." Maggie laughed and gave her scowling son a kiss on top of his head. "He was a perfect gentleman the whole time. Now stop fussing. I can handle any man."

"Just as long as *they* aren't handling *you*."

She was still laughing as she left the room and Dev shook his head. "Light flirting? Is she serious? I'm surprised Daedalus didn't trip over his own tongue on the way to the door."

"Does your mom flirting with Daedalus bother you?" I asked.

"Not really," Dev admitted. "She hasn't really shown much interest in anyone since my dad died. I mean, she's flirted and yeah, she's had some relationships but nothing serious."

"So you wouldn't have a problem with your mother dating my uncle?" Riot asked grinning.

"Hell no, I like Daedalus. I wouldn't even mind if Mom fell in love with him and wanted to marry him," Dev told him. His nose wrinkled. "But can you imagine having Darkfist as a stepbrother?"

We looked at each other and grimaced. "Eww!"

CHAPTER EIGHT

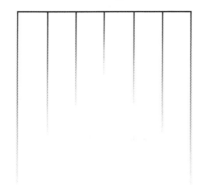

"**B**ANE, HOLD IT."

I was starting up the stairs when Demon called my name. I paused, hiding my grimace as I turned back to my brother. "That is the second time in two days—"

"I know," he said. "I'm sorry, but I wanted to tell you that we have to go back out tonight."

I frowned. "What now? We have terminated all of our targets, have we not?"

Demon inclined his head slightly. "We have. However, before you and the others came upstairs Daedalus gave me the name of another informant with information about the rogue vampires."

"That is odd," I said, surprised. "Usually, when one informant ends up dead, it deters the others from coming forward."

Demon shrugged. "Daedalus said he was contacted by someone who wishes to meet and talk to us."

"And this informant knows who the rogue sovereign is?"

"He did not say," Demon admitted. "But Daedalus did say that the informant is a vampire."

I gaped. "A vampire is going to rat out one of his own? That is a good way to end up dead."

"Not if we get to him first so let's haul ass."

I sighed and came back down the stairs. "Oh, fine. So where and when are we meeting with him?"

"He gave me Vlad's address. It is a townhouse near Banks Street."

"*Vlad?*" I repeated, grimacing. "Why wouldn't he just come to us? Why go through Daedalus?"

"I didn't ask," Demon admitted.

"And didn't really care," I suggested.

"No. If this vampire has information that leads us to the rogues then I don't care who it comes through."

"Okay," I said. "What time do you want to meet this Vlad character?"

"Be ready to go by seven."

That evening, when Demon and I met in the front foyer, I was surprised to find that my brother was still wearing jeans. I have never known my brother not to be properly equipped for a mission, even if it was not an official hunt. He grimaced when I suggested that he should change into black leather since blood does not wash out of jeans very well.

"I hate leather," he complained.

"Why?" Dev asked curiously. He had come downstairs with us and was lounging casually against the railing. "It's not like it's too hot or that it chafes."

"Leather always reminds me of Lilith."

I blinked and then Dev and I began to laugh. "I had forgotten about her," Dev said.

"How the hell could you forget *her?*" Demon grumbled.

Lilith BloodMoon is a fairy obsessed with leather and Demon. Lilith is not her real name. It is actually something less intense like Lilliana Dazzle. Most faeries name their children according to what their personalities would be. Either Lilith's parents had screwed up big time or perhaps it was just wishful thinking on their part because Lilith's personality doesn't really fit the name. Eventually it became apparent that she was one of the faeries called banshees. Anyway, she had eventually left faerie, sick of their perky, everything-is-wonderful attitudes and came out into the real world, as she put it, "to play with the big boys." She met Demon, who is the biggest, most dangerous boy on the block. Being who he is, she was thrilled.

The relationship had not lasted very long. Demon had become tired of being Lilith's play toy and suggested that she move along. She did not take kindly to the suggestion and for a few months, the love-struck banshee dogged his every step. After a few months, she grew tired of playing the game by herself and moved on to another supernatural who shared her obsessions, at least for the leather.

"She drove us nuts for nearly a year," Demon complained.

"No," Dev grinned. "She drove *you* nuts for a year. To the rest of us she was entertainment."

Demon rolled his eyes. "Give me ten minutes to change," he said grudgingly.

Five minutes later, he was back downstairs, looking very irritated but wearing the leather. I grinned at him. He pointed a finger at me. "Shut up," he said.

I held my hands up in surrender. "I didn't say a word."

Demon drove, of course, and this time we took one of his beloved cars. We both sat up straight, our wings touching. "So tell me something about this Vlad character," I said.

"You mean besides the fact that he has a fondness for unoriginal names?" Demon shrugged. "According to Daedalus, he has not been a vampire for very long and he is not affiliated with Hadrian's kiss."

That was a surprise. "I thought all vampires had to be associated with the local kiss."

He raised an eyebrow at me. "I am not."

"Yes, but *you* are Wrath. I am going on the assumption that Vlad is not a high-powered vampire."

Demon gave a short, sarcastic snort. "Hardly."

"So what is his story?" I asked.

"He called Daedalus this afternoon and suggested that he may have some information that we need," Demon told me.

"But he would not say what the information was."

"No."

I shook my head. "Why do I get the feeling that Vlad is up to something?"

Demon shrugged. "The fact is that Vlad hinted to Daedalus that he has been a naughty boy and has done something that might get him on the list. He thinks Vlad wants to make a trade—his life in exchange for information."

"Vlad actually thought you would go for that?" I asked. When Demon did not immediately respond, I stared at him. "Demon, tell me you are not seriously considering letting a target escape just so you can get a lead on the rogue vampires!"

"A *potential* target," Demon corrected. "Before you give yourself an aneurysm, let me tell you what I found out about him. Apparently, there is a young woman going about claiming that Vlad had attacked her and turned her into a vampire."

"Uh oh," I said.

"That was my first thought too. That is until I visited the young woman and she gave me this photo of Vlad." He reached down between the driver's seat and the console and came up with a photograph.

"Hold it. She had a photo of her attacker?" Demon gave me a pointed look and I grimaced. "They were in a relationship, weren't they?"

"What do you think?"

"I think I hate post-vampire regret." I studied the photograph of a smiling young man with short blond hair and friendly blue eyes. "He does not look much like a rogue vampire."

"One could say the same about Hadrian."

"This is true," I said. "So Vlad is going to trade information about the rogue sovereign so you won't execute him for something he didn't do anyway?" I gave my brother a look of approval. "That is sneaky, Fechín. I am so proud."

He grinned at me.

We arrived at Vlad's house just after sundown, the usual rising time for vampires. We would probably catch Vlad just getting out of his coffin. Demon went to the front door, knocked on the door, and announced himself. There was no response from inside. Demon came down the steps.

"Wait here," he said.

Demon disappeared around the back of the house and a few minutes later, he returned looking very irritated. "He is not here," he told me.

"Do we wait here or call another time?" I asked.

"We shall wait," my brother growled.

Uh oh.

Demon is not the most patient of men. My father always said that of the two of us, I was the more easy-going. However, after twenty minutes of waiting, even my good nature was starting to fray.

"Now what do we do?" I demanded. "He is obviously not coming home and we cannot wait here forever." I hesitated. "Well, technically, we *could* but—"

"Let's give him a few minutes more," Demon suggested. "Then, we'll go find his sorry ass and kick it for making us wait."

"Oh, goody!" I cheered as we went around to the front door again. "Road trip!"

Demon gave me an amused look. "*Goody?*"

I shrugged and grinned back. Then I blinked. There was a little old man standing on the stoop of the townhouse next door. He was dressed in a brown robe, dingy with age and wear, and slippers in much the same condition.

"Well, hell-o, human servant," I muttered under my breath as Demon came down the stairs to join me.

"Are you serious?" Demon whispered back. "If you were a hip, young vampire would that guy be your first choice as a human servant?"

The old man tottered toward us and I could see my brother's point. He could barely hold himself upright let alone fight off vampire hunters.

"You boys looking for Vlad?" the old man asked.

"Yes, sir," Demon said moving toward him with a friendly smile. "Do you know where we can find him?"

The old man chuckled. "Not specifically. I know of a couple of young women that he sees on a regular basis. He could be with any one of them. Vlad doesn't have much trouble with the girls, if you know what I mean."

Demon's jaw tightened but it was quick. He kept his expression friendly and as non-threatening as possible. "Do you happen to know which of the young ladies he might have spent the night with?"

"You mean the day?" the old man startled us by asking. He nodded. "Yes, I know what Vlad is. It isn't a very common name among *humans*." Even the old man sounded disappointed by Vlad's lack of originality.

"That is not his real name?" I asked.

The old man shook his head. "His real name is Walter. Guess that's why he chose to go by Vlad."

I didn't think it was much of an improvement, but kept my opinion to myself.

"I know he's not supposed to tell anyone," the old man continued concerned by our grave expressions. "But he's a real nice kid. He helps me get my groceries sometimes and fixes things when they break down around here, which they always do because the owner is a scumbag. I can't afford to pay to get the things fixed myself so Vlad helps out."

"I see," Demon said quietly. "Well, if Vlad comes home would you be so kind as to give me a call?" He handed the old man a card that simply had a number on it. "Tell him it's very important."

"Okay." The old man took it in his gnarled fingers and slid the card into the pocket of his robe.

As we walked away, the old man disappeared back into his townhouse. "Vlad the Helpful Vampire," I murmured to Demon.

"Something is not right about this," Demon responded. "How did the old man know what we were?"

"Perhaps it was a lucky guess." Then I shook my head. "Doubtful. It is more likely that he is a sensitive."

Demon shrugged. "That is certainly possible or perhaps Vlad warned him that we were coming...Hey!"

Demon was glaring at someone ahead of us. I turned and there was a short, thin young man standing at the end of the street. It was Vlad. He stood frozen to the spot. Better late than never, I suppose.

Demon pointed at him. Vlad flinched. "Stay right where you are," Demon called out. "Don't make us do this the hard way!"

So, of course, Vlad ran.

Demon cursed. "He is going to make us do this the hard way."

"He is just making it more fun," I told him.

He gave me a sideways look.

"For us," I added.

He grinned. "Game on then, brother."

It would not take us long to catch up to Vlad but we were not in any hurry to snag him. It was not an exceptionally busy street but there were still people about and call to the police in this neighbourhood would bring the cops fast. It was in our best interest to get Vlad somewhere more private so we could discuss things. Like *why* we shouldn't execute his ass, for example.

We chased Vlad around the corner and down the side street. He would not be able to outrun us even going as fast as a vampire can and they can move very fast. We jogged along at a safe distance so it wouldn't look as though we were chasing him. We were just two brothers out for a jog together...in leather pants and long leather coats. Nothing to see here. As identical twins, we attract a lot of attention, even when we are dressed somewhat normally. Anyone who is a twin will know what I mean.

Demon soon tired of the game. "Fly over the building," he told me as soon as we were clear of humans in the street. "Block his access to the next corner and drive him back toward me."

I nodded and darted down the next alleyway to drop my coat. I gave my wings a shake to straighten the feathers and then leaped into the air, wings flapping. Once I caught an updraft, I was able to soar overhead with less effort. I quickly spotted Vlad getting ready to veer around a corner to the right. He probably had no clue that he had been running in circles. The thing about a terrified person is that they tend to do very stupid things. Hollywood is not far off with their slasher movies. Frightened people trip over things as they run and they go into the basement by themselves in a haunted house with a killer on the loose. It is not that they are unintelligent, but because as terrified as they are, they always think they can escape. Vlad was one of those people.

I soared overhead, scanning the ground for Vlad. I didn't see him and I didn't see Demon. I frowned. Where the hell could they have gone? I circled around the block and finally spotted Demon running down an alleyway toward another side street. I followed and landed behind him. My feet hit the ground running. I caught up to my brother.

"I'm sorry," I said as I ran alongside him. "I lost him."

Demon nodded. "He must have ducked into a building. You start with the buildings in the area where we last saw him in case he doubled back. I will check the ones further up."

I nodded and ran back the other way. The first couple of doors were unlocked. I ran through the buildings, checking every possible hiding spot, but did not find Vlad. I moved on to the next street, methodically working my way back toward Vlad's townhouse. Vlad had not gone into any of the buildings. Soon I was heading back down the street where he lived. That is where Demon caught up with me.

"He could not have been so stupid as to go back home," I said to my brother as we jogged toward Vlad's house. We stopped and stared at the front door of the townhouse. It was standing wide open. "Then again..."

Demon didn't speak. He drew his weapon softly and gestured for me to follow him. I drew my sword and we quietly slipped inside the house.

It was dark inside. Vlad had not turned on any lights, but then he probably didn't need them. It was, after all, his house and vampires can see very well in the dark. It helps them sneak up on their prey. If we had been human, we could have walked right by him and not noticed it. However, we were not human and furthermore, Demon was a vampire too. I wondered if Vlad had thought of that.

Demon looked back at me and all I saw was the flash of his eyes. I saw the silhouette of his hand as he pointed toward the stairs. I nodded.

Demon had scarcely placed one foot on the bottom step when suddenly we heard an ear-splitting shriek coming from the second floor and something that sounded like a fight. We did not pause to figure out what was going on. We just ran like hell up the stairs.

The upstairs was also in darkness but we could hear crashing at the end of the hallway. I wasn't sure which room it was coming from but there weren't that many from which to choose. Demon wrenched the first door open. It was a closet. I opened the door next to it and saw a window. Someone was climbing out of it.

"Hey!" I yelled and raced into the room, thinking that it was Vlad. I went about three steps and fell over something, landing on my face in something warm and wet. My foot hit something soft and fleshy.

"Uh oh," I said as Demon ran past me and leaped out the window.

I got up and went back toward the door of the room. I felt along the wall until my hand hit a light switch. The room flooded with light and I blinked trying to adjust my eyes to the sudden brightness. I turned to look back to see what I had tripped over, already half-suspecting that I knew what it was. I was right.

Vlad lay in the middle of the floor in a pool of blood. There was a gaping wound in his chest where his heart should have been. I had a sinking feeling that I knew where the heart was.

"Aw, shit," I muttered, lifting my foot and looking down. I was standing on what appeared to be the remains of Vlad's heart. I grimaced and began searching the house, sword in hand in case Vlad's attacker had not left the premises. However, I had the feeling that unless the attacker was crazy, he or she was long gone. I checked the upstairs. There was a second bedroom and a bathroom. I checked every closet. I moved downstairs and found the kitchen. I was leaving the kitchen to check the living room we had passed on the way in when my cell phone suddenly went off scaring the shit out of me.

I had no doubt about who was calling me. I held the phone up to my ear. "Fechín, where are you?"

"Chasing shadows," he sighed.

"You didn't find the murderer either?" *Damn*, I thought. *He's good if he can elude Demon. Or desperate.*

"No. I take it our boy *is* dead?"

"No doubt about it. His heart is on the floor about three feet from his body. I would say that makes him dead."

Demon was quiet for a moment and then he said, "His heart was ripped out of his chest?"

"Yes."

"Are there any other marks on him?"

I frowned. "I didn't notice any. Why?"

"I'm not sure yet."

Knowing my brother, he would tell me what it was that he suspected when he was damned good and ready and not before. Asking questions would get me nowhere. "It must have been good information if someone was willing to kill him before he could tell us," I said. "Do you think he knew something about the rogue sovereign?"

"It seems most likely."

"Damn."

"Yes." Demon paused and then said, "He cannot have gone far. I was right behind him. I'm going to search the houses in the area."

I gaped. "Are you crazy? How are you going to do that without getting caught?"

He didn't answer. "Call Nightscare and tell him to come and pick up Vlad," he went on.

"We're not calling it in to Daedalus?" I asked, surprised.

"No." He hung up.

Grumbling, I dialled Nightscare's number and gave him the message. I shoved Vlad's body into the closet in case anyone came into the house looking for him. His neighbour might have seen him come home...

His neighbour.

On my second attempt, I reached my brother. "Brandon?" he said when he answered.

"Yes. Listen, I was just thinking about the neighbour. I am going to go and talk to him. Maybe he saw something."

"Good idea," my brother said. "Once you're done call me, and I'll let you know where I am."

"See you soon."

I closed my phone and went back downstairs cautiously. It was unlikely that

Vlad's assailant would return to the house, but I was not going to count on it. Strange things happen and I have seen almost all of them in my time.

I went next door to the old man's house and knocked on the door. There was no answer for about five minutes and I was getting worried that whoever had killed Vlad had already done away with his elderly neighbour. I was about to crash the door in to check when I heard the distinct rattle of a chain being removed and the door opened a crack. I saw a single grey eye peer out at me suspiciously. "Yes?" asked a creaky voice.

"Mr. Harrison?" I said, glancing at the mailbox for his name.

"Yes?"

"My name is Brandon. I was here earlier with my brother..."

"The vampire. I remember."

I gaped at him for a moment. Wow. He really was a sensitive if he picked up that without Demon even flashing fang. "Um, right. Look, we were wondering something. Was anyone else here looking for Vlad today?"

Mr. Harrison scratched at the few remaining grey hairs on his head, frowning. "Well, now. Let me think..."

It took about ten minutes for the old man to get to it, but the short answer was no, Mr. Harrison had not seen anyone hanging around Vlad's house today. I sighed. "Well, thanks anyway," I said, turning away.

"Wait." Mr. Harrison caught my coat sleeve. I looked back into his sad grey eyes. "Vlad is dead, isn't he?"

"What makes you say that, Mr. Harrison?"

He pursed his lips and gave me a pointed stare. "Let's cut through the crap, okay? I know who you are and I know what you do. You just came out of Vlad's house and, in spite of the fact that you tried to clean it off; you have blood on your boots."

I glanced down, frowning. I could see a small smear of blood on the toe of my boot. I grimaced. "Bloody hell."

"Since you're asking if I saw anyone hanging around Vlad's house I am assuming that he is dead and that you are not the one who killed him."

"No, sir, we did not," I said gently.

He took a deep breath. "But, you will find out who did?"

"Yes, sir, we will."

Mr. Harrison studied me for a moment. "I believe you will. Thank you," he replied. He paused and looked up at me with tears in his eyes. "You know, Vlad was a good boy, no matter what he was, and he—he cared about me."

I nodded. He closed the door softly and I walked down the steps to the sidewalk. I glanced back at his house, saddened. Vlad was all Mr. Harrison had and now he was gone. Who was going to look after the old man now? I stared at the house for a moment longer and then, mentally added Mr. Harrison's name to the long list of people under the Deadlies' personal care. It was the least we could do.

CHAPTER NINE

I DREW MY CELL phone out of my pocket to call Demon and tell him to send someone around with some groceries for the old man the following day when a movement in the shadows in the space between Vlad's house and Mr. Harrison's caught my eye. I continued to dial, pretending not to notice but I turned my head slightly, watching and waiting. It was a vampire, but not one familiar to me so it could not be Hadrian or Darkmoon.

A second later, the energy became familiar as my brother answered the phone. "Fechín."

"Come back to Vlad's house," I said curtly and snapped the phone closed.

The shadow moved again. This time it was coming toward me. I was not about to let it get any closer. "Tanith, that is close enough," I snapped.

The shadow paused and then the darkness parted like a veil allowing her to step into the light. The last time I saw her she was wearing an old-fashioned black dress. She changed her style since then and was now wearing tight black jeans and a tight fitting, off the shoulder black top. It looked good on her. Her long black hair curled loosely around her pale shoulders. Her violet eyes gleamed as she gazed at me. She was beautiful. I was glad my brother was not here to see her. "Demon," she greeted me with a smile.

"You have a lot of nerve showing up here," I told her. Then it occurred to me that she was oddly close to the murder scene. "What are you doing here anyway?"

"I wanted to see you. I *needed* to see you," Tanith said. "I wanted to be alone with you without your brother glaring daggers at me."

I glared at her. "I should think he has a damned good reason for hating you."

She was drifting a little closer to me as I spoke. I drew my weapon, but she stayed out of my reach. Pity.

"What are you doing here?" I asked again. "And don't give me that bullshit about wanting to talk to me. How the hell would you know that I was here?"

She smiled slightly. "You are so suspicious, my love. Very well. I was looking for someone else and saw you. I thought I would take the opportunity."

"For whom were you looking?"

She laughed. "I have missed you so much! I love how you talk; how you look…"

"Really."

"You know it," she said. "And I know it. If only you would stop being an Enforcer for two seconds."

"It is who I am."

"Who you are is a man who loves me and whom I love. How can you have forgotten what we were to each other?"

The trouble was I didn't think Demon *had* forgotten and that is what scared me. I had to get rid of her before my brother showed up. I still had my blade in my hand but without any real evidence that she was a rogue, I could not get rid of her permanently as much as I would love to.

I shook my head. "If you loved him as you claim you would have known that I am not Fechín."

Tanith started and then gave a long, drawn-out hiss. Her lovely features twisted into an angry snarl. "You think you are funny?"

"That's right, Tanith. I think that turning my brother into a vampire is bloody hilarious," I told her and took a step forward, my blade still in my hand. "Come here and I'll show you just how funny I think it is."

"You would dare to threaten me?" The wind came up with her voice and whipped my hair around my face.

"Turn it off, Tanith."

Tanith started and the wind died off as suddenly as it came. We both turned as Demon strode toward us, weapon in hand, eyes burning with fury. "Are you threatening my brother?" he demanded.

Tanith took a step backward. "No, Demon. I would never—"

"That is good," Demon interrupted. "Now, what the hell are you doing near the scene of a murder?"

Either she was a good actor or she had not known about the murder. She looked as though he had knocked the breath out of her. "Oh my god, Fechín!" she gasped. "Who—who was murdered?"

"A vampire by the name of Vlad," Demon said coldly. "Ever heard of him?"

Before she could answer, Demon's cell phone chirped, signalling that he had a text message. He flipped it open and checked the message. He looked up again and cursed.

Irritation abruptly forgotten, I asked, "What is it?"

Demon nodded in Tanith's direction. I looked back at her and cursed too. She was gone.

"I should have killed her when I had the chance," I snarled.

"Never mind Tanith," he said. "We have bigger problems." He held up the phone. The screen showed that he had sixteen calls from the same number.

I looked at him. "Who is that?"

"Maryrose," he told me. "That is the young lady that Vlad turned."

"She called you sixteen times?" I said, amazed. "Why?"

"She was probably trying to call me off," Demon said with a shrug.

I glanced up at Vlad's house, hoping that the Boogeys had removed his body by this time. "You were the least of this guy's worries."

"Apparently," my brother replied, dryly. "Now I think we had better get over to Maryrose's house immediately."

"What is the big hurry?" I asked.

"Before things went bad between them, Maryrose and Vlad were lovers," Demon said grimly. "And I hope for our sake that he told her what he knows and for hers that the murderer hasn't thought of that too."

Demon called Serkan while we were en route to Maryrose's house and explained what was going on. Serkan was to get her to safety when we were done with her.

Nothing sucks more than having to tell someone that her loved one was murdered. We have not had to do this very often. Usually the Satana takes care of that. We're executioners not police. I think Maryrose must have known that something was wrong when she opened the door and saw us. I sat by while my brother told her what had happened. I had to look away when she collapsed on his shoulder, sobbing as if her heart would break. Pissed off as she was with him, she loved Vlad, and his death hurt.

When she was calm, Demon questioned her about Vlad and anything he might have said to her that could lead us to his killer. Unfortunately, she knew nothing helpful. She and Vlad were not on speaking terms for the last few weeks. Serkan arrived a few minutes after we did. He waited while she packed her things. Demon and I left.

We had been driving for a few minutes when I realized that we were not heading in the direction of home. I was slouched in my seat, half-asleep, and now I sat up straight and looked around. "Uh, Demon? Where are we going now?"

He turned a corner. "Back to the werewolf bar."

"Why?" I asked, puzzled.

"To let them know that Swamp is dead."

I was not certain of his motive there. We often re-visited victims after executing their attackers. We wanted to let them know that the person who had hurt them or killed their loved one was dead. I did not understand why Demon thought that the werewolves would care. Other than knowing that Swamp couldn't come after them for ratting him out, his death wouldn't concern them. I seriously doubted that Demon cared whether these werewolves would sleep easier tonight or not.

"Why exactly are we going to the bar to tell them that Swamp is dead?" I asked finally.

Now Demon looked at me. "Because I want to remind them what the penalty is for breaking the law."

Ah. Now *that* made more sense. "Why, Demon," I grinned. "That would be... us. I thought you had already done your good deed for the day sending Serkan to help Maryrose get out of Blackridge."

He grinned back. "Good deed, my ass! This is purely for the fun of it!"

I began to laugh. Several minutes later, we pulled into the exact same spot as we had earlier in the day. I crossed the road with my brother, but he caught my arm as I reached for the door. "I go in first, Bane," he said.

I nodded and held the door as he stepped into the building first. As much as he was going to enjoy watching the werewolves twist in the wind, he was not about to allow me or anyone else to take the risk of walking into a potentially dangerous situation. Wrath is first through the door. Always.

As I stepped in behind him, the bar's patrons had already stopped what they were doing and were silently staring at us. I moved up to stand beside Demon. No one spoke. This time, we needed no introduction. They were all staring at us. Demon waited for a minute, letting them stew, wondering why we were there and who we were after.

"I thought you might be interested in the outcome of the hunt for Swamp," Demon said at last.

The werewolves looked at each other. There was a mixture of relief and fear in their eyes. They were glad we had not come there for them, but they were afraid to know what had happened to Swamp.

"My guess is that they are well aware of what the outcome is," I said casually.

The bartender, a different one this time, obviously knew of our earlier visit. He was younger and shorter than the first bartender and paler. He had pale hair, pale eyes, and very pale skin, but I figured that the skin colour was due to the Enforcers showing up on his shift.

"Is he..." the bartender began. Then he trailed off. He cleared his throat and tried again. "That is, is Swamp...you know."

"Terminated," Demon said flatly.

The bartender turned even paler if that was possible. I was fascinated. The only person that I knew of who could do that was Dev. He is a partial shapeshifter and this boy was werewolf. At least I was almost certain that he was. Over the years, Demon, Riot, and I have gained enough experience so that we can just look at someone and know whether he is a supernatural and what kind. The other Deadlies are slightly younger and usually correct in their guesses, but they still have not encountered all the supernatural species out there.

Demon turned his attention from the bartender back to the other werewolves. "Don't bother going out to look for the remains."

I would think my brother's comment odd if I had not seen the expressions on the faces of the werewolves. There was no mistaking it. They were thinking of fresh meat. Had they met Swamp? There was nothing fresh about him even before he was killed, but clearly some of them were considering going to Swamp's house and disposing of the body themselves. I shuddered.

"The Boogeys took him already," Demon told them.

Then, my wicked side, the side I share with my brother, kicked in. "They might have left the head," I spoke up.

He paused, looking thoughtful, but I saw the gleam in his eyes as he took my cue and ran with it. "That is a possibility," he said, mildly. "The Boogeys don't really care for werewolf flesh though I know they usually make the brains into pudding. I understand that it is really very tasty."

Someone gagged and bolted for the washroom.

Demon smiled coldly. "Just a friendly warning," he said. "There is a price to pay for breaking the law and we *always* collect."

Dead silence followed this announcement. Satisfied that we had made our point, Demon walked to the bar and leaned on it. He pointed a finger at the bartender. The boy hesitated and Demon sighed. "Don't make me come over there and get you."

The boy almost jumped out of his skin and hastily moved over to where we were waiting. "What is your name?" Demon asked.

"W—what?" the kid stammered.

"*What... is... your...name?*" Demon snarled.

"Sean."

"Have you worked here for long?"

"About a week, sir."

That made Demon and me smile. "Sean, let me give you some advice…free," Demon said firmly. "Quit this job right now before it is too late. These animals will chew you up and spit you out. I would hate to see you end up a name on our List or worse yet…a victim."

Sean took a deep breath. "I don't know if Linus will let me quit in the middle of my shift."

Demon gave a short laugh. "He will let you," Demon assured him. "Don't worry about that."

Demon was right of course. Linus accepted Sean's resignation with no problem at all. In fact, he seemed more than eager to get rid of the kid. It might have been more about getting rid of the two Enforcers that Sean had standing at his back. He certainly didn't seem pleased to see us in his fine establishment again. Linus even coughed up Sean's last paycheck in order to expedite the process.

Once Sean gathered all of his belongings, we walked the kid out of the bar and down to the bus stop.

"Good-bye, Sean," I said. "Do not let us see you in this part of town again."

"No, sir," Sean gasped as the bus pulled up.

The doors of the bus swung open and the kid bolted up the stairs two at a time. We watched him walk down the aisle and park himself on a seat. He slouched down, huddling on the seat. He couldn't have been more than seventeen. Looking at the kid's frightened face, I wondered who the bastard was who had bitten him. He deserved to die.

"We should have asked," I growled.

Demon did not need to ask what I meant. "He would not have told us."

I looked at him. "You think he knew his attacker?"

Demon did not answer.

As the bus pulled away from the curb, Demon took a deep breath and grinned at me. "Well, we made someone puke and probably saved a kid from becoming a future name on our list."

"It has been a good day," I agreed as we started across the road.

CHAPTER TEN

BEFORE WE EVEN REACHED the car, something small darted past us going the other way. We stopped short and stared at the building into which it disappeared. "What the hell was that?" I demanded.

"It appeared to be something small and blue." Demon sounded strange. I glanced at him. He was staring up into the sky. "Quite possibly it was edible."

I followed his gaze. Several dark shadow creatures with glowing eyes sailed over our heads. "I had forgotten about the Red Eyes."

They melted through the wall of the building after the small blue creature. "I think it is time to find out what the Red Eyes are up to, don't you?" Demon asked.

We followed the Red Eyes and their potential victim to the building. Demon tried the door and found it locked.

"How did whatever that thing was get inside if the door is locked?" I asked. Then I answered my own question. "It was a gnome."

Gnomes are definitely small and, considering the colouring of the creature, this one was probably a water gnome. Still, they can lock and unlock doors without keys. It is how they get into houses to perform small tasks of good deeds for the humans. They are one of the few truly good supernatural creatures. We have never had to execute a gnome.

"Poor little guy." I frowned. "What is he doing in Blackridge? Cities make gnomes claustrophobic."

"If we rescue him before the Red Eyes eat him you can ask him," Demon answered.

As he yanked his blade from its sheath, blue flames leapt in his eyes. I felt my own eyes flare in answer and I pulled my weapon as well. We were in hunt mode. With a grim expression, he turned and kicked in the door. The lock, a deadbolt, gave away easily under his strength. Apparently, Wrath had decided to dispense with subtlety.

Even though we see well in the dark, the Red Eyes *are* darkness so they were difficult to spot immediately. I knew enough to look for the eyes instead of the forms and found them easily. I did not see the gnome anywhere. It seemed as though the Red Eyes were searching for something and so I hoped the gnome had hidden and that we were not already too late.

I expected Demon to say something, to call out first, but I should have known better. One second he was standing next to me, and the next he had one of the Red Eyes pinned to the floor, his blade pressed against its throat.

"Don't you move," Demon hissed. I knew that he was speaking to the Red Eyes but I froze anyway. Then I felt silly and glanced at Demon to make certain that he hadn't seen me. He was still snarling at the creature pinned beneath him.

"What are you doing here?" he demanded.

"Nothing!" one of the other Red Eyes protested in a high-pitched whine that made me cover my ears.

Demon pressed on his captive's throat making him choke. "You do not want to lie to me."

The Red Eyes stared down at their trapped comrade. I had no idea that you could choke Red Eyes. It was good information to have for future reference. I was curious to see if Demon meant to kill it to make a point. I admit that I was also curious to know whether the shadowy creature would turn blue through lack of oxygen.

"Where is it?" Demon asked softly. The Red Eyes looked at each other. "*Where is it?*" he snarled making them all jump.

"We haven't found it yet," one of the Red Eyes admitted reluctantly.

The other Red Eyes began to howl and scream at their friend in protest. The sound grated on my nerves like fingernails on a blackboard. "Enough," I bellowed.

I backhanded the closest Red Eyes and sent it sprawling across the floor. "The next one to do that is the first one in line to lose his head!"

The Red Eyes fell silent and I caught sight of my brother's amused grin before it disappeared. "Thank you, Bane." He turned back to the Red Eye that he had pinned to the ground. "What were you planning to do to the gnome?"

The Red Eye made a guttural sound and Demon eased up on its throat so that it could speak. "We were just fooling with him!" it whined hoarsely. "We weren't going to hurt him!"

Before Demon could reply, the small creature popped out of a drain in the floor. "That is a big lie!" the gnome squeaked shrilly. The drain cover was still on his head as he climbed out of the drain. He removed it and replaced it over the hole. He hurried over to stand next to me, out of reach of the hissing Red Eyes.

"They said that they were going to eat my flesh and that they would cut my heart out last so that they could feed while I was still alive!" The gnome gazed up at me with indignant dark blue eyes.

I could not see the Red Eyes' expressions so I could not tell their reactions to the story, but I was certain that the gnome was telling the truth. They are not liars. I waited for Demon's signal. He gave me a slight nod.

Execute.

I whirled and stabbed the nearest Red Eye as Demon took the head of the one on the floor. He was up and we took down another before anyone else could react. Within seconds, the bodies of six dead Red Eyes lay on the floor around Demon and me. Here is an interesting fact. Red Eyes bleed black goo.

The gnome gaped up at us. "Holy shit!"

We stared down at him and then we began to laugh. Demon looked at me and gestured toward the gnome. "Ask away," he said.

"Who are you and what are you doing so far from home?" I asked the gnome.

"My name is Adrastos Livius." The little gnome bowed slightly. "I am from the Hills."

He referred to a large range of dark mountains that gave Blackridge its name. "That is quite a long trek for a gnome," Demon remarked.

"Don't I know it," Adrastos said vehemently. "But my wife, Ariadne, came here a few weeks ago looking for a missing cousin of hers. I have not heard from either of them since. I became worried so I came to look for them."

"Any luck?" I asked.

Adrastos shook his head sadly. "I can't find hide or hair of either Ariadne or Normie."

Normie the Gnome? I bit my lip to stop myself from laughing, but a snort of laughter escaped anyway. My brother gave me a stern look and I struggled to compose myself as he turned back to Adrastos. "Tell us what we can do to help," he said.

Adrastos blinked at us in amazement. "I am grateful to you, er—"

"We are Enforcers," my brother said.

The gnome bowed. "I am pleased to meet both of you." He glanced around at the dead Red Eyes and shivered. "You don't know how glad. I am grateful to you for your offer of assistance, but I think that my wife might be frightened if you were to approach her. We gnomes are rather timid." He smiled ruefully.

Demon nodded. "Then, I will tell you what we will do. We will keep an eye out and if we see or hear of them, we will get word to you."

"You are very kind, gentlemen," Adrastos said solemnly. "Many would not do as you have done for me tonight."

"I am sure that they would."

Adrastos shook his head. "No. They would see the Red Eyes chasing me and think, 'What has it to do with me?' But you came to my rescue and you did not have to do so."

To my horror, Adrastos began to cry. Obviously, it had been a very long and onerous journey for a small creature whose greatest adventure to date had been sneaking in and out of a sleeping farmer's house. I patted his shoulder. "Is there anything else that we can do for you? Do you need a place to stay? Food?"

He gave me a watery smile. "I am provided for, I thank you. I am just worried for my wife and her cousin. They are so vulnerable out here." He waved at the bodies of the Red Eyes. "What if they had found her and Normie instead of me? What chance would they have had against them?"

"Try not to think about that," Demon replied softly. "You will make yourself crazy if you do."

"I must get on with my search," the gnome said as he moved toward the door. "But I will repay you for your kindness to me tonight."

Adrastos disappeared into the night while Demon made a phone call.

CHAPTER ELEVEN

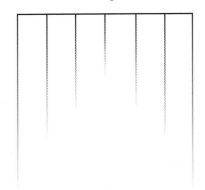

D EMON DROVE HOME TOO since he could not trust me to drive one of his precious vehicles a foot without breaking something. I was too exhausted to yank his chain about it and dozed off immediately. The next thing I knew, my brother was nudging me with his elbow. "Wake up, Bane. We are home and I am not carrying you up to bed."

I turned away from him. "And I was so looking forward to you reading me a story and tucking me in."

"Ha. Ha. Get your ass out of my car."

I smiled and opened the door.

"Now what the hell is going on?" I heard Demon sigh.

The other Deadlies were standing on the front porch watching our approach uneasily. "This does not bode well," I said to Demon.

"It usually doesn't." He sighed and started forward. I followed. We mounted the steps and paused.

"Well?" Demon demanded.

"You guys aren't going to like this," Kaz began.

"*What?*" Demon and I demanded in unison.

Kaz shook his head. He looked at Dev. "Tell them."

Dev scowled. "You tell them!" he retorted.

"Do I look crazy to you?"

No good could have come from Dev's response to that. Rather than have this deteriorate into a full-scale argument with no explanation in sight, I interrupted. "*Someone* tell us!"

"Riot," Demon gave our friend a hard look.

"Why me," Riot complained.

Demon didn't speak. He just stared steadily at Riot until he broke. "The Graces are here!" Riot blurted.

Demon and I gaped at him, horrified. "What the hell are *they* doing here?" I gasped.

Without waiting for an answer, Demon pushed past the others and stalked into the house. I trailed behind him reluctantly. I stepped into the library and entered a nightmare. I closed my eyes and then counted to five. Then I opened them again. Riot was right. It was a sea of white. The Graces had made themselves at home in our library and availed themselves of our whiskey.

The Graces are often mistaken for angels due to their large white wings. They are, of course, daemons as we are; though they certainly would deny being anything like the Deadlies. The three male Graces all wear white pants and are zipped into white shirts with openings in the back to accommodate their wings. The women wear floor length white gowns with the same kind of modifications. All of them are blond and blue eyed with the faces and forms of Greek gods and goddesses, except for one of the Graces who has long black hair. He is Conrad Star, also known as Modesty, and he is my cousin.

Conrad gave me a shy smile when I met his gaze. I smiled back briefly until I caught Zane, one of the Graces, scowling at us. Caught fraternizing with the inferior life forms, Conrad quickly looked at the floor.

I turned to Demon, waiting for him to react. I watched him slide into his Wrath persona as easily as putting on a coat. With it, the tension in the room seemed to thicken and I think we were all holding our breath, waiting for the explosion.

"Do not mind us," Demon said in a sharp, cold voice. "Make yourselves at home."

The Graces started nervously and Ambrose, who was sitting at the desk, leapt to his feet as if his ass was on fire. I bit my lip to keep from laughing aloud. Ambrose is the biggest coward alive for all his swaggering. He was just lucky that his ass wasn't actually on fire. Demon's eyes were emitting blue sparks.

Demon glanced at me but showed no surprise that I now had red daemon skin and eyes, and horns jutting out of my head. He glided toward the desk as Ambrose edged out of his way. Leaving Ambrose standing awkwardly by, my brother sat down and dumped Ambrose's glass of whiskey into the wastebasket. Then Demon stared up at him coldly. "I assume that you have a good reason for being here uninvited?"

Ambrose is Courage and is supposed to be the Graces' leader, but he couldn't coax a pack of lemmings over a cliff with a bulldozer. He glanced at Zane, waiting for him to explain.

Zane got to his feet and I had to work to keep my dislike out of my face. Zane is Intelligence and he knows it. My Deadly is Pride, but he should have been Vanity. Zane is my height but he has that beach bully type of build. He has long white hair that curls almost into ringlets and eyes as blue as the heavens. Painters and poets have used him as a model for Zeus over the years though he looks nothing like the real Zeus. I know. I have met him.

He is also the most arrogant sonofabitch I have ever met. He is a couple of centuries younger than Demon and I. "We have come to you for help." Zane said with the air of one granting a great favour. I am sure that he thought that he was too, just by permitting us to be in his presence.

"Lucky us," I murmured to Dev.

"What seems to be the problem?" Demon asked.

"Our sanctuary has been compromised," Zane informed us haughtily. "We require a place to stay."

"*Sanctuary?*" Dev muttered in disgust.

"Dev," Demon murmured. Dev subsided, but I agreed with him. Zane always was a pompous ass.

"Go to a motel!" I snarled.

"And how do we explain our wings to the motel employees?" Zane smiled thinly. "Believe me, Vanity, if we had anywhere else to go we would do so."

"Wear a *coat* over your wings...*Dumbass!*" I snarled.

Zane snarled back, extending his white wings and flexing his muscles, threateningly. He knocked a vase off the table next to him. I retaliated by flaring my wings and growling. "Do not destroy our house just because you cannot keep yours safe!" I snapped.

"Put your wings down!" Demon ordered.

Startled by Demon's tone of voice, Zane's wings retracted immediately, but I was used to my brother. Zane looked like he thought Demon was about to kill us.

He should have known better. He might throw us through the window to make his point, but it would not kill us. Still, I lowered my wings slowly and gave them a little shake to straighten the feathers. I smirked at Zane who was flushed with embarrassment and anger.

"If you two are finished with the pissing contest," Demon gave me a stern glare before turning his attention back to Ambrose. "I would like to know how your house was compromised."

Ambrose spoke for the first time. "That is none of your business, Wrath."

Demon fixed Ambrose with a look that could freeze hellfire. Ambrose cringed. "If we decide to let you stay," my brother said coolly. "We are entitled to know. We want to be sure that your being here is not going to compromise our house."

"I give you my word—" Ambrose began.

Dev snorted and spat on the floor to show what he thought of Ambrose's assurances. "That is gross," I whispered. Dev smirked.

"For crying out loud, Ambrose, why don't you just tell them what happened?" Abigail Grace, his youngest sister, added in exasperation. She was lounging in one of the chairs, her long legs draped over the armrest, rolling her eyes at her brother. I bit my lip to keep myself from laughing.

Abby is Happiness but she has a temper that is borderline Demon. Since she usually aims this temper at the other Graces, I like her. I am also strongly attracted to Abby. Since I am in love with her sister (at least some of the time) this bothers me. I am a fickle, fickle man.

She is a lot taller than the other female Graces. I guess about 5'9. While her sister, Carys, has soft curves and alabaster skin, Abby is long, lean, and tanned—more muscle than soft curves. She refuses to wear the long white dress, insisting that with her build it makes her look like a pillar. Instead, she wears white jeans and a white halter-top something like what Morgana wears. Her shoulder-length blond hair is slightly darker than her brother and sister's hair. Her eyes are also dark blue, and Ambrose and Carys' eyes are much lighter. Abby's features are not as delicate as theirs are, but she has an interesting face. There is character there, which the other two lack. I have admitted that I am very attracted to Abby, but I also like her. She is, above all, a lovely and generous person. Attracted as I am to Carys, I cannot say that I like her.

Carys rose from the sofa and laid her hand on his arm. Her head was scarcely above her brother's elbow. "Abby is right," she urged softly. "It is the only way that they will trust us."

"Then, why don't you tell us," my brother said. "Since Ambrose appear to be incapable of giving a straight answer."

Carys turned toward Demon. "About a week ago there was a plane crash," she explained. "Ambrose and Zane managed to rescue some of the passengers before the plane exploded. They were all unconscious and though many of the passengers escaped, they could not rescue everyone. Unfortunately, many humans perished."

Demon nodded. "We heard about that. One or two of the humans mentioned angels and so we figured that it must have been your work."

She smiled slightly. "It was." She went on, "When the fire departments and ambulances arrived, Zane and Ambrose left but a reporter had shown up earlier and unnoticed. He caught them rescuing the passengers and took pictures."

"Let me guess," Demon sighed. "Their wings weren't covered?"

"No, and worse yet, the reporter managed to follow them home." Her blue eyes seemed to look through him, not at him. Carys is blind.

"Which reporter is it?"

"Jay Brian Fuller."

"Oh, shit," I said with feeling.

Fuller wrote for a well-known magazine dedicated to scandal but they preferred celebrity gossip and photos to the more outlandish Bigfoot and space alien stories that were Fuller's specialty. You might even say it was his obsession. He often lurked around odd crime scenes and sometimes the Satana could not get to the scenes until Fuller left or the cops chased him off. By then, the humans had control of the body and, until it went to the morgue, the Satana could do nothing to remedy the mistake. After that, the body "disappeared" courtesy of the Boogeys. He has screwed up more crime scenes than I can count so you can see why we are not very fond of Jay Brian.

"Oh, shit, indeed," Abby spoke up with a rueful smile on her lovely face. "Fuller believes that he has found a "nest of angels" as he called it in his article."

It did not surprise me that Fuller had the terminology wrong. It is a "host of angels." Of course, the Graces are not angels so he screwed up all around.

"*He wrote an article?*" Demon groaned.

"And don't forget the pictures," Abby told him. She gave him a mischievous smile. "But something happened to the pictures. A screw up at the photo mat, I believe. So naturally, no one believes him. When Fuller brought his editor out to show him the house, we fled out the back door and so when they searched it, they came up empty."

"They broke into your house too?" I gasped.

"Yes. Unfortunately, now that his editor thinks he has lost his mind, Fuller is determined to prove himself. He won't leave," Constance added. She is taller than Carys is. Her hair is the colour of dark gold, almost the colour of Riot's skin. Her eyes are such a light shade of blue that they are almost too pale to be pretty. "He just sits outside the house with his camera waiting for us to emerge."

"How do we know that you were not followed here?" I demanded.

Carys' eyes turned toward me. "Bane," she said softly and smiled.

I opened my mouth to speak and was immediately overwhelmed with the need to reach out and touch her, caress her. Instead, I turned abruptly to my brother. "Ask a witch to ward their house so they can go home," I suggested.

"That might work temporarily," Demon agreed. "They could live at their old house while they look for new one."

"So?" I urged.

Demon eyed Ambrose. "You still don't know if you were followed here."

"We were not," Ambrose assured him.

"Prove it!" I snapped.

"We slipped out while he was off...taking care of some business," Ambrose told us stiffly.

Abby rolled her eyes. "For crying out loud, Ambrose, stop being such a tight-assed twit! He means that we bailed when Fuller went to take a piss," she translated.

I heard Dev choking back a laugh and then he covered it with a cough.

"Besides," Ambrose went on. "I would sense it if anyone had followed us." He sent a hard glare in Abby's direction when she snorted. She returned the glare.

"You didn't sense him following you the first time," Kaz pointed out.

Ambrose turned his scowl on him now. "That was because I did not know that he was there."

Kaz groaned. "He can't be that stupid," he said in an aside to Demon.

"If it is any consolation," my brother said to Kaz. "As soon as Carys mentioned Fuller, I checked to see if he was here and I didn't sense his presence. Bane?"

Everyone looked at me. I do not have vampire senses but as a Deadly, I can sense vanity and Fuller has loads of that. I let my senses wandered out of the library, out the doors and search the grounds for Fuller's big ego. Then I shrugged. "I agree. We're clear."

"You might have said so," Ambrose said stiffly.

"And you might be less arrogant," Demon pointed out, coolly. Ambrose subsided and slunk away from the desk.

"While I think it was totally irresponsible of you to lead a reporter to your home," Demon went on. "I think that we can come to an agreement."

"What kind of *agreement*?" Zane asked suspiciously.

Demon rose and walked around the desk. "We are in the middle of an investigation and could use the extra eyes and ears."

Ambrose was not the only one who was stunned, but he was the only one not rendered speechless. "Are you suggesting that we work together?" he asked.

Demon shrugged. "Why not? We are all bound to protect humans and supernaturals from danger. This certainly qualifies."

Riot had been prowling around the room restlessly. If the Graces look down on the rest of us, they consider Riot to be the lowest of the low because he is Lust. For some reason, Lust is the worst of the Seven Deadly Sins in their eyes. Knowing how the Graces felt about him, Riot took this opportunity to join Constance and Ithel, who is Generosity, on the sofa. He cuddled between them. "Well," he purred with a sultry smile. "Welcome to the family." The two women shivered as he made himself comfortable laying his arms along the low back of the sofa so it looked as though he had his arms around their waists. He laughed softly. Ambrose and Zane both bristled.

"Don't be stupid," I snapped at them. "Riot will kick your asses while you're still trying to figure out how you're going to kick his."

"He's *Lust*." Zane sneered. "What does he know about fighting?"

In the next second, Zane was pinned to the wall with Riot's hand at his throat. "Apparently, I know more than you do. You should never dismiss an opponent so recklessly. It can get you hurt."

"Okay, Riot, you have made your point. Let Foolishness go," Demon said mildly, but I saw that he was trying to hide a grin. "Well, Ambrose?" he continued. He ignored Riot who had taken his hand away from Zane's throat and was now roughly swatting non-existent lint off him. "We will give you a place to stay in exchange for your assistance in this matter."

Ambrose was still eyeing Riot in irritation as he strolled back to sit between the two women again. Constance was making goo-goo eyes at Riot. Zane and

Ambrose exchanged looks of disgust. Finding a Deadly attractive had obviously lowered her in their esteem.

"Beggars cannot be choosers, Ambrose," Carys urged softly.

Finally, he nodded reluctantly. "Very well," he agreed. "We will help you. Bring us up to date."

Demon moved back to sit behind the desk and waved at Ambrose to sit on the chair opposite. Ambrose obviously saw the chair behind the desk as the seat of authority. Now Demon had it and Ambrose did not know how to reassert himself. I went to sit with my brother. I leaned on the edge of the desk and kept my back to the others in order to hide my smile.

Demon gave them the rundown of the last week, omitting today's executions except for the last one since it had yielded a tip. Dev grimaced when Demon finished the story of Vlad and Maryrose. "So much for our big lead," he sighed.

"Poor Maryrose," Abby said softly. "I think it is very sweet of you to help her, Fechín."

I watched my brother out of the corner of my eye. He was frowning, puzzled as to how he should respond to that. I doubt anyone had ever told him that he was sweet in his entire life. Though I knew that Demon had no interest in Abby, I could not help feeling a little stab of jealousy mixed in with amusement at seeing my brother dumbfounded.

"Er. . .Thank you, Abby." Demon frowned.

"I hear congratulations are in order for you, Dev," Carys interjected.

Dev was slouched against the wall to my right and now he straightened and seemed uneasy. "Yes?"

"Maia Severn," she prompted with a smile.

"Oh. . .right."

"She loves you very much. You are very lucky."

To my amusement, Dev's cheeks turned pink. "I know. I mean, yes." He sent me an agonized look.

I shrugged. What did he expect *me* to do? However, I was surprised by the suspicious look I saw Abby give her sister. "Back off," Abby said sharply.

Carys started and turned her head toward her sister. Her cheeks turned pink. "I didn't—"

"See that you don't," Abby told her flatly.

Carys fell silent, looking embarrassed.

What was that all about?

I was about to ask when Hex came in carrying a loaded tea tray. All of us winced. The Graces may not spend much time with us but they had spent enough to be wary of Hex's tea.

Another imp trailed after Hex with a sulky expression on his face. Toad was the Graces' servant. Though he is a male, Toad is much smaller than Hex and his skin is pale pink rather than red. He would make a perfect imp girl. Toad slunk into the room, glaring at Hex' back and I figured that she had given him a stern lecture about something. I wondered what he done. Toad is rather lazy. He had probably tried to hide somewhere while she was busy preparing refreshments for all of us.

Conrad rose from his seat near the door and held it open for her. "Thank you, Conrad dear." She beamed up at him and then gave Toad a cold look.

Conrad is painfully shy and one of the more likable Graces. I am not just saying that because he is my cousin. His mother, who was my mother's sister, had married a daemon named Quicksilver Star. Quicksilver was a tall, handsome man with short curly silver hair and silver eyes. Even his skin is silver. However, his son strongly resembles the Hellblazer side of the family. Conrad has black hair, blue eyes, and daemon red skin. He looks exactly the way I do when I change forms. If he had had black wings, the three of us might have been mistaken for triplets. He blushed and quickly sat down again, not making eye contact with anyone.

"Hex, you know you are not supposed to call attention to Conrad," I reproached her in a low voice.

"Poor dear," Hex whispered back. "I wish you and Demon would take him in hand. If anyone can build up that boy's confidence, it is you two. And he certainly could use some building up." She glared at Ambrose.

"Conrad," Demon was saying in a friendly tone. "How is Aunt Charisma anyway? We have not seen her in a long time."

Conrad smiled at him, pleased. "She is very well. She said that she would call—"

"Please!" Zane snapped glaring at Conrad. "Could we dispense with the family reunion?"

Conrad closed his mouth and shrank back. Though we were all daemons, the other Graces couldn't forgive Conrad for his relationship to Demon and I.

I scowled at Zane and started to tell him what I thought of him and his superior attitude but Hex interrupted. "My darling Charisma," Hex exclaimed, delighted. She spoke to Conrad, beaming. "How is my dear girl?"

However, Zane had done the damage. Conrad murmured something and retreated into his shell. Hex cast a stern glance at Zane and I was pleased to see him flinch under her disapproval.

Hex turned to Demon. "I have the guestrooms ready for your company," she said stiffly.

"Thank you, Hex," he said. He turned and stared at Toad coolly. "Since there are twice as many people in the house now, I am sure that Toad will be more than happy to assist you."

Toad gaped at Demon. "I will?" he said.

Demon smiled coldly. "You will if you plan on sleeping inside the house and not in the woodshed."

Hex beamed at him. "Thank you. I was wondering how I was going to get this lazy ass to do his fair share."

I caught Conrad's eye and we laughed. Demon sighed and shook his head but he was smiling.

"Well," I announced getting to my feet. "It is late and I am exhausted. I will turn in. See you tomorrow." I nodded to my brother, heading for the door.

"Oh, Bane dear," Hex interrupted. "If you're going up, perhaps you will escort Miss Carys?"

I froze and looked over my shoulder at her. "I beg your pardon?"

Hex cocked her head, puzzled by my reaction. "Since you're going up, you wouldn't mind escorting Miss Carys, would you?"

I glanced at Carys. "I suppose I could show her the way," I said reluctantly.

"I wouldn't want to put you out, Bane," Carys said mildly.

I scowled. I was aware that I sounded very ungracious and I was probably earning myself a stern lecture from Hex later. "No trouble," I said shortly. I turned back to Hex. "Which room is hers?"

Hex beamed at me. "It's the one next to yours."

"I'm sorry," Carys said as I escorted her from the library. She linked her arm through mine and I led her to the staircase.

"For what," I asked gruffly, feeling uneasy. Being around her overwhelmed me, but touching her was ten times worse. It felt like my whole arm was on fire. My chest ached. This was the most unpleasant feeling ever. If this is what it was like to be in love, it sucked.

"I'm sorry that you're unhappy that I'm here."

"I am not unhappy that you are here," I told her, lying through my teeth.

Her eyes lit up and I could have kicked myself as my heart stuttered in response. "I'm glad that you don't mind," she said softly.

"I do not mind."

"Good. Then perhaps you can drop the formalities because I like being here," she said tucking her arm more firmly in mine.

I did not object to having her snuggled up against me because...well, I am a man, after all, and she is a damned good-looking woman. Under any other circumstances, I might have even encouraged it, but now any way you look at it, it would be a bad idea.

We stopped in the hallway in front of the room Hex had designated for Carys. "Here is your room," I told her and opened the door. I stepped back.

Carys held on to the doorframe. "You're going to have to lead me in and show me where everything is."

"Oh...right."

I gave her my arm again and then led her around the room. It was one of our smaller rooms but it was very elegant with its peach and gold coloured wallpaper and a small round peach rug on the floor beside the bed. I pointed out the dark cherry wood dressing table, bureau, bedside table and the large marble fireplace. I led her to the cherry four-poster bed and placed her hand on the bedpost. "This is the bed," I said tersely.

My head was starting to hurt and I was getting cranky. As a Deadly, I should have been immune to migraines, but my head felt like it was going to split and strobe lights were going off behind my eyes, half blinding me. I didn't think any amount of painkiller could wipe out this one.

She skimmed her hand down the post and felt the mattress. Her hands led her to the end of the bed and found the little peach and gold settee at the foot. She sat down on it and turned to me. I knew she could not see me but I held my daemon appearance. "Thank you, Bane."

"You are welcome," I responded shortly and backed away from her. "Good night."

"Good night," she said. Then she called me back. "Oh! I forgot my things downstairs."

If I could just go to my room and close my eyes for a while, I might finally get some rest. "I will get your suitcase and bring it up," I told her, not believing, even as the words left my mouth, what I was saying.

She smiled. "Thank you."

"You are welcome," I grimaced inwardly, careful not to show my dismay in my tone.

I went back downstairs. I paused to speak to my brother and Kaz as they came up the stairs with Abby. "Everyone else has gone to bed. Kaz and I were just locking up," Demon told me.

"I am just going to bring Carys' suitcase up to her," I replied.

"Oh!" Abby's eyes widened. "I forgot my suitcase too."

"I can bring it up for you," I offered.

She shook her head. "No, you won't. This isn't a hotel and you aren't a servant," she said with a small smile. "I'll come down and get it."

Demon and Kaz continued up the stairs while Abby and I returned downstairs. Conrad was struggling with the front door and several suitcases at the same time. There was already a large pile almost as tall as I was by the door.

"For pity sake, Conrad," I burst out. "Why are you doing this by your—" The expression on my cousin's face stopped me and I added more gently, "You should have asked *us* to help you."

Conrad shook his head. "You all have your own chores to do."

"You are *not* a—" I broke off again and took a deep breath to steady myself. "You should have found one of us," I insisted. "Next time, you come and get Demon and me, or grab Dev or Kaz or Riot. Hell, any one of us will help you." I did not point out that Toad or the other Graces should have been the ones helping him since he probably knew that already. "Promise me this, cousin, or I'll tell Demon and you know what will happen then."

"He'd kick someone's ass." A small smile lifted the corners of Conrad's mouth. "Okay, Bane. I promise."

"Thank you, Conrad," Abby said.

Abby reached down and took out two cases. "These are my sister's," she told me and set them down. She picked up another suitcase and a small overnight bag. "These are mine."

In spite of Abby's arguments, I insisted on carrying her luggage for her as well. Finally, she gave in. I eyed the remaining pile. "I take it the rest of these belong to the others?"

"Yes," Abby said.

Conrad broke in hastily. "I will take—"

I cut him off. "Take your own bag up," I told him. I would be damned if he was carting all of that up the stairs as well. "The others can bloody well haul their asses down here and get their own suitcases!"

Conrad looked doubtful. "Bane…"

"I'm serious, Conrad. They're on Hellblazer turf now and *you*, my dear cousin, are a Hellblazer."

Conrad's smile broadened. He picked up an overnight bag about the same size as Abby's was. "Good night, then."

"Good night, Conrad."

We watched my cousin trudge up the stairs. I looked back at Abby who was regarding the remaining suitcases with distaste. "It appears that my colleagues decided to bring their entire wardrobes with them," she told me ruefully. "I told them not to, but—"

"Don't worry about it." I paused and then said, "Colleagues?"

Abby looked at me in surprise. "What else would I call them?"

I didn't answer that. I call the other Deadlies my friends. Except for Conrad, I did not know what life for the other Graces was like.

Instead, I answered, "I have a few suggestions, but I doubt any of them are appropriate for a young lady's ears."

She laughed. Her pretty, blue eyes twinkled at me. "I'm sure it isn't anything I haven't called them myself from time to time."

Looking down at her, I had to smile back. When Abby is happy, everyone else around her is happy too. I have a confession…I love making her happy.

Then, I don't know what happened. One minute Abby was smiling up at me, and the next she had dropped her suitcase and was kissing me. This was not just a peck on the cheek. It was full on the mouth with lots of heat. Abby is many, many centuries younger than I am. She is even younger than Onyx and he is over four hundred years old. She is still a kid compared to me, but she was grown-up enough for her kiss to bring my body to a simmer. Forgetting everything, except Abby, I returned the kiss.

When she pulled back, she was still smiling but I was not. It took a few tries before I could speak. "That was—" I stammered. "What—"

Okay, maybe I wasn't quite ready to speak.

"Consider it a tip, Bellboy." Her hands slid over my chest.

"Uh—" I choked.

"You kiss very well," she went on. Her smile was wicked. "I thought that you would. You *are* pretty delicious."

Damn. She should have been Honesty. Suddenly aware that my hands were on her ass and I had her fitted rather snugly against my body, I released her abruptly and picked up Carys' things, heading toward the stairs.

Abby followed me. "I've wanted to kiss you for a long time," she said conversationally. "I'm glad that I did."

I stopped short and turned to look at her. "Why?"

"Why what?" She was smiling. The heat of that smile matched the heat of the kiss and that made me nervous.

"Why did you want to kiss me?" I asked, even though my brain was screaming at me to shut up and not go there.

"I like you, Bane," she informed me cheerfully. "And you're hot. There's nothing wrong with wanting to kiss a hot guy."

I gaped at her for a moment, again rendered speechless. Then I turned away hastily and continued up the stairs. I set the cases down outside of Carys' door and turned to Abby. "Let your sister know that her suitcase is here," I said. Before she could respond, I fled to my own room.

CHAPTER TWELVE

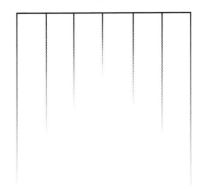

I WAS EXHAUSTED AND my head hurt but I had trouble falling asleep. Damn Abby and damn Carys! I had gone down stairs just so I could get away from one sister and instead, I stumbled into the arms of the other. I hated to admit it, but that kiss had melted my knees.

Of course, like an idiot I kissed her back. I groaned silently. Worse, I was sure that if she did it again I would most likely let her.

As for Carys—just her touch, the sound of her voice was enough to make me want her desperately. I hoped they would not be staying long. Between the two sisters, I would be a raving lunatic within the week.

I spent the next two hours tossing and turning. I could not sleep on my back because of the wings and it was too hard to sleep on my stomach since all I could think about was that hot, steamy kiss with Abby. Finally, about 2:30 in the morning, I gave up and went downstairs. At least my headache was gone. I walked into the library, thinking about finding a book to read to help me fall asleep. We collected many good books over the years, many of them first editions, but there were a few books guaranteed to cure insomnia in the first paragraph. We never throw anything out, not even the crap. We have more respect for books than that.

I had only taken a couple of steps into the room and stopped short. "Demon."

He was sitting in the library in the dark, staring into the empty grate of the fireplace. I walked over to him and turned on the small lamp at his elbow. He was holding a glass of whiskey in his hand. He glanced up in surprise when I spoke. "What are you doing up so late?" he asked.

"I had trouble sleeping," I told him. I picked up the whiskey decanter that was sitting next to the lamp and poured myself a drink. I don't usually drink alcohol since it doesn't affect me for either good or evil. I did it more to be sociable than anything. I spun one of the other chairs around to face the fireplace and sat down next to my brother. "I thought you would be sleeping."

"I thought the same of you. It appears we were both mistaken."

"You could not sleep either," I said.

"No."

I glanced at him and sipped my drink. "Thinking about Kit?"

He stiffened. "Why should I?" he demanded, but I noted that he did not deny it.

Kit was the victim of a vampire back in the 1800s. It just so happened that this particular vampire was a rogue on our execution list. He had murdered five women by the time we caught up to him and Demon came upon him while he was trying to make Kit Victim Number Six. Demon rescued her, chasing the vampire away, and then saved her life by feeding her with his own blood.

She lived with us for several weeks until we caught the vampire and during the time she was with us, I saw her falling more and more in love with my brother every day. Before I could drop him a hint and ascertain how he felt about her, we found and terminated the rogue. Kit disappeared from our lives the same night. Demon was so upset that it was years before we could mention her name in front of him.

"Are you ever going to tell me what happened that night?" I asked watching him from the corner of my eyes. "The night she left?"

Demon hesitated and then took a gulp of whiskey. "No."

I shook my head. "We all know something happened," I told him. "One minute she is living with us happily, a part of our family, and the next night she is gone without a word. It makes no sense."

He gave me a sharp look. "Drop it, Bane."

"I am sorry," I said gently. "I know how it hurt you, and I hate to see you hurting."

"I am fine," he replied shortly. "I was fine then and I am fine now."

"You were *not* fine and you *are* not!" I argued. "But if you do not wish to confide in me..." I rose abruptly.

"Bane, please," Demon said with a hint of desperation. He grasped my arm and his tone made me sit down again. "I just...I do not want to talk about Kit. You can understand that?"

"Not really. I thought that you and Kit—" He glanced at me and the pain in his eyes stopped me cold. "I see."

We sat in silence for a few minutes, as I struggled to find something comforting to say. Finally, all I could come up with was, "I am sorry."

A small smile lifted the corners of his mouth. "Apology accepted, though unnecessary." He took another sip of the whiskey and the desperation seemed to drain away, but his eyes were still serious. "I know that you all liked Kit. So did I, but she is not the same woman that we knew. She could be working for the rogue sovereign."

"You do not believe that. You knew her better than any of us."

Demon got to his feet abruptly. "Perhaps I did not know her as well as I thought I did," he said quietly and walked out of the room.

I remained in the library, staring into the empty grate of the fireplace.

At some point, I must have fallen asleep in the library because the next thing that I remember, Morgana was leaning over me brushing my hair back from my forehead. "*Bane*," she sang. "Up and at 'em, Sunshine."

I cracked one eyelid. "Sunshine?" I repeated incredulously. Though Morgana cared about all of us, she had a special place in her affections for me though I was under no illusions about it. I looked like Demon. That was the attraction.

She laughed and straightened. "Come on. Breakfast is ready and if you want anything you better get there before the Graces get to it."

I groaned as I remembered why I had ended up asleep in the library to begin with. I stood and stretched. It was a good thing that I was a Deadly. Falling asleep on a chair with such a low back is not a good idea for someone with a more human physique.

"By the way," Morgana said as I followed her out of the library. "You had a phone call this morning."

"*I* did?" I said surprised. Then I realized who it must have been. "Oh, you mean my—Serkan."

"No." Morgana shook her head. "It was a woman."

Now that was a shock. "What woman?"

Morgana shrugged. "She said her name was Cherie."

I frowned. "I do not know anyone by that name."

"She seemed to know you very well if the message she left was any indication," Morgana told me with a sly smile. "It was pretty intense. What did you do to this girl, Bane?"

I shook my head, puzzled. "I wish I knew."

Morgana laughed. "Well, perhaps the message will jog your memory. I left it on the table beside the phone." She glanced up as Abby came down the stairs escorting Carys. "You might want to pick it up before anyone else sees it."

I snatched up the message without looking at it and turned toward the group coming down the stairs. Conrad walked ahead of Carys, watching her steps carefully. She stumbled once and he caught her quickly. It was the first time I had ever seen the Graces really take care of each other.

Abby spotted me first. She smiled and her eyes locked on mine, inviting me to…I do not know what but it intrigued me against my better judgement. "Why, good morning." she purred.

Conrad looked over his shoulder and his eyes lit up. "Good morning, cousin."

Carys' face softened into a gentler, less heated version of her sister's smile. "Good morning, Bane," Carys said softly.

I muttered a greeting and was relieved when my brother and Riot came down the stairs right behind them. Demon greeted the ladies politely and then stepped over to me. "Good morning," he said. "You are up early." There was no trace of last night's despondency in his face.

"Yes," I said in a low voice. "I did not fall asleep until long after you left. Did you finally get some sleep?"

"Not much, no," he admitted ruefully. "We had better get some breakfast. We have a lot of work to do today."

Conrad and I walked down the hallway on either side of Demon, leaving the ladies to follow with Riot. When we entered the kitchen, Hex was standing in the middle of the floor, staring at the large table with a puzzled look on her face.

"Hex," Demon stepped in holding the swinging door for the rest of us. "Is something the matter?"

Hex gestured toward the table. She was still holding a large plate in each of her tiny hands and I feared that she would lose her grip and one of the plates would go flying across the room. "It's not big enough," she told us with awe in her tone. We glanced at the table. "We have seating around this table for twenty people and it is just not big enough."

"Well," Demon said with a smile. "When you factor in the fact that fourteen of us have wings and then add in Maia, no, there wouldn't be much room. I guess we will have to use the dining room."

"We have never used the dining room," Hex said, bemused.

"There is a dining room in this house?" Maia had arrived with Dev. They were lovers who were at ease with each other. It showed in the way their arms draped around each other's waists. It showed in the way that his hand caressed her hip in a casual sign of affection. She looked much better this morning, not as tired. I hoped this was a sign that she was sleeping better.

"Yeah," Dev told her. He pointed to another swinging door a few feet from the first one. "Through there."

"But we have never *used* it," Hex repeated looking as though we had asked her to serve breakfast in the old pig barn out back.

"It seems that we have no other choice today," I responded. "We have guests and we cannot ask them to stand while they eat."

Hex looked doubtful for a moment as if she had actually considered doing just that. Then she nodded and sighed. "I suppose you're right," she agreed reluctantly.

Demon and I looked at each other, puzzled. He turned to the others. "Ladies, if you would like to go through to the dining room, we will join you in a minute."

Maia walked over to push open the door and peek inside. She turned back with her mouth hanging open. "This is amazing!" she exclaimed as she held the door for Carys and Abby. "I've never seen such a big room. It must be a twenty-foot ceiling at least! I didn't realize that the house was so big and I'm here all the time. The furniture is gorgeous. It's all hand-carved in dark wood and I'm pretty sure those are antique silver candlesticks on the table." We could hear Maia continuing to describe the room to Carys as the door swung shut.

We turned back to Hex. "What is the matter, Hex?" Demon asked softly. "Why don't you want to serve breakfast in the dining room?"

One thing about Hex, she is eternally honest. She will not beat around the bush. She extended her arms. "Look at me, Demon! It is one thing to carry full plates to the table in the kitchen, but to carry them through the door too is next to impossible!"

"Hex," I said surprised. "You carry a full tea tray to the library every day!"

"But it is one tray and it *is* heavy." To our horror, tears sprang into her eyes. "If I must serve fifteen people in the dining room, it will take an hour to get the table set and food on the table. It will take even longer to clear. I just don't think that I can do it!"

"Then we'll help you," Dev told her hastily and grabbed the pile of plates sitting on the counter. He shoved them at Riot. "Take these into the dining room. I'll get the silverware. Bane, bring the coffee and mugs."

We did as Dev told us. Conrad watched us with a serious expression. I paused. "What is it?"

He looked at me. "Toad should be helping her," he said quietly.

"Then why don't you go roust his ass out of bed?" I suggested.

You would think I had told him to kick Ambrose where it counts, which wouldn't have been a bad idea either. However, Conrad shook his head and backed away muttering, "Oh, no. I couldn't do that. He's the *Graces'* servant."

I almost pointed out to him that he was a Grace, too, but perhaps he meant the Grace family's servant. "Well then," I said. "One of us will do it. You can help me set the table."

Demon smiled slightly at me as Conrad hoisted the large tray of coffee and mugs easily with one hand and sailed into the dining room with as much grace as any of his teammates.

"I will help Hex make breakfast then," Demon said as he ushered her gently but firmly toward the stove. "What do you want me to do?"

Hex gaped as Dev started giving orders. I suppose it was the fact that we obeyed him that was so astonishing. Now she was smiling again as she handed a bowl and a whisk to Demon. "Make your world famous pancakes, dear."

The rest of us carried everything into the next room while Hex and Demon began to make the breakfast. The table was set and I was heading back into the kitchen for another pot of coffee when Kaz came in from the kitchen with Zane. "Demon is cooking," Kaz told us, awed.

I had to smile at his incredulous expression. "So?"

"Demon can cook?"

I laughed. "Hell, yeah, he can cook."

"I've lived with you guys for more than five hundred years," Kaz said, shaking his head. "And I didn't know Demon could cook." He gave me a curious look. "Do you cook too?"

"Absolutely. Hex taught both of us when we were about eight. She hoped that it would keep the pair of us out of trouble."

Kaz grinned. "I suppose there is no sense in asking if it worked."

"None at all," I replied cheerfully and went into the kitchen.

The fresh pot of coffee I made was sitting on the counter when Onyx ambled in and poured himself a cup. "Where is everyone?" he asked.

"We're having breakfast in the dining room this morning," I replied. He raised his eyebrows but did not comment. "Onyx, if you are on your way in, would you take that pot of coffee with you?"

"Sure." He picked up the pot went into the dining room.

"Hey, Bane," Demon said, wiping his hands on a dishtowel. "You want to take over here for a minute? I'm going up to give Ambrose and Ithel a fifteen-minute warning."

"Go rattle their cages," I said, solemnly, as I moved toward him.

He tsked. "You always make it sound as though I enjoy harassing the Graces." We grinned at each other.

"And don't burn the pancakes." He handed me the flipper and I whistled as I stepped up to take his place at the stove.

Ambrose and Ithel arrived at breakfast inside of the fifteen minutes, though barely. They were cranky and glared at Demon throughout the meal. Apparently neither of them was a morning person.

Maia was still admiring the dining room with all the delight of someone who has just found a hundred dollar bill in her pocket. "It's enormous! I didn't even know it was here! What other rooms haven't I seen?"

Dev shrugged. "We don't use many of the other rooms. We don't have a TV obviously so the parlour doesn't get used."

Maia leaned forward, interested. "Since Demon is such a technophile, why *don't* you have TVs and DVD players?"

Dev shrugged again. "Who has time to watch? If we aren't out hunting the bad guys, which is rare, then we're training. If it's raining, we're in the catacombs beating up on cement blocks. If it's nice outside, and sometimes even when it's not, we're outside beating up on each other."

"But what do you do for fun?" Maia asked.

We looked at each other and then at her. "That *is* what we do for fun," we all said.

She and Abby burst into laughter, but Carys was frowning at Morgana. "Surely, they don't fight with you," she said.

"Don't you believe it," Morgana snorted.

"But, you're a *woman!*" Carys gasped.

Morgana gave her a look of utter disgust. "I'm a *Deadly*," she corrected haughtily. "And I can fight with the best of them!"

"Damn right she can," Demon said with a hint of pride in his tone. "Morgana backs down from no one." His eyes twinkled. "That includes me. Anyone who thinks he can bully Morgana will find out just how wrong he is the hard way. She is one of the best fighters on the team."

Morgana's mouth fell open at the compliment. She quickly turned her face away, but I caught sight of her glittering eyes and happy smile. Demon does not often hand out compliments but when he does, it is usually right when you need to hear it most and you could be sure that he meant every word.

Demon is like that.

We decided that Toad was getting his ass out of bed to help Hex as long at the Graces remained guests at our house. It was not fair to ask her to care for all of these extra people. We argued over who was going to roust Toad from bed. In the end, we drew straws. Dev won. As Dev gleefully went to wake Toad up, Demon led the rest of us to the library.

Demon sat down behind the desk as he had last night and I perched on the desk next to him, using my brother as a kind of shield. I shifted again as soon as I saw Carys and Abby on the stairs earlier and maintained that shape through breakfast. I hoped that they would find another place to live soon. It was hard to hold this shape for so long.

"That food was too good," Abby groaned, clutching her stomach. "I think I ate enough to keep me full until next week."

Demon laughed. "I am glad you enjoyed it."

She licked her lips and smiled at me. "It was tasty."

I choked on the sip of coffee I had just taken and my brother lowered his eyes to the desktop to hide a smile. "Today we have a lot of ground to cover," he said ignoring my glare. "We will split into two teams. Maia gave us the names of some people who knew Scummer. One team will interview the people on Maia's list. The other team will return to Vlad's townhouse and see if there is anything there that might give us a clue to the identity of the rogue sovereign."

He glanced up at me. "Bane, I want you to be in charge of that team. I will take the other team."

To my horror, Demon not only left me with the two biggest assholes in the group but he put Abby on my team, too. Before Demon could escape with his team, I took him aside.

"What is the big idea leaving me with Abby?" I demanded angrily.

Demon seemed surprised. "What do you mean? What is the problem?"

I started to blurt out that I was afraid that she might kiss me then realized that wasn't what I was afraid of at all. I knew I would like it and was afraid that I might respond again. That was a bad idea for so many reasons.

I shook my head. "Just forget it."

I could not fool my brother. "Bane, believe me, I am not playing matchmaker," he assured me. "I thought that Abby would be helpful keeping Ambrose in line and I know that Zane goes crazy with jealousy every time you and Carys are around each other. That is all. I swear."

That took some wind out of my sails. "Oh."

Demon laid a hand on my shoulder. "I would never leave you in a situation that makes you uncomfortable." He eyed me curiously. "What is all this about Abby?"

I grimaced. "Forget it, Demon."

"Ah, a mystery. Come on. If you can't spill your guts to your little brother, who can you spill them to?"

He had a point. Riot would just encourage it, and Dev and Kaz would think it is hilarious and tease the hell out of me. "We're twins. Two minutes does not make you younger," I muttered.

"Two minutes is two minutes. Stop trying to change the subject."

I took a deep breath. "Abby kissed me," I blurted.

Demon stared at me but did not seem astonished. "Abby kissed you."

"Yes, on the mouth...like she meant it."

"I see." He looked curious. "Why does it bother you?"

"Why does it..." I gaped at him in disbelief. "Demon, she is a Grace!"

"So?" I could see that he was trying not to smile.

"It is *not* funny!" I exploded. "What the hell am I going to do?"

"I am not laughing at you," he told me.

"You could have fooled me," I replied dryly.

"It was just a kiss, Bane. Why are you so worked up about it?"

I glared at him, not wanting to tell him the truth, but that unwavering stare broke me down. "Because I liked it a lot," I admitted finally. I groaned. "Damn, it was hot."

Demon's mouth twitched as if he was trying not to smile. "Hmm."

"What the hell does "hmm" mean?" I demanded.

"I have always wondered why you shape shifted whenever the Graces were around. I always assumed that it was because of Carys."

"So?" I crossed my arms over my chest defensively.

"So?" he mimicked me, grinning openly now. "I was just thinking that maybe it was for another reason entirely."

I glared at him. "Is that so? What reason would that be, oh wise one?"

He grinned at me and then started to walk away without answering.

"*Demon*," I hollered after him.

"Sorry. Some things you just have to work out for yourself, big brother."

CHAPTER THIRTEEN

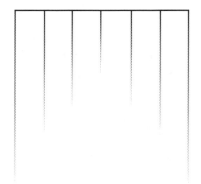

I HAD NO TIME to "work things out for myself" as my smartass (and completely unhelpful) brother suggested. He and his team took the only other vehicle big enough to carry a large number of people. The rest of us had to go in two vehicles.

"I shall drive," Zane told Riot haughtily. He held out his hand for the keys.

"No," Riot responded in the same tone. His fingers curved protectively around the keys. "You shall not."

Zane gaped at Riot. Had anyone ever refused him anything before? I doubted it. I paused on the porch to watch Riot in action.

"Then I will not go," Zane said, crossing his arms over his chest and trying to stare Riot down.

Riot was unmoved. He shrugged. "Then your ass can remain here and when Wrath gets back you can explain to *him* why you didn't go."

Zane stared at Riot for a second longer and then started for the car. I bit my lip to keep from laughing but when I glanced at Abby, I saw that she was doing the same. Our eyes met and I had to look away.

Riot and Ithel followed Zane. When he reached for the front passenger door, Riot stopped him. "The lady rides in front," Riot said.

"Why?" Zane demanded.

"Because she's a *lady*," Riot said. "If you were a gentleman, you would know that."

"Play nice, Riot," I murmured as I unlocked the vehicle we were using.

"Besides," Riot continued. "I don't like you."

Zane got into the car with a huff. Riot held the door open for Ithel who slid into the front seat, blushing. I rolled my eyes as I yanked open the car door. "I said play *nice*."

Riot darted a look at me. "That was nice."

"*That* was nice?" I raised an eyebrow at him.

"I didn't make him ride in the trunk, did I?"

I closed my eyes and fought not to grin. It would only encourage him. Some days he's worse than Dev.

"Where is the townhouse?" Riot asked.

I opened my eyes and gave him the address. "Just follow me," I said. "It'll be easier."

Riot grinned. "Oh, hell no! I know a short cut."

I snorted. "What are you going to do, cut through the farmer's cornfields? You'll end up in Summerton."

"You'll see," he said smugly. He walked around to his side of the car and opened the door, grinning at me over the top of the hood. "Eat my dust, Vanity." He got into the car and gunned the engine.

I turned hastily to Abby and Ambrose. "Okay, that is *it*. Get in. He is *so* not getting there first."

Abby was laughing as we tore out of the driveway after Riot, but Ambrose was deathly silent. When I looked in my rear view mirror, I saw him clinging to the door handle. We set off toward Blackridge and all the way into town, Riot and I kept passing one another on the road. If Demon could have seen us, he would have shot us. Once inside the city limits, Riot went left and I went straight, cackling the whole time.

"Sucker!" I crowed.

Abby glanced at me. "What?" she asked.

I grinned. "That road is all construction and it's nine in the morning. It will be backed up to Lakeside."

"That's good?" Abby asked.

I glanced at her. "That means I can slow down."

Finally, Ambrose heaved a sigh of relief. "That *is* good," he said.

Scaring my companions to death was not on the agenda for the day. If either of them swore to my brother that they would never get into a car with me again, he might come through with that threat to make me take driving lessons and it would not be some kindly driving instructor giving me my road test. It would be Demon. I slowed down and drove just under the speed limit. We still arrived at Vlad's townhouse first.

I was reclining on the hood of the car and gazing up at the sky with Abby beside me when Riot pulled up. He got out of the car and walked up to me, scowling. "Okay, okay," he said. "You've made your point."

I sat up, grinning. "Make sure you tell Demon that I got here first and I didn't even have to speed."

Abby darted a look at me.

"After I got into Blackridge, that is," I amended.

"Can we just get on with this?" Riot muttered irritably. He glared over his shoulder at Zane.

I drew my friend aside and out of reach of Zane. "Rough drive?" I asked in a low voice.

"You take that sonofabitch back with you," Riot growled. "Or he might not make it home in one piece. I swear I'll take the long way just so I can push him out on the mountain pass."

To be honest, I didn't want to drive with Zane either. We had a lot more reason to hate each other than Riot and Zane did, but Riot looked like he was beyond the point of reason by now. He couldn't kill Zane but he probably *would* push him out of a moving car. Demon would definitely disapprove.

"Fine," I sighed. "I'll take him."

Riot turned and looked up at the row of townhouses. "Which one is Vlad's?"

I pointed. "That one. Someone has to stay out here and keep an eye out for cops or anyone coming up to the door."

"Perhaps only a couple of us need to stay outside," Abby suggested. "Three of us standing here would definitely call attention."

"Good idea," I said to Abby. I turned to Zane. "You and Ithel stay out here. Here is my cell phone number. Call me if you see anyone coming to the house. The rest of you come with me," I said.

"Why does *he* go in with you?" Zane demanded, pointing at Riot.

"Because I say he does," I said coolly. "Besides, whoever remains outside has to be inconspicuous. Riot is about as inconspicuous as a Vegas showgirl in a convent."

Abby covered her mouth with her hand and turned her head away. Riot grinned broadly. "Very illustrative," he remarked.

"And true," I reminded him. "Don't forget true." I turned back to Zane. "Besides, I am not walking in there with someone I do not trust."

Zane's face turned red and, for a moment, I thought his head might explode. No such luck. "You trust them?" he asked sourly pointing at the other three.

I glanced back at Riot, Ambrose, and Abby. "Well," I admitted. "Two out of three isn't bad."

"I hope I am one of the two," Abby remarked, smiling.

Riot looked at me, a sly smile on his face. I thought about kicking him but decided it was better to ignore the whole situation. "Let's get on with this, shall we?" I replied. "We're drawing attention out here."

Riot looked up and down the empty sidewalk then raised his eyebrow at me. I scowled at him. "Shut up," I said and I turned my back on him, ignoring his snickers as I led the way into the townhouse.

It was dark inside. I had closed all of the curtains the night before so no one could peek in the windows and see the Boogeys taking Vlad's body away. We stood in the hallway and Riot closed the door behind us.

"You said you found him upstairs?" Riot asked.

I nodded. "I'll show you. Abby, have a look around the living room. Through there." I pointed. "Ambrose, there is a kitchen that way. Search everything. Be thorough."

"I know what I'm doing," Ambrose said stiffly.

Abby gave him a meaningful look but didn't say anything. Ambrose turned bright red and slunk into the kitchen muttering under his breath.

Riot and I grinned at each other. I looked at Abby, still smiling. "And I thought my brother was the only one who could do that with a look. I'm impressed," I told her.

Abby laughed. "If that is all takes to impress you, my other talents will floor you."

Riot burst into laughter as my jaw dropped. I could feel the tips of my ears turning red. "Okay, well, um..." I stammered. "This way, Riot."

I hurried up the stairs and down the hallway. "We found him in here," I told

Riot, flinging open the bedroom door and stepping inside. "He was on the floor. I stepped on him. Well, on his heart anyway."

"Gross," Riot commented.

"The assailant went out the window, we think," I went on. "We didn't pass anyone on the stairs and—"

"Bane," Riot said cutting me short. "She's downstairs, you know. You can slow down now. You're babbling."

I stopped in mid-sentence and stared. "I beg your pardon?"

"I've never seen you behave shyly around women before let alone running from them, but that was quite the sprint up the stairs. I swear you were taking three steps at a time. What's the problem?"

"There is no problem," I growled. "Focus, Riot."

"I *am* focussing." Riot grinned. "I am focussing on why you felt the need to flee from Abby like a skittish horse."

"That is *not* what you are supposed to be focussing on."

"I know but I will anyway. Teasing you is way more fun than digging through some dead guy's junk."

"I shall call Fechín," I threatened. "And tell him you are being a pain in the ass instead of helping."

Riot pouted. "You're no fun."

"Pull yourself together." I pointed to a chest of drawers. "Start looking."

Riot pulled open the top drawer. "For what—a list of rogue sovereigns living in Blackridge?"

"If there is one," I looked down at a stack of books on Vlad's bedside table. They were vampire/romance novels. I rolled my eyes.

Riot closed the drawer and opened the next one. "Geez, you sound like Demon."

"We *are* twins," I reminded him.

"But not at all alike," he said. "You're more easy-going than he is."

"That is not true. Demon is usually very easy-going. He is just—" I paused for a second and groped for the right word. "He is complicated," I said finally.

Riot yanked open another drawer and snorted. "No shit." He looked up at me. "Hey, there's nothing wrong with being like Demon. You'll probably be channelling him like crazy on the ride home with Zane the Prick."

I grimaced. "Do *not* remind me."

"So," Riot said. "Do you want me to take Abby instead?"

He said it so casually, but he didn't fool me. I glared at him as he slid open another drawer and pretended to look inside. "No, I do not want you to take Abby," I said sarcastically. "You are not pawning both the assholes off on me."

"Bummer," Riot sighed as he closed the last drawer and moved on to the bed.

We tore the bedroom apart. It wasn't pretty when we were done but there wasn't a crevice left unchecked. We found nothing of interest.

"The bedroom is clear," I said. "Let's check the rest of the floor."

"You're too generous," Riot said kicking aside a pile of clothes on the floor. "The place is a wreck."

"We might have had something to do with that," I pointed out.

"No," Riot said. "It pretty much looked like this when we walked in."

I couldn't argue with that. Apparently, housekeeping was not one of Vlad's fortes.

"Vlad appears to have been a bigger packrat than you are and that's saying something considering that you have been accumulating shit for over 1000 years," Riot went on.

"You're hysterical," I growled. "You're just too funny for words. Now shut up and check the bathroom."

The only other bedroom was clear and I was just starting to check the hall closet when Abby appeared at the top of the stairs. "Bane," she said quietly. "There is a man downstairs who says that he needs to talk to you."

"What man?"

"He says that he was Vlad's neighbour."

I closed the door of the closet, surprised. "Mr. Harrison?"

She shrugged. "He did not give his name. He is an older gentleman."

I nodded. "That is Mr. Harrison. Did he say why he wants to talk to me?"

"He said he thought of something after you left last night and he figures he owes you and Vlad," Abby said. She paused, frowning. "Why does he owe you?"

I could not imagine, but I was not going to look a gift horse in the mouth, especially if he might possess vital information about the rogue vampires.

"Riot," I called out. My friend stuck his head out of the bathroom. "Vlad's neighbour wants to talk to us."

We went downstairs and Abby led us to the kitchen where Mr. Harrison sat at the table. Ambrose was leaning against the counter, his arms crossed over his chest, frowning as if he smelled something bad. Zane looked up as we came in. "This man came to the door and said he wanted to talk to one of the Deadlies. How does he know who you are?" he demanded.

I ignored Zane. I owed him no explanations. Instead, I focused on the old man. He was dressed in casual clothes today. He wore a pair of jeans that sagged on his lean hips and had on a green flannel shirt. They were faded but clean. On his feet, he wore a pair of well-worn brown shoes. He looked at me and started to speak, but then stopped, staring past me as though he had seen a ghost. "Who is that?" he asked in a whisper.

I looked back over my shoulder. There was only Riot and Abby. "This is my friend, Kane, and this is Abby," I told him, wondering which of them had caused the look of bewilderment on the old man's face.

"He..." The old man pointed at Riot. "He looks like Johann."

Riot looked at the old man and then at me, quizzically. I shrugged. I didn't know who that was either.

"Never mind," the old man said suddenly looking embarrassed. "I only came over because I thought of something after you left last night."

I sat down at the table. "Okay, Mr. Harrison. Tell me."

"Well, I didn't think of it at the time because he was so—I don't know—ordinary," Mr. Harrison said. "But there was a man lurking around here last night just after you took off after Vlad."

"You didn't recognize him?"

Mr. Harrison shook his head. "No. As I said, he was just some man. He was pretty forgettable physically, if you know what I mean."

I shook my head. "Tell me."

Mr. Harrison frowned. "He had brown hair, kind of scruffy looking, but then it was no worse than any other young man I've seen. He wore jeans and a jean jacket. There was nothing distinctive about him. He wasn't handsome or ugly; he looked about thirty-odd, but could have been older or younger. He was someone you might pass on the street and not even notice."

"I think I understand," I said. "Was he fat, thin?"

"Rather thin."

"Good. Was there anything about him that stood out?"

"No. He looked just like any other human." Mr. Harrison stopped and frowned. "No wait. There was one thing. He was *not* human. I didn't think of it at the time. The feel of him was different but it wasn't anything I'd ever felt before. I know shapeshifters and vampires. I can even sense daemons, but I don't know what *he* was."

I questioned him a little further about the man. The man had not gotten into a car as far as Mr. Harrison knew. The old man had not gotten close enough to see if he had scars. The denim clothes were faded blue. However, the last item set off alarm bells. Mr. Harrison had noted that the man wore green and white runners. I looked at Riot. His eyes widened and I knew I was not mistaken.

"Mr. Harrison," I said. "Would you be willing to repeat all of this to my brother?"

"The vampire that was with you last night," Mr. Harrison said, nodding. "Of course I will if you think it will help you find whoever killed Vlad."

"Good." I opened my cell phone and after staring blankly at it for a few seconds, trying to remember how to send a text, I finally typed something in and hit the send button. Then, I crossed my fingers hoping I'd sent it to Demon and not to the Antarctic.

A few seconds later, a text came back from Demon. *On my way.*

"He'll be here in a few minutes," I announced, closing the phone.

Mr. Harrison glanced toward the window, doubtfully. "But, it's daylight!"

I did not want to get into the details of my brother's abilities so I just assured Mr. Harrison that Demon would be fine. We spent the next few minutes waiting in silence, but I noted that Mr. Harrison had not taken his eyes off Riot. Riot noticed it too, but he pretended not to. He is used to being the centre of attention.

Finally, Mr. Harrison spoke. "It's uncanny."

Riot turned his head to look at him. "Johann?" he asked with a slight smile.

Mr. Harrison nodded.

"You were good friends?" Riot asked gently.

"Yes," Mr. Harrison replied. He paused, staring at his hands linked in his lap, and then he looked up at Riot. "We were very good friends. We were—" The old man hesitated and broke off, clearly unsure how much he should reveal.

"I see," Riot said reassuringly.

"Does that bother you?" Mr. Harrison asked, watching Riot intently for a reaction.

Riot shrugged. "I am Lust," he said. "I've been told that I resemble men and women, gay and straight. One woman told me that I looked like a horse." He paused and then added, "She scared me a little."

"She was a *gambler*," I explained hastily when Mr. Harrison's jaw dropped. "She liked to bet on the races."

"I would have felt better if she told me that I strongly resembled hundred dollar bills," Riot remarked.

Mr. Harrison chuckled. At least he did not look like he was going to have a stroke now. The horse comment almost did him in, I was certain.

A few minutes later, I heard the front door open and Demon strode into the kitchen a few seconds later. Conrad followed with Carys. Maia was with them. "Where is Dev?" I asked.

"Keeping out of trouble I hope," Demon responded. "I left him and Kaz downtown with Constance."

Riot snorted.

Demon looked at Mr. Harrison. "How nice to see you again, Mr. Harrison," he said gently. "My brother tells me that you have some information for us."

Mr. Harrison described again the man he had seen hanging around outside Vlad's house. "He didn't appear to be interested in the house." Mr. Harrison added, "In fact, I thought at first he was lost. Then he seemed to wander away. I forgot about him after that. I *am* sorry I didn't remember about him before."

"Do not worry about that," Demon assured him. "You remembered now and that may help us. Thank you, Mr. Harrison."

Mr. Harrison got to his feet slowly, as though it hurt to move. "It was the least I could do for Vlad but I was not sure how to get in touch with you." He paused. "Then, that man came to my house this morning and—and, well…thank you."

"Think nothing of it," Demon said with a smile. "If you need anything, you call the number that he left with you."

Mr. Harrison nodded. "I will and thank you again." He left, moving slowly, almost painfully. He was wheezing and his colour didn't look very good. If his appearance counted for anything, Mr. Harrison might not require our care much longer.

I looked at Demon who was studying the old man critically. He glanced up at Riot. He mouthed the words, "Call Claire." Riot slipped out of the room to make the phone call to the doctor.

"That doesn't give us much to go on," Ambrose said after the old man was gone. "It was a pretty generic description. Any number of men could fit it."

"But few of them might be supernatural," Demon pointed out. "And we can exclude shapeshifters and vampires since Mr. Harrison said he would recognize them."

"He *says*," Ambrose said scornfully.

"He knew what I was last night," Demon said. "He says the man wasn't a vampire or shapeshifter and I believe him."

"Demon," I said

Demon turned to me. "You said that there was something else about the description that caught your attention."

"Yes, the green and white running shoes. Scummer was wearing one last night but the other was missing."

"This man was wearing two," Zane said.

"But the rest of the description fits Scummer too," I said.

"Except that Scummer was dead at the time this man showed up here," Demon added.

I nodded.

Demon's eyes narrowed thoughtfully. "It could be a coincidence," he said. "But I do not think so."

"I do not think so either," I said. "But how is it possible?"

"I am not certain." Demon looked at me. "Are you finished here?"

I nodded. "I do not think that there is anything here."

"Very well," Demon said. "We will return to the house to discuss this."

We left the house and everyone returned to the cars while I locked the house. I joined the others on the sidewalk just as Abby asked, "Mr. Harrison thanked you for something you did for him. What did you do?"

"Vlad was Mr. Harrison's caretaker of sorts," Demon explained. "When he was killed we took over the responsibility. One of our contacts came over this morning and brought him some groceries. It was my brother's idea."

Abby smiled at me and my heart leapt in my chest. I could have strangled my brother. "Well, we could not leave that old man alone with no one to take care of him," I muttered. "I just wish we could have done more. He deserves to enjoy what is left of his life."

"You have done a wonderful thing for that man." she assured me. "You cared about him. I could make him happy with a touch, but it would be false happiness, temporary. You gave him something real." Gently, almost shyly, she kissed my cheek.

I stared down at her in astonishment and then glanced at Demon and Riot.

They were grinning. I glared at them. Riot looked away quickly, at least attempting to hide his laughter, but Demon wasn't intimidated.

"Let's head home," he said still grinning at me. "We have a lot of things to get done today."

CHAPTER FOURTEEN

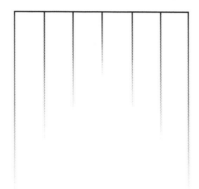

IT WAS AFTER TWO when we finally finished lunch and Demon debriefed the rest of the team on Mr. Harrison's information. Everyone seemed just as puzzled as we were about how a dead man could appear twenty-four hours after his own death and kill someone, especially since he was not a vampire. Demon, I think, had some idea but was reluctant to say anything. I found that a little unnerving. It was as if he didn't even want to suggest his idea and that meant it had to be something incredibly serious.

After lunch, Demon took me aside and told me that he had decided to take Abby and Conrad with him that afternoon leaving me with the rest of the Graces. I was horrified. "What the hell did I ever do to you?" I demanded.

"I was stuck with Carys and Constance all morning," he growled.

"You also stuck me with two of the biggest assholes in the bunch. At least leave me Conrad."

Demon shook his head. "He was the only helpful one. The other two are useless as hell as interviewers."

I crossed my arms over my chest. "Not my problem."

"Oh, just suck it up," Demon told me. "They will do less damage if we leave them here with you than if we have Constance whining about how tired and hungry she is through every interview."

I gaped at him. "She did not."

"She did. Carys just sat there looking pretty. I think she is used to everyone else doing the work. Her brother and Zane are so overprotective because of her vision that no one expects anything of her. It is too bad because she is probably smarter than Zane and Ambrose put together."

I sighed. "You win. I will take the Graces."

I was seriously irritated as I watched Conrad and Abby leave with the other Deadlies. I did not want to consider *why* it ticked me off that Abby was leaving. I just knew that I would rather have had Abby on my team than Carys.

I turned toward the library and out of the corner of my eye I saw Toad slinking into the parlour, probably to hide from Hex until she was done cleaning up from lunch and I was damned if he was getting away with it. The Graces had done nothing but take advantage the second they walked through our door and I would be damned if Toad was going to take advantage of Hex. She already done all of the work preparing and setting up for the meal by herself.

I followed Toad into the parlour just as he stretched out on the sofa and put his feet up. "What the hell do you think you are doing?" I snarled.

To my satisfaction, Toad promptly fell off the sofa and scrambled to his feet, wide-eyed. "I—I was just—" he stammered.

"Follow me," I said curtly and stalked out of the parlour with Toad trailing behind me. I didn't have to look back to know that he was doing as he was told. From his reaction, I already guessed that he thought I was Demon. I was going to use that to my advantage. Perhaps it was a little unfair to Demon, but under the circumstances, I think he would forgive me.

"Hex," I said opening the kitchen door. She turned to look at me and I saw her eyes widen. She knew who I was, of course. She had known me from infancy and if there was one person that Demon and I could never fool, it was she. However, I think she knew what I was doing and when she saw whom I was doing it to, she smiled.

"Yes, dear?" she said. She was careful not to use any names. That way Toad could not accuse her of lying if he ever figured out that I had conned him.

"Toad is going to clean up after lunch," I said. "He will clear the table, wash the dishes, and sweep the floor and any other chores you think need to be done. You are to sit back and make sure he does the job up to your standards. He does not leave this kitchen without your permission." I glared at Toad. "Is that clear?"

"Perfectly, dear," Hex said serenely.

Leaving a sulky Toad and a smug Hex to their assignments, I returned to my teammates who were still waiting in the library. Ambrose hovered around the desk indecisively. I walked past him and sat in the chair while he was still thinking about it. You snooze, you lose.

"You two can research Hadrian," I told Ambrose and Zane. "He became a vampire about four hundred and thirty five years ago. Though he has been living in this country for about two hundred and fifty years, he is originally from Britain."

Zane and Ambrose looked at each other. "Finding his family shouldn't be too difficult. We can start at the Standish estate."

"What estate?" Riot echoed incredulously. "He grew up in a shack in some dumpy little village."

"Standish?" I repeated, frowning. I shook my head. "His last name was Smauker, not Standish."

The five Graces gaped at us. "But, Hadrian always claimed that he was nobility..." Ithel began.

"I do not care what he claims," I snapped. "I am telling you that he was born to Margie and Harry Smauker in a small village in Lancashire in 1597."

"How do you know, Vanity?" Zane snapped.

I snarled at him. "What would I gain by lying?"

That shut him up. I directed my attention to Ambrose because, while he was as big an ass as Zane was, right now I did not want to beat the shit out of *him*. "There may not be records for his birth, but you may be able to find something on his parents' death. Margie died in 1609 and Harry in 1623."

Ambrose nodded. I turned to Carys and Constance. "Darkmoon may be a bit harder. We do not know what her original name was. She was Phoenician and grew up around Carthage. I do not know the date of her birth or the date she became a vampire. She may have been a noblewoman which would explain Hadrian's obsession with her."

"Give Hadrian some credit," Riot broke in. "He's not just interested in her social status. There are some other obvious benefits to being her mate."

I glared at him. Riot smiled mildly. I returned to Carys and Constance. "We think she may have lived in Carthage sometime in the 500s or 600s AD."

"Then there definitely won't be any records," Carys sighed.

"Sorry," I told her. "You can use the laptop computer. It may give you some information or at least tell you where to start."

I nodded. Constance hesitated. "But neither Carys nor I have ever used the computer before."

I sighed. That meant that I would have to leave Riot in charge of the computer. I could take Constance with me and pawn Carys off on Riot. Somehow, the thought did not relieve me.

"I can use a computer," Ithel said.

Riot and I looked at her. She blushed slightly. "Abby thought it would be a good idea if one or two of us learned how to use one. So she, Conrad, and I taught each other."

"Very well," I said. "You are in charge of the research on Darkmoon."

Pleased, she got to her feet. "I'm on it. Constance, why don't you and I work on the computer? Perhaps Carys can help Riot and Bane."

"Zane and I will begin calling some of our contacts in Britain and see what we can come up with," Ambrose said and they walked out of the room.

Ithel sat down at the desk and Constance joined her, pulling up a chair. Carys turned toward me and waited. I was still aghast. What had just happened?

"What about Tanith?" Riot prompted me.

I shook my head and sat down next to Carys. Riot joined us. "I know more about Tanith than I do the other two. Because of—" I broke off.

Carys seemed puzzled but Riot scowled. "I know it's wrong but I'm really hoping that she turns out to be the bad guy so we can execute the bitch," he said.

I agreed whole-hearted with that sentiment. "Get in line," I told him shortly. "First we have to do our research." I leaned forward, my elbows on my knees. "Tanith is European. I do not know exactly which country. She was born about 500 AD or thereabouts. She became a vampire at age thirty. She was a queen or princess in her country wherever that is."

"A princess shouldn't be too hard to track," Carys pointed out.

"But nearly every region in every country had someone who was considered royalty. A lot of them used the titles "prince" or "princess." And we don't even know which country let alone which region," I reminded her. "We could get a hit on some male relative rather than her."

"Unless she did something of great importance or was involved in some kind of major war," Riot added. "It will be hard to find her specifically."

"Then where do we start?" Carys asked.

I rose from my seat. "We start looking into European royalty in the 500s."

Do you know how freaking hard it is to get a list of monarchs from 500 AD? It is damned near impossible unless you know who you are looking for and when and where they lived. The only research we ever do is when we are hunting down a target. That usually involves searching all known addresses and interviewing friends, enemies, and family members. We did not have anything like that for Tanith and I was not sure where to begin.

Carys suggested the local library since our computer and phone lines were already in use. That meant I had to drop my illusion for the second time that day. I did so reluctantly but waited until the last possible second to do it.

I drove to the library after a brief but successful struggle over the keys with Riot much to Carys' amusement. I pulled up in front of the library to drop off Carys and Riot and then went to park the van. When I got inside, Riot handed Carys over to me since he was already hard at work on the computer. He spent a lot of the time trying to ignore the two female librarians who hovered around him waiting to assist him should he require it. Carys and I went to look up books on the Middle Ages. There were just over a dozen of them. Carys and I carried an armful each to a nearby table and sat down.

After six hours of research, I closed the book with an exclamation of disgust. "Nothing," I grumbled.

"It does seem a challenge to get information," Carys said removing the headphones she was using to listen to an audiobook.

"It is worse than challenging. It is hopeless," I said putting my head down on my forearms.

I felt Carys' soft hand on my head, stroking my hair. "Bane," she said softly.

I looked up and started to remind her not to call me by my real name in public, but the soft look in her eyes stopped me cold. Her lips parted and her fingers skimmed over my mouth as she leaned forward. Then, gently, her lips touched mine.

It was a sweet kiss, not hesitant but not demanding. Finally, Carys drew back from me and I stared at her. She looked slightly dazed.

"That was a great kiss," she said bewildered.

I was stunned. I felt...nothing at all—not love, not lust—nothing. How could this be? I could only stare at her, wordlessly.

Suddenly, Carys got to her feet and snatched the CD player from the table. "I am done with this book. I will ask the librarian for another."

She hurried away. I stared after her, confused. When she returned twenty minutes later, it was as though we never kissed. She put her headphones on and did not speak to me again until it was time to leave.

Riot joined us just as the library was getting ready to close. Carys and I took just about every book on the Middle Ages that the library had to offer. "Well, that was a complete bust," he sighed. "I didn't get much of anything." He looked down at the piles of books in our hands. "Looks like you two scored though."

I shook my head. "These are just a few of the ones we didn't get to. We can take out only a certain number of books on a certain subject at one time, so we will start with these. We don't know what is in them yet."

"I could grab a few more," Riot suggested.

"No," I said. "We have enough here to last for a few days."

"Try weeks," Riot said taking one of the books from my pile and looking at the title on the spine. He wrinkled his nose and replaced the book. "Just a little light reading."

"Not so light," Carys grimaced. "These books must weigh ten pounds each."

"Well, then, allow me to carry them for you, Miss Carys," Riot said gallantly and swept them out of her arms.

I remembered Demon's comment about Carys sitting around looking pretty and felt a surge of annoyance with her. She had carried those books from the shelves to the table and to the front desk without any assistance. The delicate female act was definitely getting old, but I kept my mouth shut.

Riot and I moved toward the line-up carrying about six books apiece. The librarian who was checking out the stragglers looked up, caught sight of Riot, and promptly forgot what she was supposed to be doing. The little old lady, whose romance novels she was in the process of checking out, frowned at her and rapped her knuckles on the counter top. The librarian started, blushed, and went back to work. The older woman turned around again to see whom the librarian was staring at and when she saw Riot, her mouth pursed up sourly. Riot and I grimaced at each other.

The other librarian had been pretending to put away books on the shelves in Riot's vicinity for the last twenty minutes. Now she hurried to the other computer and waved us over frantically. "I can help you here," she announced with an eagerness that was wholly attributable to wanting to get Riot closer to her.

Out of the corner of my eye, I saw the first librarian pick up her pace in order to the get elderly lady out of the way so that *she* could wait on us. She was out of luck. Riot took the books over to the other desk. I followed. As the old lady was leaving, a group of teenage girls took her place and plopped down ten books each on the counter, which promptly slid off the counter and into a jumbled pile on the floor. The librarian watched in disgust as the girls began to sort out which books belonged to whom and fumbled through their purses and wallets searching for their library cards. Our librarian had a triumphant smirk on her face that did not endear her to her co-worker.

The woman who checked out our books was efficient even while she checked out Riot. He chatted with me in a quiet voice and refrained from making eye contact with her during the process until he had to hand over his library card.

The librarian took it and studied the name. "Kane Williams," she said aloud. The other librarian and the teenagers were listening with interest. "I don't think I've seen you in here before, Mr. Williams. Are you interested in the Middle Ages?"

"No, but Brandon is," Riot gestured toward me.

Obediently I handed over my card too. "Kane is just helping me out by taking out some books under his name so that I can have a lot out at one time."

The librarian stared at me for a minute, transfixed by something. I was not sure what it was. Then, she turned back to Riot. "It's very nice of you to help a friend, Mr. Williams," she said. "But we don't suggest it in case your friend forgets to return the books on time. Then you'll have a big fine against your card."

"No problem," Riot told her. "We've been friends forever and I know where he lives."

The librarian seemed puzzled when I snorted and then began to cough to cover my laughter. Riot elbowed me, but maintained a pleasant smile on his face for the librarian's benefit.

Finally, she finished up with our books and we left at the same time as the teenagers. Riot held the door for them. They giggled and whispered, and all but batted their eyelashes at him as they hastened down the front steps. One actually checked out his ass.

"She can't be more than fifteen," I muttered to Riot.

He shrugged. "Remember, I don't look my age to her. I probably look like that kid from the wizard movie."

The first librarian had come up behind us to lock the door. As Carys and I started down the steps, we heard the woman speaking to Riot. Carys cocked her head, listening. Riot murmured something to the librarian and Carys frowned. I couldn't hear what he was saying but whatever it was, it made the librarian turn pink and smile at him. A moment later, he jogged down the steps to join us, smiling too.

"We didn't get a lot but we have a good start," I commented as I slid into the driver's seat of the SUV that Demon did not know that he had loaned me.

"I'm exhausted." Riot sighed. "Who knew that working on computers could be so tedious?" He climbed into the back, rested his head against the window since there was no back to the seat, and closed his eyes.

I glanced at Carys who was sitting in the passenger seat next to me. She turned her head slightly to address Riot. "You didn't flirt with the females in the library all day and then as we were leaving, you did."

In the rear view mirror, I saw Riot crack open one eye. He closed it again. "Who said that I flirted with them *then*?"

"You mean you didn't?"

"Does it matter?"

"I'm just trying to figure you out. Why didn't you flirt with them?"

Riot opened his eyes. "Well, first of all, four of them were underage," he pointed out. "And secondly, one of the librarians was married. I don't chase women who are committed to other men."

"What about the older woman?" I teased.

Riot grinned. "She was pretty hot for an old chick. But somehow I got the feeling that she disapproved of me."

I laughed. "She did look as though she had just been sucking on a lemon. That is unusual. Women don't typically disapprove of you."

"Women often disapprove of me. That's half of the attraction."

"The bad boy that Mother warned them about," I intoned dramatically.

Riot chuckled. "Yeah, that's usually it."

"So what did the woman want?" Carys persisted.

He frowned at her. "Why do you need to know?" he asked.

"There's no call for sarcasm, Lust." Carys frowned too. "I'm just asking a question."

"I just don't know why you are asking it but if you really must know, it had nothing to do with me."

I glanced at him in the rear view mirror. "It didn't?"

Riot shook his head, grinning. "She was asking about you."

I blinked. "Me?"

Riot waggled his eyebrows at me. "Apparently you have a very sexy voice and she wanted to know if you were married."

"*Me?*" I repeated, astonished.

Riot laughed. "Anyway, she and her co-worker wanted a double date with us and I graciously thanked her but said no."

Carys frowned. "Because she was married?"

"Yes," Riot replied in a cold voice. "Why do you find that so shocking?"

"I beg your pardon," she said stiffly. "But you're Lust. Why would it matter to *you* if the woman is married?"

I didn't like the way she said it, as if Riot was inferior to her somehow because of who he was. "Don't you feel bad about using women to feed your lust?" Carys went on.

Riot's expression grew cold. "Using?" he repeated.

"Not using," I corrected hastily and shot a warning look at Carys, which was stupid because she could not see it.

"Well, you inspire lust so you can feed from it," Carys continued.

"Don't you inspire love in order to feed?" he asked.

"That's different."

"Why?"

She made a sound of impatience. "It's *love*. It's something good and pure," she said in a reverential tone. Then her face took on the same expression that the old lady had. "Lust is...not."

I gaped at her in disbelief. The look Riot shot at her was not at all friendly and frankly, her narrow-minded view of Riot stunned me. I wondered what she thought of me. I glanced at him in the rear view mirror again. There were golden sparks shooting out of his eyes. "Let us drop this subject," I said firmly.

"Thank you," Riot snapped, glaring at Carys. He leaned his head against the window again and closed his eyes.

She seemed to sense our displeasure. "Kane, I apologize," Carys said quietly.

Riot opened his eyes and lifted his head. "Really," he said coldly.

Carys smiled. "You mustn't be angry."

"Mustn't I?" he repeated sarcastically. "Well, let me tell you, Miss Carys, I don't think you have any clue what real love is."

Carys jerked in surprise at his harsh tone. "What are you talking about?" she said sharply. "Of course I do! I *am* Love!"

"Have you ever felt real love, Carys?"

"What?"

"Have you ever been in love?" he repeated. "Have you ever felt real love? Has your heart ever stuttered in your chest because the person you love walked into the room? Have you ever felt the need to kiss them just because they smiled at you? Have you ever looked at someone and thought I could spend the rest of my life just gazing at this woman?"

His wistful tone caught my interest. "What woman?" I asked, glancing at him in the mirror again.

He waved his hand dismissively but did not meet my gaze. "Or whatever."

Carys hesitated. "Well—"

"What about lust?" he interrupted, his voice changed from wistful to suggestive. "Have you ever felt lust, Carys? Have you ever wanted someone with such intensity that you would dare anything, *be* anything he wanted just to have him touch you and to be able to touch him? Has anyone ever made your body tighten with need just from the sound of her voice?"

His example had changed genders again. There was clearly someone in particular on his mind. Whoever she was, she had Lust all stirred up. I could feel his voice vibrating along my skin. Immediately, an image of Abby wrapping her arms around my neck popped into my head. I could feel the warmth of her mouth on mine. Oh, hell. I turned and glared at him over my shoulder. "Tone it down."

He smiled slightly.

Carys sucked in her breath. "Stop that!" she snapped.

Riot leaned forward. "Why?"

"It's disgusting!"

"Most people who are in *love* would disagree with you," Riot told her quietly. "And if people didn't feel lust—didn't want each other—how would they propagate their species?"

"People who love each other don't need lust for that," she insisted.

"You are wrong. Love and Lust go hand in hand in any solid relationship," I told her coolly.

Riot's eyes met mine in the mirror and he shook his head incredulously. Then he sat back, rested his head against the window, and closed his eyes again.

We drove home in cold silence.

CHAPTER FIFTEEN

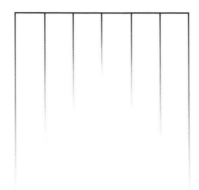

B Y THE TIME WE arrived at home, I had another splitting headache. This was becoming an unpleasant habit. As soon as we pulled into the driveway and I had turned off the engine, Riot got out of the car without speaking. I watched my friend wrench open the front door and then slam it closed as he disappeared inside. My head reverberated with the sharp sound of the slamming doors.

Carys was furious. "What did he mean that I don't know what real love is? It's who I am!"

"I think he just meant that when two people love each other, they often feel lust for each other too," I explained with more diplomacy than I was feeling. My head was killing me and I was pissed off too.

Carys shook her head. "That's ridiculous."

"It *isn't* ridiculous," I snapped throwing open my door. "And maybe Riot was right."

I came around the SUV to give her my arm. My heart jumped as soon as she touched me. All I could think about was that gentle kiss and my head start hurting more. We walked toward the house together and I felt Carys' bewilderment. "Is something wrong?" she asked.

"No."

"Yes, there is. We were getting along fine and now your body language has changed. You're pulling back from me."

I shrugged. She didn't understand and I didn't think I could explain it to her. She had her set ideas about what was and was not love. I admit to disappointment. I had always known that keeping her at arm's length was a good idea and Riot's conversation with her had just cemented that belief. A part of me felt that something had died and yet, another part felt relieved. However, it was still going to be difficult to get over her when I felt like she was the only woman in the world for me.

"Is it because you're not good enough for me?"

I stopped in my tracks, pulling her up short. I was speechless.

"*I* don't think that," she added hastily. "But I know what my brother thinks and Zane. I wondered if perhaps you felt that way too."

Before I could respond to her, Ambrose opened the door. He glared at me. "There you are, at last!" he snapped. "Carys, have you eaten dinner yet?"

"No," she began.

Ambrose glared at me. "It figures."

"Ambrose!"

"Forget it," I told her sharply and dropping her arm, I moved past them into the house.

"Where are you going?" she asked fretfully.

"To the basement," I snapped. "I feel the need to beat something and I am sure that you would rather I beat on cement blocks than your idiot brother!"

I stormed away, leaving the pair of them in the hallway.

Until recently, the basement had housed Tanith and her entourage. We were protecting them as well as trying to keep an eye on them. At the time, it seemed that she might have been the rogue sovereign. It was still possible. I had not found much information yet, but I still needed to talk to my brother. I hoped that he could give me more.

In the meantime, I had some anger issues to work out. The workout room consisted of several cement punching bags, as well as barbells that had poured concrete weights. Each one probably weighed the same as a large elephant. After all, we are the Deadlies. A human could not have lifted one of those barbells. I picked one up easily and hurled it across the room, leaving a small crack in the wall.

I felt my brother's presence before he said anything. "Bane."

I paused and then swung at the cement block hanging from the ceiling by a thick chain. It moved about a foot and then swung back. I backed up a bit before it made contact with my body and sent me to the floor. That would be damned embarrassing with my brother watching.

Demon stepped into the room but stayed well back from me. He did not speak.

"When did you get home?" I asked flatly.

"A few minutes before you did," he said.

We were both silent except for the sound of my fists slamming into the concrete block. "What happened?" he asked after a while.

"What makes you think anything happened?"

"This temper is not typical of you. I am usually the one down here trashing the place. Besides," his voice changed to a low, long growl. "I could feel your anger from the other end of the house."

I stopped, breathing hard. "Sorry," I said guiltily. "If I had known that you were in the house, I would have held it in."

"You do not have to apologize. It is nothing that I cannot handle."

I had heard *that* before. I struggled to pull myself together. "Riot did not tell you about Carys?" I asked.

"You tell me," Demon said. His tone was milder and I relaxed.

"Carys insinuated that since Riot feeds from lust he is somehow inferior to her," I told him.

At first, he did not speak. I heard him moving closer. "That made you angry."

"I was angry but I am not angry now."

"No, you are not angry at all. You often come into the catacombs and beat the shit out of the punching bags when you are ecstatically happy."

I should have known better. I cannot lie to my brother. "All right," I snapped. I took a deep breath. "I *am* angry. I admit that I do not like her writing him off as being nothing because he is a Deadly!"

He considered me in silence for a moment. "I doubt he is much troubled by what she thinks of him. He has more important things on his mind right now."

"Like what?" I asked curiously.

"You should ask him, not me." He eyed me. "Something else is bothering you. What is it? What did Carys say to you?"

I could not look him in the eye. "She said that I was not good enough for her."

When he did not answer, I glanced up. Demon was gaping at me, speechless. His expression was almost worth reliving that little stab through the heart. It is not often that I get a chance to shock my brother. I smiled. "Why, whatever is the matter, Demon?"

"I cannot believe she said that," he replied finally.

"She did say that *she* does not believe it but it appears that Zane and Ambrose have pointed it out to her repeatedly," I told him bitterly.

"Did you believe her?"

"No."

"Damn them," Demon said softly.

I sighed, suddenly tired of the Graces, the rogue vampires and most of all, of love. "They are Graces, Demon. They have been brought up to believe that they are better than the Deadlies."

"That is not true of all of the Graces. Both of Carys' parents have been perfectly kind to us."

"They have short memories apparently," I said. "To be fair, Carys did not mention that any of the others feel this way."

He shook his head. "I thought Carys was more open-minded than that."

"It appears we were both wrong."

"I am sorry about Carys, Bane."

We were both quiet again, staring at the floor. Finally, he looked up at me. "Do you want me and the others to kick them out of our house?" he asked. "I can tell that Dev is just itching to connect his boot to Ambrose's ass."

Leave it to my brother to make me laugh about this. "They have no place else to go," I pointed out, reluctantly. "So I suppose we are stuck with them living here until they get another house."

Demon grimaced. "I must admit that the extra eyes and ears have been very helpful, but I would kick them out in a second if I thought it would make you feel better."

I had to smile. "I know that and I appreciate the sentiment, though I am sure that you would enjoy every second of it, too."

He smiled back. "Only marginally."

"Liar."

His grin widened. "In the meantime, I think I can help you out."

"How?"

"I will make certain that you do not have to deal with Carys. I can rearrange the teams."

"You do not have to do that," I protested.

"But, I will anyway."

"I am a big boy, Demon. Honestly, I can deal with this."

"But you should not have to deal with it," he replied. "Anyway, I came down here to get you because everyone is waiting upstairs in the library for the debriefing. Do you think you can face them without throttling anyone?"

"I can if you can." I gave the cement block one last punch. It cracked and I followed my brother out of the room.

I reached the steps before Demon and was about halfway up when I realized that he was no longer with me. I glanced back. He was standing at the bottom step still, staring at the floor. His breathing was rapid and raspy.

I frowned and went back down. "Demon?"

He looked up sharply. His pupils had dilated and his face was extremely pale. "Demon!" I gasped in alarm, clasping his shoulder. "What is it?"

Suddenly he took a deep breath and the panic disappeared from his face. "By the way," he said, calmly. "You had a phone call."

"Oh?" I watched him carefully, trying to see past that blank expression.

"Hex left the message on the phone table in the hallway." Then, he moved past me and went up the stairs as if nothing had happened.

I grabbed the phone message off the table and shoved it into my pocket. My fingers felt another piece of paper inside that same pocket and I remembered that I had another phone message from someone named Cherie earlier. Well, it would have to wait. I followed my brother into the library where the others were waiting for us to report on our findings. I began with our research first.

We had learned very little about any royalty in Europe, at least from the time period we suspected Tanith had lived in. "Are you certain that she was a noblewoman?" I asked Demon.

He was sitting behind the desk with his feet propped up on it again. He nodded. "Tanith was certainly a lady or princess of some kind. Her family will probably have some kind of record of her. Keep trying."

"Did she have a last name?"

He shrugged. "If she did, she never mentioned it to me."

That was no help, but grumbling wasn't going to help either, so I kept my complaints to myself. Demon turned to Ithel. "Did you get anything on Darkmoon?"

She frowned. "No. There is no record of anyone by that name is Carthage. Though there was a family called De Lunascura."

"That is 'dark moon' in Italian," Demon said. Ithel nodded. "Fantastic. It's a lead. Find out all you can about the De Lunascura family."

"Okay."

Demon looked over at Ambrose. "What did you and Zane get?"

Ambrose shook his head and made a face. "Nothing. Either no one in that village knows anything about Hadrian Smauker/Standish or they are afraid to tell."

"Probably the latter," Zane added.

Demon nodded and glanced around the room. "Anyone else?"

No one answered for a moment and then Conrad spoke up. "I have something."

"*You?*" Zane laughed, scornfully.

Conrad glared at him, his blue eyes snapping. "Yes," he replied, coldly. "*Me.*"

Zane seemed taken aback by Conrad's reaction. I silently applauded my cousin and glanced at Demon. There was evidence of his influence here. Hex was right. One day in Demon's company and Conrad's self-confidence had soared.

Demon addressed Conrad as if Zane had not spoken. "What do you have, Conrad?"

Conrad purposefully turned his back on Zane who seemed more than a little shocked by the snub. "Well, I spoke with a fairy that came from the same county that Hadrian's family had lived in. It seems that they did live on the estate of the Standish family," Conrad explained. "There was some reason to believe that Hadrian Smauker was actually a by-blow of the son of the house at the time."

"That is why he believes he has a right to the name," Demon suggested.

"Most likely, though it seems like flimsy reasoning to me since it was all a rumour and the lord of the estate was also reputed to be Hadrian's father." Conrad went on, "Anyway, there was a marriage between Hadrian Lucius Smauker and guess who? It was a woman by the name of Elissa Minerva De Lunascura!"

Dev was in the middle of taking a drink from his can of pop. Suddenly he choked and began to laugh. Demon grinned. "I have a hard time picturing Darkmoon being called Elissa Minerva."

"I agree. It is too pretty for her." Conrad laughed. I could feel the pride coming off him in waves. No, I did not feed from it. He was family and he deserved to feel pride in his accomplishment. It certainly was not excessive. He was still Modesty after all.

Conrad continued with his report. "Hadrian claimed that his wife was the daughter of some Count in Italy. It seems that within a few months of their marriage, the other villagers became suspicious since they never saw her during the day. Servants talked, I guess. Anyway, Hadrian and Elissa fled the village and no one ever saw them again. That was in 1628. Then in 1759, Hadrian and Darkmoon surfaced in Blackridge."

"Did the fairy give a description of Elissa De Lunascura?"

Conrad frowned. "This is where it gets puzzling. No one seems to know what she looked like."

"It doesn't matter. The information you came up with is brilliant, Conrad," I said. He flushed with pleasure at the compliment. I suspect that he did not get very many of them.

"All we need is the smoking gun to prove that Darkmoon is Elissa De Lunascura," Demon added. "Great work, Conrad."

He blushed even more. "Th—thanks, Demon," he stammered, but I could see that he was pleased.

"They never saw *her* during the day?" I repeated. "What about Hadrian?"

Conrad looked thoughtful. "You know, the fairy never said that there was anything unusual about him."

"Perhaps Darkmoon is the one who turned him," Demon suggested. "It sounds as though she didn't turn him until after they were married and even then it was not done until much later."

"I wonder why," I remarked.

"We could always ask Hadrian," Riot said. The rest of us stared at him incredulously. He grimaced and shrugged. "Right. What was I thinking?"

"Now what do we do?" Ambrose demanded, clearly affronted that he had been left out of the conversation of which Conrad was the star.

"Now we look into the past of Elissa De Lunascura," Demon told him. "We need to find out if there is anything that can prove that she is Darkmoon aside from the coincidence of the name."

"We could do what Riot suggested and ask Hadrian outright," Kaz pointed out.

"And when he refuses to answer on the grounds that it is none of our business?" Demon asked.

Kaz grinned. "He'll tell you anything if you phrase the threat the right way."

Demon rolled his eyes. "Well, I would rather not give Darkmoon or Hadrian the heads up that we are investigating their pasts and give them the opportunity to hide anything useful." He turned to me. "Have you tried looking up Tanith on the Internet?"

"I did." Riot stepped forward. "All I came up with was that the name Tanith comes from Carthage and that it was the name of a goddess..."

"Carthage?" Demon interrupted. His feet dropped to the floor and he sat up straight.

Riot's eyes widened. "I never thought of that. Tanith and Darkmoon come from the same country."

"And the same region," Demon added thoughtfully. "Anything else?"

"I'm afraid not," Riot said.

"Okay, keep trying. Find out more about the goddess," Demon suggested.

"You think Tanith is the goddess?"

"Doubtful. If she is a goddess, a vampire bite would have killed her."

Riot nodded. "Oh, right."

"She could have earned that reputation simply because she is a vampire and exhibited some kind of power in public. That is often how people who were not actually gods and goddesses got the name," I pointed out.

"That is true," Demon said. He got up and came around to lean against the desk next to me. "Keep searching for information about the goddess. It might still lead us to Tanith."

"We didn't have much luck in our interviews." He went on, "Everyone we spoke to either didn't want to tell us anything, couldn't tell us anything, or gave us descriptions that were so different as to be useless in identifying the rogue. The only thing we do know for certain now is that the rogue vampire is a female."

"So, that narrows it down to either Tanith or Darkmoon," I said.

"Or an outsider that we have yet to hear about. We have had three different people tell us that the rogue sovereign is an "older woman with short blond hair and blue eyes" or "a twenty something male with brown curly hair and green eyes." That doesn't describe either Tanith or Darkmoon."

"One guy told me that the sovereign was an alien with an orange mohawk and glowing lime green eyes. He also said she probed his ass," Kaz muttered. "But I think he was drunk."

"Gee, *you think?*" Dev snorted.

"Is it possible that they're lying to protect themselves or the sovereign?" Ambrose asked.

"It is probable that they are lying," Demon told him. "We will keep trying, but unless someone comes forward and gives us the name of the sovereign, we are going to have to get our information from other sources."

He got to his feet. "We will start again fresh tomorrow. We have more information to go on now. Let's start asking questions about Darkmoon and Elissa De Lunascura." He turned to me. "Bane, you keep working on Tanith."

I nodded.

"And let's all get some sleep. I have a feeling that tomorrow is going to be another long day."

CHAPTER SIXTEEN

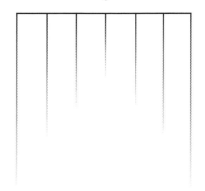

I FELT THAT I was beginning to understand my brother's insomnia. I could not sleep. I could only think about what Carys had said to Riot. She was so patronizing and arrogant. I had always thought that Carys was one of the more tolerant of the Graces. Clearly, I was mistaken and that really bothered me. No matter what Carys told me, I believed that she, like Ambrose and Zane, thought a Deadly was beneath the Graces. I also believed that she had not meant to let that little bit of information slip but why it mattered, I didn't know. It made me wonder whether I was wrong about the other Graces too. I was certain that Conrad did not feel that way about us. Abby seemed to like us, but was that a lie as well? Did she believe that the Graces were superior to the Deadlies? *That* also bothered me.

About midnight, I gave up and remembered my phone messages. I turned on the light and took the papers out of my jacket. They were a bit wrinkled from being shoved into my pocket. I smoothed them out and suddenly remembered that Cherie was the waitress from the werewolf bar. I grimaced as I read and was thankful that Morgana had taken the first one and not Hex since it was the most graphic. It brought some interesting images to mind. Funny, the woman in those images was not Cherie.

Damn it.

I stuffed the messages back into my pocket and got out of bed. There was no way I was going to sleep now. It was late or I might have called the number. Instead, I left the bedroom and headed downstairs for the kitchen.

The lights were off except for one over the sink. I stood there trying to figure out what it was I wanted. It wasn't really food, but at the moment, it was my only option. I opened the fridge and started looking for leftovers.

Suddenly, I heard the kitchen door swing open behind me. I looked up and froze. "Abby."

She stopped too. "Bane?"

"What are you doing up?" I asked.

"I couldn't sleep. You?"

I shrugged. "I couldn't sleep either."

"I see," she said with a smile. "Well, I know what was keeping me up. Why are you awake?"

I didn't answer right away. I just realized that Abby was wearing a short nightie and my imagination was running away with me. "I was hungry," I told her hoarsely.

"Me, too," she said and stepped into my arms.

Her fingers slid along my arms, up to my shoulders and then she kissed me. Or I kissed her. I'm not sure which. All I know is; I lost my head.

My fingers slid underneath the nightgown, over her hips and I lifted her onto the kitchen table. She moved her hips to the edge of the table, her legs on either side of my hips. Somewhere, in the back of my mind, I knew this was a bad idea. I told my conscience to shut up.

"Abby. . ."

"Please. . ." she whispered back. Her fingers were tugging at my jeans.

Suddenly, the overhead light flashed on. "Shit, sorry," someone said.

It took me a second to pull myself together. "Kaz," I said and stepped away from Abby. "What are you doing here?"

"I live here."

I glared at him. "I meant in the *kitchen*."

"I thought I heard noises." He was grinning at me. "If I had known what they were, I would have stayed out."

Blushing, Abby slid off the table. "I guess I'd better go back to bed," she murmured and slipped past Kaz and out of the kitchen.

Kaz looked back at me. "Sorry, Bane."

I sighed and shook my head. "No. It was probably good that you showed up when you did or we might have done something that she would regret tomorrow."

"*She* would regret? Just her—"Kaz started to say but I walked out of the kitchen before he could finish.

When I woke up, bright sunlight was streaming in through the window. I groaned and rolled over. My eye caught the time on the old ship's clock on the nightstand and I sat up with a groan. It was past nine. Hex is a stickler about her meal times. Breakfast is promptly at seven and cleared at eight. If you are not at the table, you do not eat.

I dressed hastily, wondering how much grovelling I was going to have to do to get breakfast out of Hex. I barrelled out of my room and nearly knocked Abby over. I grasped her waist to keep her from falling. She smiled up at me, her hands slid up my arms and she wrapped her arms around my neck. "Good morning." She kissed me on the mouth.

I know that I should not have done so, but I kissed her back. I was still disturbed about last night and she had kept invading my dreams. Her mouth was as warm and soft as I remembered, and so was the bare skin that peeked between her halter-top and her jeans. It felt very, very nice under my fingers. The kiss didn't *feel* like a lie. I backed her into the wall and lifted her against me, deepening the kiss. Her legs wrapped around my waist, pulling me tight against her. We both groaned at the same time and that broke the spell.

I drew back from her slowly and stared into her beautiful blue eyes. "Oh, shit," I said and released her quickly.

"What?"

"We're in the hallway, Abby!"

"Oh," she said breathlessly. "Well, my bedroom is right here." Abby lifted her hand to touch my chest.

I groaned. "No, no, no. Flee. Flee, Bane..."

I bolted for the stairs, shifting back into my daemon persona. About half way down, I stopped short.

At the bottom of the stairs, Demon and Maia stood talking quietly. I wondered if they had just witnessed my serious lapse in judgement. Since they did not look up or acknowledge me, I assumed that they had not. Carys stood by the library door, looking slightly put out. I think they had left her out of the conversation purposely. Demon was still angry with Carys for the way she had treated Riot and me. You are never disrespectful to a Deadly. Ever.

Maia noticed me first. "Good morning, Bane, Abby."

"Good morning." Abby's voice was right behind me. "I hope everyone slept better than I did." I dared not turn around to look at her.

My brother murmured a greeting and headed for the door before my feet touched the bottom step. I frowned after him.

Maia moved to stand in front of me, directing my attention to her. "With the information that Conrad gave us, we've decided to get to work right away since we've all had a chance to eat. Zane and Ambrose are on the phones already making calls to Italy and Britain," she told me as she began to back away down the hallway.

"Wait," I said, following her. "You are not going with Demon?" She was talking fast and that always makes me suspicious.

"Riot, Constance, and I are going through the books you brought home yesterday," she explained, ignoring my question. "You can help Abby on the computer after the two of you have had your breakfast."

It took me a minute to realize that this meant I was working with Abby *alone*. I knew whose idea this was, in spite of his assurances that he was not trying to play matchmaker. I spun around to give my brother a piece of my mind only to discover that he was long gone. I turned back to argue with Maia just as she closed the door to the dining room.

Suddenly, I was alone in the hallway with Abby.

Reluctantly, I turned back to face her. She was smiling at me. I scowled. "What?"

Her smile grew wider. "I dreamed about you last night. Do you want to hear it?"

"Crap," I said stiffly.

She laughed, eyes sparkling. "At least you didn't say no."

"I need coffee," I growled stalking toward the kitchen.

Abby, undeterred by my attitude, followed. "Are you always this cheerful in the morning?" she asked. "You know, if you had just followed me upstairs last night, you probably would be in a much better mood this—"

"Seriously, Abby," I interrupted. "No jokes allowed before coffee. It is a house rule."

"Who's joking?"

I pushed open the swinging kitchen door and held it for her.

Two steps into the room I stopped short as Hex turned to glare at me, her arms folded across her chest. "I suppose you want breakfast?" she demanded.

I felt like a two-year-old getting a scolding from nana. "Yes, please," I said in the meekest voice that I could muster. Behind me, I heard Abby giggling. I will say this for Abby—you cannot stay angry with her. If you can, you are tougher than I am. I had to fight hard not to smile. Hex would not appreciate that.

My apologetic expression did not fool Hex for a minute. "My rules are not made to be laughed at." I started to protest but she wagged a tiny finger at me. "They are established to keep this house organized and running smoothly. It creates extra work for me..."

Etcetera.

The lecture went on longer than it took to make a plate of toast, a fresh pot of coffee, and some eggs. I had told Abby to go on ahead while I stood in the doorway, balancing my plate and coffee mug, waiting for Hex' lecture to wind down, but Abby waited with me, smiling. She seemed to enjoy Hex's tirade as much as I did.

"I am very sorry, Hex," I told her when she finally stopped long enough to draw breath. I added hurriedly, "And now I had better get to work. Demon will expect some kind of result today. Let's go, Abby."

We fled down the hallway. Abby's face was bright red and I appreciated her efforts to keep herself under control until we got inside the library. We set down our plates on the desk and she immediately burst into laughter.

"Thank you for restraining yourself in front of Hex," I said.

"She's too sweet!" Abby laughed, wiping a tear from her cheek.

"She is an imp," I reminded her, pulling out a chair for her. "And she works for the Deadlies."

Something in my tone made her stop laughing. She sat down in the chair, staring up at me curiously. "Should that make a difference to me?"

"It matters to your brother and Zane."

"Those two," Abby snorted contemptuously and rolled her eyes. "Please tell me that you aren't listening to the garbage they've been spouting about Deadlies being lesser daemons than Graces! It's such bullshit!"

I was startled by her language, but not displeased with the sentiment. "Not all the Graces think so," I pointed out.

Abby scowled and it made me smile. *She is gorgeous even when she is pissed off.*

I shook the thought away. What the hell was I thinking about a Grace? Even if Abby wanted me, it was nothing more than lust. There was no way her brother was going to allow such a thing. Besides, I had enough problems contending with Carys. I scolded myself again for my fickleness. What kind of man was I that I could lust after one sister while I might be in love with the other?

A confusing thought suddenly darted into my head. Which one did I lust for and which one did I love? To my utter astonishment, I wasn't sure.

I was aware then that Abby was speaking to me. I pulled myself together in time to hear her say, "I don't know who else you could have been talking to. As far as I know, everyone else thinks Zane and Ambrose are full of shit too. I think you'll find that the rest of us don't have any illusions about who does the real hard work around here."

"That is not true," I told her. "The Graces help people. How many lives did Ambrose save after that plane crashed?"

Abby's smile grew as I spoke. "What's this?" she teased. "Are you defending the Graces' honour?"

The sight of her smile made me smile. "I just want to be fair," I replied, slightly embarrassed. "Remember, my cousin is a Grace."

"Oh." Abby pretended to pout. "Is that all? You're defending Conrad. No one else?" she added hopefully.

I laughed and tapped her nose with my finger. "Okay, okay. You're all right too...for a Grace."

She gave a gasp of mock indignation. "Bane, I'm surprised at you! How prejudiced!"

"I suppose it is," I agreed still smiling at her. I bowed slightly. "Please accept my sincerest apologies, Miss Abigail."

"Apology accepted, Mr. Hellblazer."

I could not seem to stop smiling at her. I leaned down but caught myself before I could kiss her again. I pulled out a chair at the desk for myself instead. "Shall we eat our breakfasts and then get to work before my brother returns breathing fire?" I asked dropping the formal tone.

Abby looked interested. "Can he really do that?" she asked.

"No."

"Damn. I was hoping that he might set Zane on fire," she said wistfully.

I laughed.

Working with Abby was as hard as I thought it would be. She was a good worker. That was not the problem. You can probably guess what was. I watched her as she worked at the laptop, which my brother had set up on the desk before he left. If she found something she thought might pertain to Tanith, she sent to the printer. I collected the sheets, read them through, and marked anything of interest or anything questionable that Demon might be able to answer for us. It was so tedious that I would rather have gone back into the kitchen and had a whole pot of Hex' tea than continue with this research. Instead, my mind kept wandering back to last night, thinking about my dreams, and wondering about hers. The desktop started to look inviting. So did the floor, the sofa, the chairs, the bookcases...you name it.

By noon, I was more than ready for a break. I stood and stretched. Abby looked up and I caught her staring at my chest, smiling. "Lunch," I told her. Her grin widened. I pretended not to notice but caught myself staring longingly at the desk again.

"We just ate," she pointed out.

I sighed. "Did you learn nothing from Hex's lecture this morning? We have rules here, you know, the better to keep us all organized against our will."

Abby had risen from her chair and now she applauded lightly. "You do that very well." She smiled.

I led the way out of the library, relieved that some of the sexual tension had eased. "What's that?"

"Demon."

I laughed. "Riot said the same thing to me yesterday. Like I told him, we *are* identical twins."

"But not very much alike other than appearance and the fact that you both look good in jeans."

I glanced back at her. "Abby, don't."

"It's so hot when you get that look in your eyes," she added.

I could not help but laugh. "Okay, enough!" I shook my head. "Damn, you're good."

Her smile turned sultry. "Babe," she purred. "I'm the *best*."

I ignored the twinge in my stomach. "Has Riot been giving you lessons on flirting?"

"Am I doing it right?" she asked hopefully.

I laughed again, but she *was* very good at flirting. "You are an apt student," I admitted and she seemed pleased.

I pushed open the kitchen door and held it for her. Hex looked up as we came in and then checked the clock. Satisfied that we were on time and not messing with her precious schedule, she silently went to the cupboard and got out the plates. Abby and I loaded up on sandwiches and salad.

"We should have been a little bit late." Abby whispered to me. I poured us both some ice water. "I miss the lecture that comes with the meal."

I laughed softly. "There are more lectures where that came from," I assured her. "Just do everything Dev does. You will get all the lectures you desire."

Just then, the others came in to get their meals. Maia walked over to us. "How is it going?" she asked in a low voice.

I shrugged. "There isn't much except that Tanith is the name of a goddess of war and she is also a fertility goddess."

"She is associated with Baal," Abby added. "And people sometimes sacrificed children to her."

Maia looked horrified. "Children? How could they do that?"

"It was a different time, Maia," I reminded her.

"If Tanith was killing children, then Demon can execute her for that alone," Maia said.

"Tanith did not kill the children herself. The humans did that." I did not point out that Maia's mother is a goddess and may have had a few people sacrificed in her name as well. "Anyway, humans do not sacrifice other humans to the gods anymore."

"Good!" she said fiercely.

"Remember that we have no proof that Tanith is the goddess," I went on. "Her parents could have named her in honour of their goddess."

"Perhaps they should have sacrificed *her* instead," Maia said. I agreed wholeheartedly and then Abby and I returned to work in the library.

Three hours later, our sandwiches were gone, the ice water was gone, and so was my patience. There was nothing about Tanith. There was nothing concrete anyway. All we had were fifty-five pages of questions. I finished highlighting the fifty-sixth page and tossed it on the pile. I put my head down on the desk in frustration. It was as though this woman had appeared out of nowhere. Maybe the man Kaz talked to was right and she was an alien.

Suddenly, Abby spoke. "Bane?" Something in her voice put me on alert instantly. I looked up at her. She was staring at the computer screen with wide eyes and her mouth hanging open.

"What is wrong?" I said rising from my chair.

"It's her," Abby said faintly.

"It is who?"

"I was just messing around," she went on in a small voice. "I just put the name in to see what would happen. It was a total accident."

I came around the desk to have a look at the computer screen and there she was.

Tanith De Lunascura.

"I'll be damned," I murmured. "They are related. I wonder..."

Suddenly I went cold. I reached over, snatching up some of the notes on the desk and began scanning them quickly. When I got to the page I wanted, I read it through, at last finding the highlighted information that, until now, had seemed inconsequential. It was Darkmoon's birthdate. My heart nearly stopped.

"Oh, shit," I said.

CHAPTER SEVENTEEN

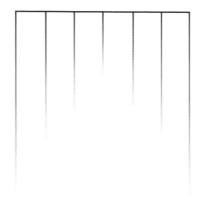

I CALLED DEMON ON his cell phone, refusing to talk to him over the phone about what Abby had found but insisting that he come right home.

"What is wrong?" he demanded, alarmed. "What have you found?"

"It is not an emergency," I said and then thought about it. "Well, perhaps it is, but no one has been injured, so you can take your time getting here." Even as I hung up, I knew he would be racing back here at top speed. I only hoped that a cop would not pull him over. I pitied the officer that tried to stop him.

Abby came up behind me and touched my shoulder as I hung up the phone. "Hey," she said softly. "Are you okay?"

"I am a little worried. There is some information that was...unexpected," I admitted. "I'm more worried about how Demon's going to take this."

Abby seemed surprised. "Why?"

"How could he not be under the circumstances?" I asked.

"What circumstances?" she asked.

"I would rather not say until I speak to my brother."

Abby and I stared at each other. "I knew that you and Demon seemed to know Tanith from before but it was more than that?"

"Yes. It was more than that," I repeated.

Abby still seemed puzzled. I hesitated, not sure how much I should reveal to her. Then I decided to trust her. "Tanith and Demon were lovers," I told her. "She is the one who turned him."

"*Demon*?" Abby gasped, sitting up straight. "Oh, no! Do you think he's still in love with her?"

"I hope not for his sake, especially in view of this." I waved a hand at the computer.

"How can you not know if he still loves her or not?" she asked curiously.

I laughed in spite of my anxiety for my brother. "Brothers do not usually discuss their love lives with each other, Abby. That being said, I did ask him and he said—well, he told me that he didn't want to talk about it only in less polite terms."

Abby laughed too. "I can imagine. Demon doesn't beat around the bush, does he?"

"Hardly," I responded dryly.

"Perhaps it is nothing," Abby suggested hopefully. "I mean, it could have been a popular last name."

"Maybe," I said, but I didn't believe it.

I paced the floor of the library while we waited for my brother and the others to return. "Should we call Ambrose and the others?" Abby asked after a few minutes of watching me.

"No," I said gruffly. "I would like to tell Demon without an audience, if you know what I mean."

"Are you worried about his reaction?" she asked quietly.

"Yes. He loved her. Maybe he still does. I do not know for sure. Even if he does not, this will upset him. If he is in love with her—" I shook my head.

It would devastate him.

Shit.

Abby got up from her chair and approached me. She moved in front of me, stopping my back and forth progress across the room. Very gently, Abby reached up and kissed me on the mouth. She drew back, keeping her arms around my waist. It felt good and right to have her arms around my waist. To be honest, it felt so right that it was scaring the hell out of me.

She smiled up at me. "Do you realize that you've dropped the illusion?"

I was startled. "I have?" I glanced in the mirror behind the desk and realized that she was right. "I didn't realize."

"Why do you feel the need to hide who you are?" she asked quietly. "I mean, honestly! I already know that you and Demon are identical twins."

I didn't really want to explain that the whole shapeshifting deal I went into around the Graces was to remind them of what I was. After all, they were well aware that I was a Deadly. I probably did not need to rub their faces in it, but some immature part of me really delighted in doing it. "Well..." I began hesitantly.

The door opened and Ambrose walked in with Zane. I moved away from Abby casually so it wouldn't look like she had been comforting me.

"Would you please knock before you bust into a room?" I demanded. I was a little annoyed and partly relieved that they had interrupted us. Abby was a Grace, as I reminded myself, and I had no business holding her in my arms. The thought made me scowl and now I had a target for my frustration. On the plus side, their presence kept me from saying something to Abby that could be potentially humiliating.

Ambrose gave me a look of disgust and then turned to his sister, ignoring me. Zane was less stupid. He kept one wary eye on me the whole time. There are some benefits to having Wrath as a twin. Those who don't overlook you, tend to paint you with the same brush instead. I was tempted to do something Wrath-like to scare the shit out of Zane just because I didn't like him. I felt very noble when I abstained.

"We're finished for now," Ambrose told Abby. "We've had some luck in gathering information. We probably know everything there is to know about Hadrian by this time. Are you finished too?"

"Yes," Abby replied.

Ambrose half turned his head toward me, the disgust still evident in his face. "Did you find out anything about this Tanith woman?"

"Whatever we have discovered, you will find out when the others do," Abby told him quietly.

Ambrose turned his head toward her sharply. "Then you did find out something."

"We will discuss it later, Ambrose," Abby said firmly.

"Don't be ridiculous! I'm your brother and your leader. You can tell me."

Abby shook her head firmly. "No, Ambrose. Demon is the leader here. We'll give the information to him first and let him decide what the others need to know."

The two men glared at me. "She never used to lie and keep secrets from us."

Zane sneered at me but he was speaking to Ambrose. "I told you that this was a mistake. This is what comes of associating with the Deadlies."

"Zane!" Abby gasped.

"You two idiots," I shot back with disgust. "Zane is the most conceited asshole I have ever met and you..." I turned to Ambrose. "You are a self-righteous jerk! You treat my cousin like crap and Abby like a two-year old, but they have more guts and intelligence than the lot of you put together."

Ambrose stepped between Zane and me. I don't know whether he meant to prevent a physical altercation or if he was simply so angry that, he couldn't wait to confront me. "How dare you lecture me about my sister!" he hissed.

"What does a Deadly know about a Grace?" Zane sneered.

Somehow, in my anger, my mouth got ahead of my brain. "I know she kisses like a succubus!" I snapped.

Oops.

Zane, Ambrose, and I froze as my confession slowly sank in. I didn't dare look at Abby. Ambrose turned white and then red. "You defiled my sister?" His voice was raspy with rage.

"No. She defiled me!" I blurted. Then I tried to correct myself, hastily. "I mean, she kissed me, not defiled..." I grimaced and covered my eyes with my hand. "I am now going to stop talking before I hurt myself."

Abby decided that this would be a good moment to kiss me again and this time, in front her brother and Zane, but they may as well have been part of the furniture. She certainly did not act as though we had an audience.

She drew back from me and asked, "Do I really kiss like a succubus?"

"You can't tell?" I asked incredulously. I was holding her so firmly against me that I was sure the answer would be rather obvious.

She gave me a half-shy, half-flirting glance from under her eyelashes. "Well, maybe I can after all." She smiled, snuggling closer.

I sucked in my breath sharply, aware that Ambrose and Zane were still in the room, gaping at us, and wishing them both to the other side of the universe. "Abby, stop that."

She began to laugh.

"*You bastard!*" Ambrose screamed and made a move as if he was going to launch himself at me.

That would be a very bad idea on his part. I tensed, ready to take him on, but the door of the library flung open, distracting us. Hex stood in the doorway, hair in disarray and eyes wild with fear.

I still had my arms around Abby. I released her now and took a step toward the imp, concerned. "Hex?"

"Bane, come quick!" she gasped out. "She says he's in danger!"

I did not take the time to ask whom. I bolted out of the library and stopped short as the blond woman standing in the foyer spun around to face me with frightened golden brown eyes. "Kit?"

"Bane!" She moved toward me. Her eyes were desperate. "Where is Demon?"

"He is not here," I told her, wondering at her distress. "But, he is on his way home."

"Call him!" She grasped my arms tightly.

"What?"

"He's always loved technology so he probably has one of those cell phone thingies, hasn't he?" she demanded.

She knew my brother well. "Well, yes, but—" I broke off when I heard a vehicle pull into the driveway. "That is probably him now."

Kit didn't wait. She burst out of the house and ran toward Demon, screaming his name. He came around the front of the SUV and stopped, frowning. "Kit, what are you doing here?" I heard him ask.

That is when I heard the first shot. It smashed into the doorframe of the house. Another bullet went through the window and smashed the vase sitting on the table in the hallway. Hex screamed.

"Hex!" I grabbed the imp and shoved her into Abby's arms. "Take her back into the library!" I said to Abby. "Get down behind the desk and stay away from the windows!" I did not wait to see if she obeyed. I hunched down behind the door as Dev burst in carrying Ithel in his arms. He flung himself against the wall beside me. Ithel clung to him, sobbing.

Kaz ran through the still open door threw himself on the floor on the other side of the foyer. A bullet narrowly missed him. It embedded itself in the railing of the staircase. "Sonofabitch!" Kaz yelped.

"Where is Maia?" Dev demanded.

"Dining room," I answered. "Ithel, go into the library! Stay on the floor and away from the windows!"

Dev detached Ithel from his neck, gently, and urged her into the safety of the library. "I'm going to check on Maia." He ran off down the hall, keeping low and close to the wall.

Demon flew through the door, carrying Kit and Carys as bullets smashed the other window. I heard the solid thuds as they struck the wooden front porch. He and the two women crouched beside Kaz. Riot appeared next to me. "What the hell is going on? Who is shooting at us?"

"I don't know," I replied.

"Where is Onyx?" Riot asked, looking around.

I glanced around too, and suddenly realized that Onyx had not made it inside. I looked back at Riot. He paled and looked panicked.

"Demon," Riot said in a hoarse voice. "Where the hell is my brother?"

I looked around too and met Demon's horrified gaze. "And Conrad?" I gasped.

I eased cautiously forward to peek out through the window next to the door. Onyx was lying on the ground, not moving, with Conrad hunched over him, protectively.

"Oh, shit!" I gasped.

"Onyx!" Riot yelled, and lunged for the door.

"Stay here!" I shoved him back. Demon, Kaz, and I burst out of the house and into the fray.

As we raced across the driveway, bullets struck the ground around us. I reached the two men first and hunched over them, my wings spread like a shield. A bullet struck the ground to the far left. Whoever the snipers were, I was damned glad that they were such poor shots.

Kaz ran up to us. "Get Conrad out of here!" I ordered.

He yanked Conrad off Onyx. "Come on!" he shouted.

My cousin looked up at us, his face white and tense with pain. "I can't," he said quietly. "I've been shot."

A bullet struck the ground just in front of us. I cursed. They were getting closer. "Where?" I demanded.

"My leg."

Demon was suddenly beside us. "Kaz, get going! Bane, help me with Onyx!"

Kaz scooped Conrad up and flew toward the house. Demon and I scooped Onyx under the arms and began to fly toward the house. The bullets were zinging past us. As we reached the house, something struck me low in the back. I pitched forward, dropping Onyx. I fell sideways into the house.

What the hell. . .

"Demon!" someone yelled. "He's hit!"

. . .is going on?

CHAPTER EIGHTEEN

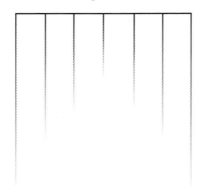

I REGAINED CONSCIOUSNESS, SLOWLY. It felt as though I was coming out of a thick fog. I had not realized at first that I had even passed out, but as my mind became more alert, I started to take notice of some details. For instance, I noted the fact that I was lying down, on my stomach. There was no pillow under my head and everything was dark.

I heard someone stir beside me and tried to lift my head but it wouldn't move. I groaned in frustration. "Bane?" I heard Demon say.

"Have I gone blind? Everything is black," I muttered.

"Try opening your eyes," my brother's amused voice responded.

I cracked one eye open and saw him sitting in a chair beside me, smiling down at me. "Asshole," I remarked and closed it again.

He laughed.

"I cannot move my legs either," I informed him.

"That will come back," he assured me still smiling.

"What happened?"

"You do not remember?"

I tried to shake my head and then remembered that it seemed to be temporarily on strike. "No."

"It is probably best that way for now."

"Was I hurt? Is that why I cannot move?"

"Yes."

I took a moment to assess the damage. "I feel pretty good for someone who has been hurt."

"Claire gave you some drugs."

"Dr. Claire has some damned good drugs," I told him through my happy haze. I closed my eyes since the light seemed to irritate my head more. "But she should save them for sick people and not waste them on a Deadly."

"Be grateful that you have the drugs. You would be a very unhappy Deadly right now if you did not."

"I was shot?"

"Yes."

"In the back. Is that why I am on my stomach?"

"Aside from the wings, yes. Claire wanted you to lie completely flat while you healed."

My memory of it was still foggy but I remembered that I had not been the only victim. I opened my eyes to look at him. "How is Onyx?"

Demon gave me a half smile. "He is fine. The bullets did not hit anything vital. He is definitely showing his Deadly though. He is cursing up a storm because he will not even have any interesting scars to show off."

I gave a snort of laughter. "Is Conrad all right?"

"Yes." Demon gave a sly smile. "The females are all fussing over him."

"That must be driving Zane and Ambrose crazy. And you?" I asked noting the white bandage wrapped around his right upper arm.

"It is just a graze. I will be healed soon."

"Was anyone else hurt?" I asked, my voice growing thick from the meds.

"No, Bane."

"Does Dad know?"

"Yes. I called him. Now go back to sleep."

"Good idea," I told him and drifted off again.

I woke up sporadically over the next few hours. Sometimes on my own and sometimes the others woke me to shove more tranquilizers and pain pills down my throat. Dev enjoyed it more than was necessary in my opinion.

When I awoke again, it was dark. I looked around, half expecting to see my brother. However, the room was empty. I lay still for a few minutes, gathering up whatever wits Dr. Claire's drugs had not overpowered.

"Ah, you are awake."

The familiar voice startled me, making me jump and for a moment, I panicked since it was impossible for that voice to be here...

"Mom?" I gasped as a small, dark-haired woman moved into my line of sight.

She smiled slightly. "No, darling."

It still took me a minute to process. "Aunt Charisma." I sighed, relieved that I was not losing my mind. "Hello."

Her long slender fingers reached out to brush my hair out of my eyes. "Hello, darling."

I closed my eyes and sighed. In appearance, Charisma did look just like my mother, Belladonna. They were, like Demon and me, identical twins. Charisma was a succubus as my mother had been. Her beauty would make you forever her slave, in spite of her red daemon skin.

Charisma gazed down at me. Her eyes were flame-blue like my mother's, like Demon's and mine were. "How are you feeling?" she asked, sitting down on the edge of the bed.

"Better," I told her. "Did you come to see Conrad?"

"And you." She smiled. "And Hex and Demon."

"Is Conrad really okay?" I asked. "I mean, he has never been shot at before. He must be scared."

"He's a Hellblazer," Charisma said darkly. "Whatever those Graces may say, Belladonna and I raised our boys to be fighters."

Uh oh. "What did Ambrose say?" I sighed.

"Nothing," Charisma said with a wicked grin. "He was too busy cringing in the corner of the library."

"Let me guess," I said, grinning. "He was not hiding from Demon."

"Good guess, darling."

Few people could stand up to Charisma when she was in full throttle. I sighed again, this time with disappointment. "And I missed it. I don't suppose you would want to kick his ass again so I could watch?"

She laughed. "No."

"Aw, come on!"

"Now, behave yourself, Bane," Charisma replied. "I am about to change the subject."

"Aunt Charisma—"

"Your sister is here."

Demon and I have only one sister. She is much younger than we are by several hundred years. I gaped at her. "Ansey? When? How?"

"Your father called her."

"Is she still here?"

Charisma smiled slightly. "Do you think she would leave without seeing you?"

I sat up and started to throw the blankets back. Charisma placed her hand on my chest. "Where do you think you are going?"

I stared at her. "To see my sister."

"Not yet."

"But I have not seen Ansey in months—"

"She will still be here ten minutes from now, Bane." Charisma folded her hands in her lap as I sat back. "I wanted to speak to you about Abby."

Aw, shit. "What about her?" I asked warily.

"You realize that this girl is desperately in love with you."

"Aunt Charisma—"

"I like Abby, darling. I would not see her hurt."

"I have no intention—" I began and then broke off. "This is not a subject that I want to discuss with my aunt."

"I did not intend to discuss it," Charisma went on quietly. "I just thought that you should know. In case you did not know...or perhaps did not believe her."

She eyed me for a moment but thankfully, she didn't say anything more about Abby. She got to her feet. However, there was one thing I had not asked. "Wait."

Charisma paused and sat down again.

"Kit..." I began.

Charisma's expression changed and she bit her lip. "You mean the young woman who came to warn you of the attack?"

She would not look at me and I suddenly felt cold. "Aunt Charisma, what the hell has he done?"

"What do you mean?"

"Demon is not keeping her as a prisoner, is he?" I asked agonizing over the possibility that my brother had done something incredibly stupid. "I mean, he does believe that she came to warn us, right?"

Charisma's frown vanished, replaced by a knowing smile. "She is not a prisoner and I think Demon knows very well that she came to warn him. However, you and your brother do tend to be rather hard-headed."

"Must be a Hellblazer thing," I suggested.

"Don't be a smartass, darling."

"Sorry."

"Your brother has behaved like a gentleman. He has given Kit Abby's room."

I slid a look at her from the corner of my eyes. "Then where the hell is Abby supposed to sleep?"

She shrugged. "Well, probably where she has been sleeping for the last four days." She patted the bed. "Right here."

I gaped as she rose again and walked out of the room, laughing softly.

As soon as the door closed behind her, I got up and started to pull on my pants. There was a tap on the door. "Come in," I called out.

I expected that it would be Demon or one of the other Deadlies, maybe my father, but the door opened and Abby came in. I had my pants on, thank goodness, but I had yet to button up. Still, I flinched when I realized it was Abby and I quickly turned around, scrambling to finish buttoning my jeans.

"Abby!" I exclaimed. "I guess I should have asked who it was first."

She crossed the room to me. I felt her hands slip around my waist. She pressed her cheek against my back and held me tightly. I was so surprised that it took me a moment to react. I gently placed both of my hands over hers and we stood like that for a moment, neither of us able to speak.

Finally, I turned around and slipped my hands around her waist. Abby lifted her hands to caress my chest and gently kissed where her fingers touched until she reached my chin and then my mouth. My hands slid up her back and my fingers found the snaps holding the white leather straps in place. They came apart easily. She shrugged, letting it drift to the floor. Then she stepped back into my arms and kissed me again.

Her fingers reached up to touch my hair tentatively and then her hands settled on my shoulders and slid around my neck, pulling me closer. I broke the kiss long enough to say, "Just like a succubus."

Abby laughed and kissed me again, her mouth demanding more. I lifted her against me and carried her to the bed. She fell back onto it taking me with her.

Her fingers were already unbuttoning my jeans. She pushed them down and I kicked them aside.

"This time?" she whispered against my lips.

"Oh, yes," I told her as one of her long legs slid up over mine. "This time..."

And that is all I am going to tell you.

In romance novels, the hero is always horrified when he realizes that his lady is a virgin and that he has just taken advantage of her. However, I am no romantic hero so to say that I was horrified to discover that Abby was a virgin would be a stretch. I was surprised, but not particularly upset.

Abby was snuggled against me, stroking her fingers over my chest. "Don't get shot again."

I smiled. "I shall do my best to avoid it."

She sat up and stared down at me. "It's not funny."

"No," I replied. "It's not. I am sorry."

She spoke again, her voice soft. "You don't know—you actually died, Bane. You stopped breathing and you had no pulse. I thought I had lost you before I even had the chance to have you." She turned her face into my chest. "In that moment, the fact that you are an immortal didn't seem to make a difference. All I could think about was that you were dying and I loved you."

Talk about a kick to the gut. I think I stopped breathing then. Abby started to laugh. "That's so sweet. You're speechless again."

I scowled at her, or tried. It is very hard to scowl at a woman who is Happiness itself. "I am not speechless," I protested. "But I thought I wasn't—" I stopped before I could finish that sentence. This was probably a bad time to point out that I was a Deadly after all.

Abby was not about to drop it, however. "What?" she asked. I didn't answer. She glared at me. "You didn't think you were what?"

Oh, hell. "Forget it, Abby."

"I will *not*. You didn't think you were—what?"

I still hesitated. I wasn't entirely sure where she stood on the whole Grace vs. Deadly thing. She *said* she loved me. I cursed again silently.

What the hell. Nothing, ventured. "Let's be honest, Abby. Ambrose doesn't think a Deadly is good enough for a Grace," I answered finally.

"What does it matter what Ambrose thinks?" she demanded. "It only matters what I think. After this, you can't possibly believe that I feel that way!"

"There has been a lot of "this" over the years," I told her. "You would be surprised how many women feel that way after..."

Abby's eyes narrowed. "How much of *this*?" she demanded.

Oh, boy. Someone had handed me a shovel and I was digging myself a hole fast. "Not that much," I assured her hastily.

"How much?" she demanded again.

"Less than Riot, more than Dev."

"That tells me nothing."

"That is the idea."

"Hmm."

I grinned. "And certainly there has been no one like you."

Abby sniffed and crossed her arms over her chest. "I should hope not."

"Forgive me, my lady, for ever doubting your sincerity," I said with great formality better suited to the ballroom than the bedroom. I touched her cheek.

Abby smiled and tapped her chin with her finger pretending to think about it. "I suppose I can forgive you if you can forgive *me* for having an ass for a brother."

I began to laugh. "Deal."

I sat up and pulled her across my lap, into my arms, and leaned back against the headboard. "I am truly sorry for thinking, even for a second, that you could be as bigoted as Ambrose."

"I understand where you got the idea. It isn't as if we haven't heard that crap every day for the last hundreds of years. But, Bane, I never believed that. I've always felt—oh."

"There is something else on your mind?" I asked.

"Carys," she admitted as if reluctant to remind me of her sister.

"What about her?" I asked, surprised.

"You're in love with her." Abby watched me from the corner of her eyes, afraid I think to read my expression.

"I am beginning to wonder if I ever was," I admitted.

Abby looked up at me and frowned. "Why?"

"I just cannot see her as someone that could make me feel like this."

Abby sat up again, straddling me, and stared at me. "Like this?" she squeaked. "What do you mean? What are you trying to say?"

149

I smiled. "What do you think I'm trying to say?"

"Just say it. I need to hear it. Please."

I wrapped my arms around her waist and pulled her in close. "I love you, Abby."

She leaned forward, resting her forehead against my shoulder, and sighed. "Bane..."

CHAPTER NINETEEN

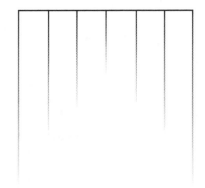

I AWOKE TO A knock on the bedroom door. I tried to roll over but there was something curled against my back. I cracked open one eye and turned my head as far as I could. Abby was nestled against me, half-lying on me. I grinned.

There was another knock and this time the door opened. I had little time to do more than yank a blanket over Abby and me. It was Demon. My brother took in the situation at a glance. "We are meeting in ten minutes," he said. "Will you be ready to come down then?"

"Uh, sure," I responded intelligently.

"Good morning, Demon," Abby's sleepy voice greeted him.

"Good evening, Abby," my brother corrected her without the slightest change in his tone. He gave me a slight smile. "Ten minutes." He closed the door.

We met in the parlour or living room as the more modern humans might call it. Demon felt that I might be more comfortable sitting as opposed to leaning against his desk as I usually did. There were not enough chairs in the library for fourteen people plus my father and sister who, Demon assured me, was still waiting to see me.

When Abby and I came into the room with Demon, Ansey jumped off the sofa and rushed into my arms. "Bane!" she exclaimed smiling up at me.

"Hello, dolly," I said affectionately and gently stroked my hand over her hair.

Ansey rolled her eyes. "Really, Bane, you act like I'm six years old."

While Demon and I are a mix between Belladonna and Serkan, Ansey is all Hellblazer. She has the red daemon skin and long black hair. She is petite, barely five feet tall. However, her eyes are not blue. They are deep green, like emeralds.

"We are your big brothers," I reminded her. "Demon and I will always take care of you."

To my surprise, Ansey's smile disappeared and she stepped back from me, her face averted. "I know." She glanced at Demon. His expression was neutral. Too neutral. It made me suspicious.

"What…" I began.

"Okay," Demon interrupted me. "Shall we get started?"

"Just a moment," Ambrose said. He rose from the sofa and moved to the middle of the room as though taking centre stage. "I have something important to say."

Demon scowled at him. "Can this not wait?"

"No, it cannot." Ambrose turned around, addressing only the other Graces. "It has become clear that the vampires have discovered where the Deadlies live. This house is no longer a safe haven for us. After much discussion with Zane, we have decided that, for our own safety, we should find another place to stay."

Abby gasped. Ambrose was watching Demon eagerly it seemed, waiting for a reaction. Perhaps he was waiting for Demon to fall to his knees and beg the Graces not to leave us. If that is what he expected, he was sorely disappointed. Demon did not even flinch. "Of course, you should do whatever you feel is necessary to ensure the safety of your team."

"It is most certainly necessary. One of the Graces was shot because he protected a Deadly. While I applaud his attempt, we should not be risking our own safety over a—" He broke off abruptly as Riot, Kaz and Dev got to their feet.

"What were you about to say about my brother?" Riot asked in the most dangerous tone I have ever heard from him.

"It seems Ambrose has forgotten that it was Deadly who hauled the Grace's ass out of the line of fire," Dev pointed out, glancing at Kaz.

"That is true, Ambrose," Ithel added. "And it was the Deadlies who rescued Constance and me." She sent an adoring look toward Dev.

"Uh oh," I muttered to Demon. "Maia is not going to like that."

Neither did Ambrose. He scowled at Dev who tried to appear oblivious to Ithel's adoring eyes, but there was a spot of colour in his cheeks.

"We will pack now and be gone within the hour," Ambrose said through gritted teeth.

Ithel, Constance, and Conrad all hung back as Zane and Ambrose led Carys to the door. I was still standing in the way. "Would you kindly move?" Zane asked me with gritted teeth.

Ambrose looked over his shoulder at the others and frowned. "I want to be out of here in an hour so let's not waste time."

"Where are we going to go?" Constance demanded. "Going home is still too risky." She was standing close to Riot. Perhaps her reason for wanting to stay had nothing to do with a desire to help us. It sucked for Conrad because he had a bit of a crush on Constance but in a way, I was glad. He could do much better than a stuck-up Grace who would always look down on him.

"We will go to the Grace mansion," Ambrose told her. "My parents will take us in for a while." Demon and I looked at each other and rolled our eyes. The Grace "mansion" was smaller than our house. I was betting that Mama and Papa Grace would be less than pleased to have seven extra bodies in their house.

"But, we were helping the Deadlies," Ithel said hesitantly, casting another look at Dev. He was purposefully keeping his eyes on Ambrose.

"The vampires know where they live! This is no longer a safe place!" Ambrose snapped. "Do not be foolish, Ithel!"

"I'm not," she protested, but she was weakening. Ambrose was their leader, for better or for worse. She glanced back at Dev and then reluctantly started forward. Constance followed her, sulking.

Conrad remained lounging in his chair. "Conrad, come!" Zane called out.

I bristled. "Do not speak to my cousin as though you were calling a dog," I said coldly.

Zane ignored me. "Conrad!" he snapped.

"No," Conrad said firmly.

"Conrad, don't be stupid!"

Conrad got to his feet slowly and crossed his arms over his chest. "The Deadlies helped us when we needed them. How can we be so cold-blooded as to abandon them now?" he asked and then scowled at Zane. "And don't ever call me stupid again."

I just barely restrained myself from applauding. Instead, I just enjoyed the stunned expressions on Ambrose and Zane's faces. "How dare you speak to me like that you—" Zane snarled.

"We appreciate your offer of assistance, Conrad," Demon interrupted Zane as he stepped between him and Conrad. He kept his back to Zane, dismissing the other man coolly. "Thank you."

Zane did not like the snub but Ambrose seemed to take it as a personal attack. "Fine!" he snarled. "Stay here forever if you like! I don't really care." He turned to his sister, still standing at the door beside me. "Abby, go and pack your things."

"I'm not going either," she told him softly.

"Abigail," Ambrose grimaced. "Do not be difficult! The Deadlies can take care of themselves!"

She shook her head. "Conrad is right, Ambrose. The Enforcers took us in. Kaz rescued Conrad and he didn't have to. He could have been hurt too." Her voice was getting louder and more distressed. "And Bane was hurt trying to protect us! And now they're in danger and we're just going to *walk out*?"

"They are immortals, Abigail," Ambrose said glancing dismissively at me. "You take this much too seriously."

"I didn't see either you or Zane rushing out there to help," his sister snapped, her teeth gritted. "How *dare* you insinuate that the Deadlies are inferior to us?"

"Abigail, you are young and don't understand these things," Ambrose told her in a condescending tone.

"Ambrose," I interrupted coldly. "You are such a pompous ass."

"And you are nothing more than a *monster!*" Ambrose snarled at me. "You feed from the sins of others! You encourage them!"

I stood straighter, bracing myself for an attack as Ambrose took a step toward me. Abby moved between us. "If you're going to go, Ambrose, go!" she yelled at him. "But I'm *not* coming with you."

"Forget it, Abby," I said coldly. "He does not understand the Deadlies and does not want to. He would rather live with his delusions of superiority."

Ambrose's face was white with fury. "Very well, Abigail," he said stiffly. Then he turned to the other two Graces. "Constance, Ithel." He started toward the door.

Constance and Ithel looked at each other and then began to walk out of the room. Conrad caught her arm. "Don't," he said softly. "Constance, please don't do this. You don't have to follow Ambrose."

"Let...go...of...me," she hissed.

Suddenly I heard something that raised the hairs on my neck. Demon was growling. I darted a look at my brother. His eyes glowed, his fangs bared. "Oh, shit," I said.

Everyone followed my gaze and froze. Reluctantly, Conrad let go of Constance's arm. She stalked out of the room without looking back.

Ambrose smirked at the look of devastation on Conrad's face. "I guess she didn't like you as much as you thought she did."

"All right, Ambrose." Demon's voice was a deep growl. "I would say that you've worn out your welcome several times over. Get your things and get the hell out of our house."

Ambrose gave Carys his arm and hastily led her from the room with Zane on their heels. For a moment, I wanted to go after her and beg her not to leave me. I frowned. What was going on here? Two minutes ago, I had felt nothing for her and now I felt like my world was crashing down around me. It didn't make sense. I was in love with Abby, not Carys.

Conrad looked as if he was feeling the same way. He had walked away to the window and stood staring out until the door closed after them. Now, he turned from the window and quickly walked out of the parlour, head down.

"Conrad..." Abby started to follow him.

I caught her arm when she got to the door. "Wait. Let him have a minute to himself."

Serkan put his hand on my brother's shoulder. "Are you all right now?" he asked.

"I am," Demon said, his voice returning to normal. He looked at me, frowning. "But Bane does not look well at all."

"Bane?" my father asked. "Are you okay? You are very pale."

"My head really hurts." I had not had a headache when I came downstairs and now my head was pounding.

Serkan walked over to look at me. "How long has this been going on?" he asked, as he felt my forehead and checked my eyes.

"Off and on for a couple of days."

"Did this start before or after our arrival?" Abby asked suddenly.

Everyone looked at her and then at me. I frowned, thinking. "After," I said, slowly. "But as much as I dislike your brother and Zane, I doubt that the Graces gave me the headache."

"Don't be so sure about that," Abby replied grimly.

"What do you mean?" Demon asked. Before she could answer, loud voices in the hallway distracted us.

"Now what?" Demon strode to the door and went out into the hallway.

For a few minutes, we listened in silence, straining to figure out what was going on. Then suddenly, the voices grew louder and there was a loud crash like a body hitting a wall.

"Oh shit!" Kaz exclaimed. "Demon's killed the Graces!"

We raced into the hallway and found Zane sprawled against the far wall at the bottom of the stairs. Conrad was glaring at him. Demon was standing next to Conrad, a cool expression on his face.

"Demon," Serkan exclaimed. "What happened?"

Zane struggled to his feet, screaming. *"How dare you? How dare you touch me?"* He made a move as if to attack, but I wasn't sure which one he was going after—Demon or Conrad.

"You don't want to try that," I broke in, fiercely. The others, including Abby, moved in to form a wall between Zane, Conrad, and Demon.

"Zane," Ambrose's voice called. We looked up to see him standing at the top of the stairs with the three women. The four of them glided down the stairs. When they reached the bottom, Ambrose stared coldly at Zane. "What is going on here?"

Zane didn't answer so Demon did it for him. "You should teach your bootlicker some self-control," he said and crossed his arms over his chest. "One should never bad mouth a Hellblazer in front of another Hellblazer."

Ambrose gaped at Demon and then he realized that Demon meant Conrad. His nose wrinkled as though he smelled something bad. I would have suggested that it was his own attitude, but my father was gripping my wrist tightly. "Bane, do *not* say a word," he hissed softly.

"Party pooper," I muttered.

"We're ready to go," Ambrose said stiffly.

Demon moved around us. "I trust that we will not have to meet again for a few hundred years."

"Or *ever* as far as I am concerned," Ambrose replied haughtily.

The front door creaked open of its own accord. Demon inclined his head slightly. "Don't let the door—"

"Hit you in the ass on the way out," I finished cheerfully. "That is a pretty nifty trick," I went on, addressing my brother. "I wish I could—"

"Open doors by remote control," Demon finished my sentence. "Yes, it is a pretty cool power, but in order to have it—"

"One would have to be a vampire." I went on, "It hardly seems—"

"Worth it," Demon continued. He grinned. "Still, it is a—"

"Hell of a lot of fun." We finished the sentence together.

"Exactly," Demon nodded.

Demon and I were speaking quite rapidly and Ambrose's head was moving back and forth during the conversation as if watching a Ping-Pong game in fast forward. When it ended, he gave his head a shake and looked utterly bewildered. Demon and I tend to have that effect on people. The other Deadlies were laughing. They weren't even trying to follow the conversation. They learned early that it is better for their sanity just to let it happen. The only two people in the room who understood the conversation were Demon and I.

I don't know if it is a twin thing or a Bane and Demon thing. We have just always done it. We try hard not to because people tend to get confused. They are so busy trying to figure out which twin is talking that they end up forgetting what the conversation was about in the first place. However, I admit that we did it on purpose this time. Ambrose had it coming and if Dad wasn't going to let me kick his ass, then at least I could temporarily short-circuit his brain.

Ambrose gave his head one final shake, trying to clear it. Then he took his sister's arm again. "Come, Carys," he intoned in a dignified tone.

Demon caught my eye and grimaced. "Is he—" I began.

"Bane," my father muttered.

"For real?" Demon finished. "I swear he must watch—"

"All the old black and white movies from the forties for his vocabulary..."

"The B-movies," Demon added.

"The D-movies," I suggested.

"Both of you knock it off!" Serkan said sternly.

Demon and I looked away from each other, biting our lips to keep from smiling. It was like being twelve years old again and Dad was scolding us for raising hell. If we made eye contact at this point, we would have burst out laughing. Ambrose stalked toward the door, dragging his sister along.

"Wait." Carys refused to move, forcing her brother to stop as well. She turned toward us, her sightless eyes staring past us. "Abby, please reconsider," she pleaded. "Bane is just using you to get back at me for what I said to Kane."

I shook my head in disbelief. "You have a very inflated opinion of yourself, you know that?"

"Kane?" Abby repeated puzzled.

"She means Riot," I told her.

Abby's eyes moved from me back to Carys suspiciously. "What did you say to Riot?" Abby demanded coldly.

Carys seemed at a loss. I doubt that she meant to admit so much. She shook her head. "It was nothing. They misunderstood—"

Abby looked at me. "What did she say?" she demanded. Her eyes went to Riot when I didn't answer. "Riot?"

Riot took her hand gently. "Don't worry about it, Abby. I don't give a shit about your sister's opinion of me anyway."

The colour drained out of Abby's face. "Never mind," she said coldly. "I can probably guess what she said to you."

Without waiting for Riot's response, she spun around to face her sister. "Carys, what is wrong with you?" Abby shouted. "How dare you insult the Deadlies when we are guests in their home?"

Carys gasped, stunned by her sister's ferocity. "Abby, I didn't mean—"

"Oh, yes, you did! Bane was good enough to feed from though, wasn't he?" Abby went on coldly. "You had no problem with encouraging his feelings for you so you could feed from him, did you?"

She had been shouting, but when she turned to me, her voice was quieter but still tight with anger. "I believe that is why you were getting headaches, Bane. You were never in love with Carys. She forced those feelings on you so she could feed from you."

I was astonished. "She can do that?" I knew that we could inspire our particular sin in humans, but we didn't have to really. That the Graces could do it too, was news to me.

"Oh, yes she can. She did it to you, she did it to—" Abby broke off.

We all stared at her. "To whom?" I asked.

"It doesn't matter," Abby said. "But it appears that if the Graces and the Deadlies try to feed from one another, it gives the victim a terrible headache."

"I never meant to hurt you!" Carys blurted. She stopped and covered her mouth.

For a second no one could speak. Finally, Riot found his voice. "You fed from your own sister?" he said in a hoarse voice. Then he was yelling. "And you had the nerve to treat *me* like a parasite?"

"How did she manage that?" I demanded. "Did she force you to love someone?"

As soon as the words were out of my mouth, I wished I hadn't said them. "Oh," I said softly. "I see."

"No, you don't," Abby said, shaking her head. "Carys didn't force me to fall in love with you, but she did take advantage of the fact that I was." Her voice softened. "I guess the feelings were too strong for her to resist."

"This is ridiculous!" Carys snapped. "Abby, you cannot be in love with Bane."

Abby snarled at her sister. "You don't get to tell me who I love! What I want to know is did you know that Bane loved me and not you this whole time? Is that why you forced those feelings on him? You couldn't stand the fact that he found me more attractive than you?"

Carys stiffened. "That's ridiculous," she said again.

"Or perhaps the real problem is that you fell in love with him yourself and then couldn't bear that he didn't feel the same about you."

Carys opened her mouth and then glanced at me. She closed her mouth again.

"I'll take that as a yes." Abby gave her a derisive smile. "It isn't enough that you fed on me, but you had to try to rob me of his love too?"

"He's a *Deadly!*" Carys snapped. "He is entirely unsuitable—"

Abby lunged at her sister with such ferocity that my hand actually went out to grasp her arm to keep her from attacking Carys. Abby did not attack her, however. She glared at her sister in silence, her teeth gritted in anger.

Finally she spoke. "I am ashamed to be related to either of you," Abby said bitterly. With that, she turned and walked into the library, slamming the door behind her.

Carys was staring blankly ahead, face pale, eyes big and breathing harsh. I thought that she was going to pass out but I couldn't even feel an ounce of pity for her. Now that I was no longer under the influence of her, I felt nothing but anger and humiliation.

"You did all of this because you were trying to keep me away from your sister?" I said incredulously. "You knew that we loved each other and yet you still—You're Love! How could you—"

"I didn't mean to cause you any harm, Bane," Carys told me, uneasily.

"Really?" I snarled.

Carys burst into tears and Ambrose took her arm. "Come, Carys," he urged in a more gentle tone. He slipped a comforting arm around his sister. I didn't know he had it in him.

Carys clutched his shirt. "Ambrose," she sobbed. "We can't just leave her like this!"

"There is nothing more that we can do," he told her. "Abby will have to find out the truth about the Deadlies the hard way. Come along, Ithel, Constance. Zane, bring the luggage." He tossed the last carelessly over his shoulder as he and the women left the house.

Zane stood for a moment, gaping after him. He looked at Conrad. He was used to passing the job on to the other man. Today, Conrad just stared at him, stony-eyed. The "dog" had turned. Zane was damn lucky that he wasn't bitten.

Zane's mouth turned down in anger and he began snatching up the bags until he was so loaded down that he could scarcely move. There was one bag left sitting on the floor, but Zane's hands were full. He stared at it, puzzled.

"Zane," Ambrose called from outside impatiently.

Zane gave the bag a kick toward the door. It was too much for Dev who gave a suppressed snort of laughter before he ran off down the hallway into the kitchen. We heard him say something to Hex as the door swung shut and then there was a burst of laughter from inside.

Zane glared at the kitchen door and then gave the bag a savage kick. It banged against the door. Zane paused then, realizing that he couldn't open the door. "May I have some assistance please?" he asked stiffly.

I took pity on him while the other Deadlies stood there enjoying his humiliation. He glared at me and didn't bother to thank me as I held the door for him. He kicked the bag out onto the front porch. We all sighed in relief as the door closed behind him.

"Okay," Demon said quietly. "Let's get back to business."

I caught my brother's arm before he entered the library. "Give me a minute with her."

He considered me for a moment and then nodded, stepping back. "We'll be in the kitchen."

As Demon led the others into the other room, I opened the door to the library.

CHAPTER TWENTY

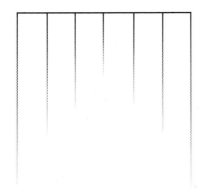

I STEPPED INSIDE THE library, closing the door quietly behind me. Abby stood looking out of the window facing away from the front of the house, so that she didn't have to see her brother and sister leaving. I stood for a moment, watching her, not quite sure what to say.

"Abby?" I said at last.

She leaned her forehead against the windowpane. "I'm sorry," she said hoarsely.

"You have done nothing wrong," I told her quietly.

"I lost my temper. I never lose my temper."

I leaned one hip on the desk and crossed my arms over my chest. "Perhaps it is understandable, under the circumstances," I suggested.

Finally, she met my eyes. "You have more right to be angry than I do."

"You mean because Carys was feeding from me? She fed from you too."

"But my feelings were natural. Yours were not. It was wrong for her to do that." She eyed me, doubtfully. "Why are you smiling?"

"Because I am irritated."

She frowned. "You're smiling because you're irritated?"

I shrugged. "I am pissed off that she used both of us and I am annoyed with *myself* for not figuring it out sooner. I knew that I wasn't in love with her and I still didn't clue in. I am not usually this dense, I swear."

She smiled slightly. "You couldn't be expected to think she would do something like this. To be honest, I never suspected it until you mentioned the headaches just now."

"You really thought I loved her."

"Yes."

"I don't."

She smiled. "I know."

"I admit that I was beginning to have serious doubts about my faithfulness though."

She laughed. "You'll have to make it up to me."

"I will do that with the greatest pleasure." I smiled. "But, I hope I am not going to have to pay for that foolish partiality for the rest of our lives."

Abby grinned at me. "I love it when you talk like that."

"Like what?"

She started walking toward me, hips swaying in a most attractive and distracting manner. "All formal and old-fashioned."

"Well, I am over a thousand years old, Abby," I reminded her. "Besides, I only do it because you think it's sexy."

She stopped in front of me and stared at my mouth. "Oh, yeah?"

"Oh, yeah," I repeated.

"How old are you anyway?" she asked.

Instead of answering, I kissed her.

When Abby and I joined the others in the kitchen a little later, they were sitting at the table eating sandwiches. They looked up as we came in. Demon got to his feet. We grew up in a time when you stood up when a lady entered the room. The other Deadlies looked at each other and then slowly got to their feet as well.

Abby smiled at Demon and then looked at me. "Did I mention that I think chivalrous men are sexy?"

"Forget it. He is not nearly as chivalrous as I am."

Demon smiled at her as he took her hand. He bowed slightly and lightly kissed the back of it. Abby grinned at him. "I don't know, Bane. He seems pretty chivalrous to me and you know what a sucker I am for all that dark hair and those blue eyes." Her voice had gone all dreamy. I thought that she was teasing me, but still...

"Knock it off!" I snapped at my brother.

Laughing, he motioned for us to sit on the stools next to him. I perched on the stool right next to my brother and Abby took the one on my right. Kit was sitting on Demon's left. She was pale and looked like she hadn't slept in days. She glanced up, saw me watching her, and quickly looked down again.

"Okay," Demon said, shoving the plate of sandwiches at me. Dev snatched another one before it got out of his reach. "Let's start with what we have learned about Hadrian, Darkmoon, and Tanith."

I started to take a bite of my sandwich. "Oh," I said. I set the sandwich down on the table, hungry as I was there was something more far important to do right now.

Demon turned to me. "Would you like to start?"

"Not exactly," I said quietly, rising from my seat. "Demon, I would like to speak with you privately first."

"Why?"

I glanced around the table. "It is important and the information is not something I think you would wish to have revealed...*Now.*"

He was silent for a moment and then he smiled slightly. "Bane, I saw the website."

"You did?" I said wincing. "Did you happen to see the—the—"

"Paper with Darkmoon's birthdate on it?" he finished. "Yes."

"Do you think she is—?"

Demon interrupted me. "Kit says they are sisters."

I heaved a sigh of relief. "I cannot tell you how much that worried me."

Demon looked at me, amused. "You and me both, brother."

The others were frowning at us. "Hey," Kaz said at last. "Do you want to let the rest of us in on it?"

Demon and I looked at each other. "Not really," we said together.

"Let's get back to business, shall we?" Demon turned to Kit. "Tell them what you told me about Tanith and Darkmoon being sisters."

Kit looked down at her hands. "I overheard Darkmoon talking about Demon to the vampires who came here and attacked you. She said that she wanted them to warn Fechín away and not to let her sister find out."

"Tanith's birthdate and Darkmoon's are fairly far apart," I said.

"Yes," Kit said. "They are half-sisters. I guess Darkmoon was a late addition to the family. Their mother died soon after Darkmoon's birth. The father passed away a few months later. Tanith left her sister in the care of another family since she was unable to be awake during the day to care for the baby herself."

"What I want to know is," Kaz said. "How the hell did they find us?"

"I swear to you that I didn't bring them here," Kit told him, vehemently. She shot a look at Demon and I guessed that my brother had probably accused her or that he had given some indication that he thought she was guilty. For a smart man, Demon is a world-class idiot sometimes.

"I didn't think that you would," Kaz assured her, glancing at Demon as well. "But you weren't the only one who knew where to find us."

I had wondered that myself. Setting Kit aside and I was reasonably certain that we could, there was only one other option.

Dev actually spoke the words. "It had to be Tanith."

"It could have been one of the others," Onyx suggested. "There were several vampires here as well."

"But most of them travelled here inside of coffins." Dev shook his head and then shut up abruptly as if he suddenly remembered that Kit had *not* travelled in a coffin.

"Besides," I went on hastily, hoping to divert my brother's attention from that fact. "If Tanith didn't want Darkmoon to have the information, her flunkeys sure as hell wouldn't give it to her. It had to be Tanith."

Kit began to fiddle with the glass in front of her, turning it around and around in her hand. "I can't see her doing that."

"Why?" Demon urged.

"Well," she began reluctantly. "Tanith wouldn't have approved of Darkmoon's plans. Darkmoon knew it so she had to get her information from someone else."

"She wouldn't have approved of Darkmoon shooting at us?" I raised an eyebrow.

Kit did not look up. "She wouldn't have given Darkmoon your location knowing that she was going to shoot at and possibly injure Demon."

I thought I detected a bit of jealousy in her voice.

"Why didn't you try to stop her?" Dev asked curiously.

"Darkmoon is a sovereign and I'm a mere beschermer," Kit told him, bitterly. "She would have me killed in a heartbeat."

"So you did what you could," I added. "You walked into the lion's den to warn him before the vampires got here."

"And I was too late," she said harshly. She lifted her eyes to mine. "I am so sorry, Bane."

"You did not shoot me."

"It was still my fault."

Demon's eyes filled with concern and he reached out to take her hand. "Don't think that way. You came out here to warn us and you didn't have to."

Kit looked at him steadily and placed her other hand over his. "Yes, I did," she told him quietly.

The concern in his eyes disappeared instantly and he drew back from her. Hurt flashed in her eyes and disappeared as quickly. I would have kicked him but I was not recovered enough to outrun him.

"Anyway," he went on turning to us. "We went looking for Tanith and Darkmoon the same night that you were shot." He made a face. "Ambrose, Zane, and the other Graces declined to join us. Conrad was on the injured list, but Abby came."

Abby scowled. "No one shoots at the man I love."

I could feel the heat flood my face. I caught the others grinning at me and scowled. It was definitely time to change the subject. "So you went and rang the doorbell but no one was home?" I asked.

"Right," Demon said. "Kit had a few other places that she knew of that we could check. We even went to a few of Hadrian's hideouts."

"Hadrian." I sat up straighter. "Do you remember when we went looking for Tanith that night after she left Dad's house? She went to one of Hadrian's bolt holes and didn't appear to be concerned about being caught there."

"I figured that Hadrian knew who Tanith was, but perhaps not. Maybe it was Darkmoon who sent her there," Demon replied thoughtfully.

We all looked at Kit. "I'm sure you're right," she admitted. "At the time, I didn't know why we were there or why Tanith chose the stapan's hideout. I thought it was a foolish move, but—" she shrugged. "It's my job to protect the sovereign, not to question her judgement."

"Or her sanity. Does Hadrian know about Tanith?" I asked.

"He does now," Demon said with grim satisfaction. "I told him when I went to his place looking for Darkmoon."

Dev burst into laughter. "You should have seen Hadrian's face when Demon walked into his house and he realized that Wrath knew where he lived!"

The others laughed. "I miss all the good stuff," I complained.

"He is still claiming that neither he nor Darkmoon is the rogue sovereign," Demon told me.

"Perhaps he is telling the truth and it actually is Tanith," I suggested.

He shook his head. "I don't think so."

"Demon, she fed from you. You were not a willing participant so clearly she has that inclination," I reminded him bitterly.

"One time she fed from an unwilling victim," Demon told me.

"That we know of, and the fact that it was my brother does not endear her to me!"

He sighed. "Honestly, Bane, I doubt that she did it to anyone else. She did what she did to me *because* it was me."

"She wanted to be with you forever." Dev batted his eyelashes and made kissy-kissy noises.

Demon scowled at him but I shook my head. "He was already immortal so that doesn't make sense," I pointed out.

"Whatever her reason," Demon interrupted. "It was not her intention to kill me but to turn me into what she was. The humans found in the zoo were not turned. They were murdered. They were used and then tossed to the animals like they were garbage."

"Okay," I said, alarmed by my brother's fierce tone and dark expression. "Accepting this is all true she could still give permission and not be killing the humans herself."

"True. However, it amounts to the same thing in my book."

"Mine too," I agreed.

"I have to admit," Kit broke in grudgingly. "I have been Tanith's *beschermer* for two years and I have never seen her feed from an unwilling victim or allowed any of her people to do so." She paused. "And other than Scarletti, she has not changed anyone either."

"But some of her people are clearly part of the rogue faction," Riot interjected.

Kit was frowning. "Is something bothering you?" Demon asked her.

"I just can't see Tanith allowing her people to go rogue," Kit told him. "Unless—" Her expression changed and she suddenly closed her mouth.

"Unless what?" Demon asked curiously.

She just shook her head, but she had an idea. Why she didn't want to tell us, I wasn't sure.

"So it's got to be Hadrian or Darkmoon," Dev declared. "Or both."

"Oh, I wouldn't put Tanith out of the running entirely," Demon said softly. "She is clearly in contact with her sister and Hadrian was not aware of Tanith's existence let alone that she had come to town. I think that Tanith is in this up to her neck. So when we find her, she loses her head too."

CHAPTER TWENTY-ONE

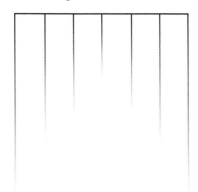

EMON'S PLAN WAS TO search every inch of Blackridge until we found Tanith and Darkmoon. He didn't think they would leave. He was convinced that they had a purpose in Blackridge other than murdering humans. We just did not know what that was.

"We'll go hunting tonight." Demon glanced at the clock. It was getting on eight-thirty, almost dark enough for the vampires to start waking up. "Bane, it would be better if you remained behind just until you feel better."

"I am well enough now," I insisted. "I am healed, Demon, really. You'll need all of us to cover Blackridge thoroughly now that the Graces..." I trailed off with a look of apology at Conrad and Abby.

"Don't mind me," Conrad said. "I'm with you on this one."

"Me too," Abby said and hugged me.

"We could use all the eyes and ears that we can get," Demon said. "But it won't do you or us any good if you are so worn out that you cannot do anything for a week after."

I scowled at him. "Hey, Mother Hen, what kind of a wimp do you take me for?"

Demon's mouth twitched and I narrowed my eyes. He didn't dare smile. "One more night of rest," he urged. "Just one more and then you can run circles around Blackridge to prove that I'm being an overcautious mother hen, okay?"

I knew Demon well enough to know that pouting was not going to help, but I did it anyway. He grinned. "Were you aware that the man you're in love with has the mentality of a two-year-old?" Demon asked Abby.

She began to laugh so I stuck my tongue out at him.

Riot was standing at the end of the table. He crossed his arms over his chest. "Have they always been this bad?" he asked Serkan.

My father grinned and nodded. "Hell, yes! They have been trouble from the moment that they could walk and talk," he sighed dramatically.

Demon and I looked at each other and then stuck our tongues out at Dad, too. He rolled his eyes and sat next to Kit on the stool that Demon had vacated.

"What will you do now?" he asked Kit.

Kit studied the tabletop in silence and then looked up, not at my father but at Demon. He and I were harassing each other by tugging each other's hair and wings. "I have decided to be Demon's beschermer," she announced quietly.

Demon was about to flick my ear with his fingers and stopped mid-flick, staring at her in dismay. "I have no need of a beschermer!" he exclaimed.

"Well, *I* beg to differ." Kit contradicted him with stiff politeness. "With Darkmoon sending snipers after you and who knows what Tanith has in store, I would say that you need protecting more than anyone here."

Demon was speechless. It was rather an intriguing sight.

"I think that is a brilliant idea." My father gave Demon a hard look.

"You would," I murmured.

"Serkan," Demon gasped at last. "This would not—"

"She can't go back to Tanith that is for certain," Serkan said firmly. "And you did say that you could use all the help you could get."

"But—" Demon stammered.

"Looks like you are hired, Kit," I cut in, grinning wickedly at Demon.

Demon scowled at all of us. "Now just a minute..."

"Good. That is settled." Serkan ignored his protests and turned to Kit. "I think there will be no problem with you retaining Abby's room." He raised an eyebrow at me.

"Umm," I muttered, embarrassed. "No. I do not think Abby will object."

Abby grinned at me. "Not in the least."

"Thank you, Abby, but as a beschermer I need to be close by so that I can get to Demon quickly in case of danger," Kit explained.

Hex set a plate of biscuits in the middle of the table. Dev snatched one up immediately. "Well, the only other room that close would be Bane's or Dev's," Hex said. "Their rooms are on either side of Demon's room. There is a connecting door."

"Bane and I can take the room that Kit is in now," Abby suggested hastily.

"It's perfect," Kit agreed.

Hex beamed at all of us. "Excellent! Bane can move his things tonight while you're all out and by the time you return I will have the room prepared for Kit."

We all looked at Demon. He was still scowling but knew he been outmanoeuvred. He shook his head and threw his hands into the air in surrender. "I give up!" he declared as he walked toward the door. "Let's work."

I caught my father's eye once Demon's back was turned. He winked.

Moving my things was a bigger deal than I first thought it would be. We had managed to move Maia's entire apartment in less time than it took me to get everything out of my closet. She had nothing on me.

Standing up to my knees in old books, old weapons, empty sheaths and other junk, I surveyed my belongings. "I am a damned pack rat," I announced to Maia and Abby in disbelief. The two women remained behind to help me. "Seriously, I may need a twelve step program. Hello, my name is Bane Hellblazer and I am a pack rat."

They giggled. I hefted an old sword in my hand. The sheath was long gone, but the blade was so dull it couldn't have cut melted butter anyway. I gave it a casual twirl. "Still has pretty good balance," I remarked. "I should have kept it sharpened."

"Why didn't you?" Maia asked, looking up from a stack of books that she was packing into a box. "You seem to have an enormous number of sheaths here and no swords to go in them. What happened to all of them anyway?"

"Broke them," I told her. "Usually over someone's head."

"Ugh." Abby's nose wrinkled. "Enough said."

"Besides, this sword won't fit in any of these sheaths. I tried."

"Then why don't you get rid of the sheaths?"

"I might get a sword that fits one of them."

Maia grimaced. "I thought *Dev* was Sloth."

"It is not slovenliness!" I protested. "It is practicality or frugality…or something like that."

"Whatever you say, Bane." Maia rolled her eyes and went back to packing the books. I grabbed a full box and started across the hallway.

"I'll take the empty sheaths to the basement, how about that?" I called over my shoulder. When I came back to grab another box, I saw that they had labelled it "Bane's Practically Useless Shit."

"Oh, now that was unnecessary," I told them. They giggled again and I took the box to the basement.

We were just finishing when the others came home. I was carrying the last box to the basement and Dev spotted the newest label "Bane's Sheaths that Aspire to Someday Hold a Sword."

Dev grinned and pointed at the box. "I should have warned them."

I shifted the box to my hip. "They are getting more creative with each box," I told him. "But we are done a lot sooner than I thought."

"Dude, it is three AM!"

"I know." I nodded, pleased. "I was thinking nine o'clock. Tomorrow night."

I heard laughter behind me as I went down the basement stairs and into the catacombs. I put the box down in the room I had chosen for storage and returned upstairs to find Demon waiting for me. The others had gone to bed, I assumed.

"How did it go? Find out anything?" I asked.

He shook his head. "I did not really expect to find them tonight. They will be expecting us to be out looking for them. They will lay low until we give up."

I grinned. "What happens when they realize that we are not going to just give up and go away?"

He grinned back. "A few weeks of us continuously hitting every supernatural-run business in the city and the other supernaturals will start hunting them and phoning in leads just to get us out of their bars and shops."

"You mean like we did with Vervain Swamp, only subtle."

"They cannot leave their hiding place for fear that someone rat them out to us so they will not be able to feed either. Between fear of capture and hunger, they will make a major mistake. In fact, I am counting on it."

"In the meantime, the humans will be safe," I said.

"Temporarily," Demon pointed out. "Eventually they will have to come out of hiding to feed. I would rather find them before they get too hungry or too desperate."

"So what is next on the agenda?"

"Tomorrow night you and I are going to hang out in the Black Candle Tavern."

"Not Kaz?" I smiled.

My brother rolled his eyes. "He would be of no use there. He would spend the entire night making out in a back room with Rowan."

"Good point."

"He is going to re-check Hadrian's bolt holes with Riot. If Hadrian and his people see us in their space often enough, I am hoping someone will become alarmed enough to turn them in."

"Hadrian certainly will not."

"Not personally. I am counting on one of his people to do the job for him."

"That would be treason," I said. Even I knew enough about vampires to know that.

"Not if he is a good and forgiving stapan." Demon paused. "That is what I would recommend."

"And probably will."

He grinned again. "Probably."

I studied him silently, considering. Then I asked, "What do you think Tanith wants from you?"

He shrugged. "Perhaps she wishes to distract me from Darkmoon. Maybe she thinks that she can intervene when it comes down to the execution."

"If she believes that then she does not know you as well as she thought."

"She never did," he said, quietly.

Demon suggested that since we were going to have a late night, we should try to catch a few hours' sleep. Since Hex had plenty of warning, she was able to set the mealtime back a few hours, though not without a good deal of grumbling. That meant no lecture. Abby was disappointed until Dev made the mistake of tossing a tea towel onto the counter. It slid off and landed on the floor, sending Hex into scolding mode. While Dev stood calmly in the middle of the kitchen getting a scold, Abby watched with amusement. Do not feel too bad for Dev. There was a gleam in his eyes proving that he was having at least as much fun as Abby was.

Once Hex wound down from her lecture, we all went upstairs to bed. We were supposed to nap, but I confess that Abby and I probably had twenty minutes of sleep out of three hours. After our nap, I roused Abby and while she was still finding her clothes, I went downstairs, meeting my brother in the hallway. He was alone.

"Where is Kit?" I asked. "I thought she would be glued to your side seeing as how she is your beschermer."

Demon glared at me, but didn't answer. I decided not to press him too far. He was obviously uneasy about her being in the house. I hoped he would be able to confide in me eventually.

We entered the kitchen to discover that we had another visitor. In all of the excitement and subsequent state of unconsciousness, I had forgotten about Maia's mother.

Ceridwen is half-witch, half-goddess. She was currently sitting at our kitchen table sipping coffee as casually as if she lived here. Dev and Maia sat across the table from her, watching her with bewildered expressions. I didn't know why Maia looked so disconcerted, but I guessed that they had gotten Dev out of bed far too early or my friend was simply thunderstruck. Ceridwen had that effect on people.

Ceridwen is a very beautiful woman and Maia looks a lot like her. Ceridwen is a bit taller than her daughter is though she has the same curvy figure as Maia. Her curly hair is longer but the same shade of brown. Her eyes are sea foam green whereas Maia's are dark, but they are the same shape. They have the same mouth, the same smile, and the same high cheekbones. I have known Ceridwen for years and now seeing the two women together, I could see right away that they were mother and daughter. I was a little surprised at myself for not seeing it before.

She glanced up as we came in and her eyes lit up. "Demon and Bane," she greeted us warmly. "I had forgotten how outrageously handsome you two are!"

I was too embarrassed to speak but Demon, cool as ever, simply replied, "Thank you, Ceridwen. It is a pleasure to see you again."

She laughed. "Ah, Demon, you are as polite and reserved as ever! Why not just ask me what I am doing in your house?"

Finally, he responded with a grin. "Because I *know* what you are doing here." He glanced at Dev and Maia.

Ceridwen followed his gaze and smiled. "Oh, yes! I am absolutely delighted with Dev!"

"Mom," Maia admonished. "You've hardly spoken to him!"

"The poor boy hardly looks awake yet," Ceridwen said graciously. "I did not wish to throw too much at him at once."

Dev mumbled something. He did seem rather sleepy. "You will have to forgive him," I told Ceridwen. "Dev is not very coherent for the first few hours after he wakes up."

Dev's eyes opened a bit more and he scowled at me. "Asshole."

"See? He is delusional." I sat down on a stool next to him calmly. My brother placed a cup of coffee in front of me, grinning. He held the coffee pot up to Maia in silent offer.

Maia pushed her cup forward. "Please," she said. "And throw in a double shot of whiskey while you're at it."

Demon laughed softly as he poured Maia's coffee. Ceridwen reached across the table to pat Dev's hand. She just managed to reach his fingers. "Well, I am delighted with Dev anyway. After speaking to his mother, I knew that I would be and Maia has told me so much about him that I feel as though I know him already."

She drew her hand back and took a sip of her coffee that Demon had just refreshed. She set the cup down and turned to Demon. "So tell me, *who* is the delicious energy?" she asked.

Maia choked on her coffee and Demon frowned slightly. "I am not sure that I understand."

Ceridwen smiled as Dev handed Maia a paper towel. "Someone in this house has an energy that is downright tasty. Who is it?"

The kitchen door flew open and Riot stalked in. Ceridwen's smile turned sultry as she picked up her cup again, smiling. "Ah," she purred.

Riot stopped short and stared at her. "Hello."

"*Hello,*" Ceridwen replied. There was an invitation in her voice that was hard to miss.

Women did not often hit on Riot in his own house. On the street, in stores, in bars, at the playground while their children played a few feet away—yes—but he did not run into amorous women in our kitchen on a regular basis. He stared at her in obvious bewilderment. Demon and I hid our smiles by taking a sip of coffee. Dev grinned, enjoying Riot's embarrassment.

Maia was completely aghast. "*Mother!*"

"Well, now," Ceridwen went on, all of her attention zeroed in on Riot. "Who might you be, handsome?"

"Riot," he replied. She raised an eyebrow. He looked embarrassed. "I mean, Kane. Arkane Hellcurse."

"The chief's son?" Ceridwen asked, surprised.

"No. I'm his nephew."

Ceridwen's expression cleared. "Ah, yes. You are Mortius and Balia's eldest son. You are Lust." When he nodded, she leaned toward him with that tempting smile still in place. "That explains everything."

"Riot," Maia sighed. "Allow me to introduce my mother to you. This is Ceridwen."

"Oh I see," Riot mumbled. We all stared at him. His cheeks were slowly darkening until his skin appeared tarnished. It was his version of a blush. He turned to Hex, abruptly. "Is there any more coffee?"

Hex assured him that there was and poured him a cup while he stood with his back to the table, waiting. When he joined us, he was composed again.

Ceridwen's eyes followed him until he sat down. He studiously ignored her smile. Ceridwen turned back to Demon. "I had another reason for coming here, besides seeing my daughter and meeting Dev."

"A reason beyond tracking down the delicious energy," Demon said with a straight face while Dev choked on his coffee and I snickered. Riot glared at us.

Ceridwen laughed. "Yes. You had asked for information regarding two gnomes lost in the city?"

Demon nodded. "Ariadne and Normie."

Dev choked on his coffee again but he didn't comment. Perhaps he was behaving for his future mother-in-law. She glanced at him with amusement. "Yes," she said, nodding. "It is a most unfortunate name for a gnome."

Dev grinned at her. "I didn't say anything."

"Where did you see them?" Demon asked, bringing her attention back to the matter at hand.

"I saw them at the Quinlan Memorial Gardens."

"They are hiding out in Emily's garden?" Demon asked surprised.

Jesse Quinlan was the man who founded Blackridge and Emily was his wife. Demon and I had been living here for about five years before the Quinlans' arrival but we did not object to sharing the area. We never met Jesse in the fifty years that they lived in Blackridge but Emily, being a witch, sensed that we were living in the area. We became friends. The Memorial Gardens are actually on the old Quinlan homestead and had originated from Emily's own garden.

"I expected that gnomes would hide out somewhere less populated," Demon continued. "Emily's garden must have over a hundred people tramping through it on a daily basis."

"She must be turning in her grave," I agreed. "Having her beautiful garden turned into a tourist trap."

"Perhaps the gnomes have come to repair the damage done to it during the day," Riot suggested.

"They probably are but I doubt that they came all the way from the Hills to do it," Demon rose. "I am heading over to Wolftown to find Adrastos and tell him where his friends are."

Riot quickly drained his coffee and got up too. "I'll come with you. Between the two of us, we might be able to find him faster."

"Good idea," Demon said as Morgana came into the kitchen. "Morgana can come with us."

The surprise and pleasure in her face was expressive. I hoped my brother knew what he was doing. I half suspected that he was using her as a barrier between himself and Kit. If he was, I was going to rip a strip off him later. That was not fair to either of the women.

"I will come too," I said and started to get up.

He insisted that I remain behind. "You will be exhausted before tonight and that is when I will need you most. Just take it easy for the day, Bane."

I had no choice but to agree. However, Demon was not getting off that easily. "Then I need two minutes of your time," I said sternly. "Come to the library."

Demon eyed me suspiciously. "Okay."

"Well, I should be going." Ceridwen rose from her seat. "I just wanted to meet Dev and let you know about the gnomes. Oh, and, Maia, you have an appointment to look at wedding dresses tomorrow afternoon at two."

A panic-stricken look came over Dev's face and Maia patted his hand as Ceridwen breezed out the back door of the kitchen. "Don't worry, Dev," Maia assured him. "I'll try to talk her out of it."

"What about you?" Demon asked pausing at the kitchen door. "What kind of wedding do *you* want?"

Maia shrugged. "I don't like the idea of white gowns and traditional weddings either. Frills and frou-frou make me cringe. I would be content with a simple hand-fasting ceremony."

"So would I." Dev groaned. "But between my mother and yours, you're going to end up with a gown with a twenty foot train, and rose petals falling from the sky."

Maia laughed and kissed him. "Oh, the horror! I'll tell you what, you work on your mother and I'll work on mine."

"That's my girl." Dev sighed in relief and leaned over to kiss her again.

Demon and I left them to their meals that Hex was just serving up. Demon stepped back to allow me to enter the library first and then closed the door behind us. "Well?" he asked curiously.

"What the hell are you doing?" I demanded.

"You tell me," he responded surprised. "What?"

"I am talking about Morgana!" I snapped. "You spend half your time avoiding being alone with her and now all of a sudden you are taking her with you on a mission?"

"Bane, she is part of this team."

"I know that, but I have to wonder why you are so anxious to take her with you all of a sudden."

"I am not anxious." He scowled. "She complained before about being left behind. She is right. I asked her to be a part of this mission. What is wrong with that?"

"There is no other reason?"

"Of what are you accusing me?" he demanded, fast losing his temper.

"Are you trying to use Morgana to keep Kit at a distance?"

"Do you really believe that I could do that to a friend?"

"I do not believe that you would do so intentionally," I admitted. "But think about how this might look to Morgana. She is in love with you, Demon."

He sighed. "I know that my behaviour toward Kit has not been terribly gracious thus far, but I would never hurt Morgana by making her think that I was in love with her."

I nodded slowly. "Just be aware that this could end in a lot of hurt feelings and tread carefully, brother."

CHAPTER TWENTY-TWO

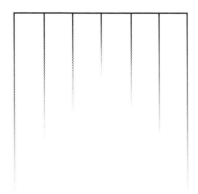

WHEN DEMON AND HIS team returned a couple of hours later, the rest of us met them at the door. Morgana came in first, pushed past us, and stormed upstairs. We all watched her go up the stairs in silence and then we all looked back at Demon.

He sighed. "Do not ask." He turned and we followed him into the library.

"I do not have to," I said sympathetically. "You took my advice."

"Yes," he said grimly.

"Things did not go well."

He shot me a look. "You think?"

I thought it was time to change the subject. "Did you find Adrastos?" I asked as we settled ourselves around the library.

"Yes. We found him readily enough," Demon told me. "It was the other two that we had some trouble finding, but Adrastos is reunited with his friends."

"Are they headed home?"

"Not yet," Riot answered in amusement. "It seems Normie the gnome has bigger aspirations than tending a farmer's flock at night."

Demon sent him a sideways look. "Farmers no longer need gnomes to tend their flocks anymore. They have barns with automatic feeders and shearing machines."

Riot shrugged and grinned. "Normie wants to help humans on a bigger scale, a kind of superhero gnome."

We began to laugh. Demon rubbed his forehead with his fingers as though he was developing a headache. "It is not funny. Adrastos and Ariadne are trying to convince Normie to go home with them and he is digging in his heels. He has decided that he wants to work for the Enforcers."

That announcement made us stop laughing. "*A gnome?*" Dev said incredulously.

"Adrastos almost got eaten!" I protested. "A gnome would only be bait out there!"

"Not to mention the fact that he's a *kid!*" Riot added.

Demon shrugged. "I told Normie that he had to be born an Enforcer and that it was not just something that you could train for, but he is determined to be one of us. I do not know how to convince him that it is a bad idea." He waved a hand, dismissing the gnomes. "Anyway, we left Adrastos and Ariadne to it."

The library door burst open and a very angry Kit stalked in. She didn't hesitate. She walked right up to Demon and got in his face. "What the hell do you think you're doing?" she shouted at him.

Demon crossed his arms over his chest. "Pardon me?" he frowned.

"You do not leave this house without your beschermer!" she yelled stabbing the air with one finger. "Is that clear?"

He sighed and uncrossed his arms. "Kit," he began gently. "We both know that I don't need—"

"Don't you use that condescending tone with me, Demon Hellblazer!" she snapped interrupting him. "Have you forgotten that Darkmoon tried to have you killed?"

"I cannot be killed," he reminded her.

"Oh, I know all that!" She threw her hands in the air. "That's not the point! Darkmoon is out to get you and you hired me to protect you—"

"Wait just a second!" he protested. "*I* did not hire you! I was outvoted."

"I think we should give them some privacy," I whispered to Kaz.

He was watching them with wide eyes as he leaned toward me. "Just when it's getting good?" he whispered back.

I grasped his arm firmly and ejected him from the room, glaring at the others. I was pleased to see that they obeyed, although they grumbled all the way.

An hour later, I walked by the library and didn't hear anything. I stood in front of the door, wondering if the argument was over or if this was just a lull in the storm. I knocked on the door, hesitatingly. "Demon," I called out.

"Come in," my brother's voice answered gruffly.

I opened the door and stepped into the room. Demon was standing at the window looking out over the side garden. I took a step toward him. "Hey, is everything okay?" I asked tentatively.

He glanced back at me. "It is fine."

I considered him for a moment. "Well, you look like hell."

"Thank you," he responded dryly.

"Kit gave you royal hell, huh?" I asked, smiling.

He scowled at me. "I am so glad you find this amusing, Bane."

I shrugged. "What can I say? I am on Kit's side."

His eyebrows lowered. "Hey!"

I joined him at the window. "Look, Demon, I may have been the one who was shot but they were aiming at *you*. I do not take kindly to people trying to put holes in my brother. It appears that Kit does not like the idea either."

"Beschermers tend to get blacklisted if they allow their charges to get killed."

"That is not what she was upset about and you know it," I told him sternly.

"Bane, I really do not want to talk about this."

"But, Kit—"

"*I said I do not want to talk about this!*" Demon snarled and stormed out of the room.

Later that evening, Demon decided that Kaz and Dev were going to go hunting around Hadrian's hideouts at the docks. Riot and Onyx were heading for the ones downtown, including the apartment building where an execution had taken place the week before. Demon did not want Kaz and Dev down there because Kaz, Demon, and Dev had a run-in with a gang and there might be trouble if the little thugs recognized them. Demon had hypnotized the ringleader so technically the kid should not remember Dev and Kaz but the others had run off before Demon had a chance to hypnotize them too. We couldn't take any chances.

Morgana teamed up with Conrad to check the south end bars. Hadrian also had an empty house there for the vampires who were not able to make it home before dawn. He did not know that we knew about it.

Yet.

"Abby and Bane will be coming with me to the Black Candle," Demon said when he finished giving the others their assignments. "And Kit," he added quietly.

"Kit is going?" Morgana spoke up shooting a dark look at her.

"Is that a problem, Morgana?" Kit asked coolly.

Morgana turned to face her. "You aren't an Enforcer. Why are you going?"

"Because I said so," Demon snapped before Kit could answer.

Morgana looked from Demon to Kit and then stalked out of the room. She slammed the door behind her making the whole room shake. Conrad winced. "Thanks so much, Demon. What the hell have I ever done to you?"

"She is a good partner to work with," Demon told him. "You just have to be assertive. Tell her to knock off the prima donna act and she will be fine."

Conrad winced. "Before or after she guts me like a fish?"

Demon grinned. "Come on, Conrad. Where is that Hellblazer courage I saw kicking the snot out of Zane yesterday?"

I turned to Conrad. "*You* clobbered Zane?"

"We all thought that it was Demon," Dev added.

Conrad shook his head. "He said something completely obnoxious and I lunged at him but Demon got between us."

Dev seemed more confused. "But Demon said never bad mouth a Hellblazer to—"

"Another Hellblazer," Conrad finished. "I know."

"Which Hellblazer did he bad mouth?" I asked.

Conrad gritted his teeth. "It was not Demon," he replied, looking pointedly at me.

I bristled. "Oh, let me guess," I said sarcastically. "It was something about me being unacceptable as a boyfriend for a Grace?"

Conrad started to speak, probably to agree with my assessment, but Demon cut him off. "It does not matter, Bane. He was wrong."

"You should have let Conrad finish the job," I told him.

"Next time," Demon said. "Let's go and get ready."

Morgana was nowhere in sight when we got into the hall. I assumed that she was sulking in her room. We followed Demon and Kit up the stairs. She walked beside him going up and not behind like the rest of us. "Oh yes," I murmured to Dev and Kaz over my shoulder. "Any woman who can stand up to Demon in one of his rages and not back down is the perfect woman for him."

"And how do you intend to convince Demon of that?" Kaz whispered.

"I thought about it and I have come to the conclusion that I may have to beat it into him."

"Let Kit do it," Dev grinned. "I'm pretty sure she could take him." I heard Kaz laughing softly.

I started to follow Abby into our bedroom, but Demon caught my arm and steered me into his room across the hall. I caught a glimpse of Abby's surprised expression as Demon closed his bedroom door.

"What is the big idea?" I demanded.

He ignored my question and went to take his knives off the top of the wardrobe.

"All of my weapons are across the hall," I reminded him.

He spoke at last. "No, they are not." He held out the two knives in his hands. "These are yours. I took them from your room earlier." He flung them at me at a speed that would seem superhuman to anyone else. It would have skewered a human, but I caught them easily by their handles.

"Why?" I asked as I slipped the knives into the sheaths on my belt.

He spared me a glance while he removed a long sword from the wardrobe. "For the same reason that I told Maia to wait in the kitchen while Dev changes."

Oh.

I glowered at him, but he was unmoved by my hostility. "Just get your battle gear on," he told me, grinning.

Ten minutes later, we were both downstairs, blades strapped to our backs, daggers strapped to our thighs and upper arms. Our long hair braided and out of the way, we were ready to go. One thing about Demon, when he is getting ready to kick ass, he does not mess around.

Morgana came down a couple of minutes later. She did not greet us or even look our way. She stayed on the other side of the foyer and pointedly ignored us. I guess she was still pissed off. She had come to Demon's bedroom while we were still getting ready, clutching her leather halter-top to her chest and when I answered her knock on the door, she had mistakenly assumed that I was he. She asked me to help her with the buckles on her top. I told her to turn around and she dropped it on the floor. I stooped to pick it up and when I straightened again, I found her breasts in my face. That was when Demon came out of the bathroom and asked if she was finished fooling around. She had been furious and stormed off down the hall, carrying the halter-top in her hand. I admit that I may have made things worse when I called out, "Wait! Don't you want my help doing up the buckles?"

She did not find it amusing.

"It served her right," I muttered to Demon.

Don't get me wrong. I like Morgana. She is a friend, and I did not want Demon to hurt her, but she just could not live with the fact that he wasn't interested. It made her very hard to live with sometimes.

Onyx and Riot came down together. Ever since Onyx was injured, Riot had hovered over his younger brother doing the mother hen routine. Riot insisted on teaming up with his brother. Riot even waited for him outside his bedroom door. Onyx didn't seem to mind right now but I had a feeling that it would get old very quickly. After all, he was over four hundred years old, hardly a child.

When they reached the bottom step, I realized that Abby was right behind them. The minute I saw her, I understood why my brother had refused to let us dress together. She was not wearing white at Demon's request. If we had to execute someone, she would need clothes that hid blood. Morgana loaned her a black halter-top, black thigh-high boots, and a pair of black leather pants. Her blond hair flowed down her back. She had weapons strapped to her arms and back. She looked like a warrior goddess. She was gorgeous. I was speechless.

"Hi." Abby greeted me shyly. "Do you like it?"

"Oh yes," I said hoarsely. "I will enjoy taking it off you even more."

Abby laughed and I pulled her into my arms and kissed her deeply. She stopped laughing and her arms slid up my arms to twine around my neck.

"All right! All right!" Demon muttered after a few seconds.

I lifted my mouth from Abby's and glared at him. "Jealous."

Demon did not reply. Something else had caught my brother's attention. He was staring at Kit who was standing on the bottom step. She was dressed much like Morgana and Abby. I loved Abby and I thought she was beautiful, but Kit was...*wow*. She had her long blond brown curls pulled back in a ponytail. Her body was proof that she spent a lot of her time doing hard work. She was all lean muscle and moved with the grace of...well, Demon. After all, he had trained her to fight. It looked like his lessons took.

She gave us an absent-minded smile when we greeted her, but her eyes were all for my brother. Demon's reaction was rather intriguing. He was stunned to silence much to my amusement. Then abruptly he began to pace, staring at the floor.

Demon was hot and bothered. I caught his eye and grinned at him. He growled at me and then refused to meet my eyes again.

Ten more minutes passed and Demon stopped pacing long enough to frown at the clock. "Where the hell is Dev?" he demanded. We all looked at each other and shrugged. He grimaced. "I'll go and get him."

He started for the stairs. Hex appeared in the hallway. "Oh," she said. "Is Maia out here? I was looking for her. Her mother is on the phone."

"She is supposed to be in the kitchen," I told her.

"Well, she isn't. I just came from there."

Demon's head snapped around and his eyes narrowed as he glared up the stairs. "*Dev!*" he bellowed and raced up the stairs.

Five minutes later Demon marched Dev down the stairs. He was scowling, Dev was grinning from ear to ear, and Maia was scurrying behind them, blushing.

"I can't believe that he just walked right in when we were—I mean, oh my god!" Maia gasped. Her face was so red I thought she might burst.

"Thank goodness we didn't get dressed together," Abby murmured to me.

"I do not *think* he would have busted in on us," I said doubtfully.

Demon was glaring at an unrepentant Dev. "Now that we are all here, let's work. This is going to be a long night."

Dev rolled his eyes but couldn't quite wipe the smile off his face as he turned to Maia. "Go talk to your mom," he told her and then made a face. "See if you can talk her out of this big wedding."

Maia kissed him lightly on the mouth. "I'll do my best, Dev."

"I still think we should elope."

"My mother would turn you into a toad."

Dev hesitated and glanced at Kaz. "I'm almost positive that Rowan could turn you back," Kaz told him doubtfully.

Dev sighed and turned back to Maia. "Keep working on her." He kissed her again.

Demon laughed and started for the door. Kit fell into step beside him. She reached for the door handle. "Let me go first."

His brows came together in a frown. "Why?" he asked.

"I'm your beschermer," she reminded him, patiently. "I always go through the door first."

"The hell you do."

She gave him a look. "We talked about this. The beschermer goes through the door first. I take the bullets from now on, Demon."

Demon stared at her. His face turned white and then his eyes slid toward the basement door, his hands clenched into fists.

"Demon," I called his name softly. He did not respond and I touched his arm, concerned. "Hey."

He seemed to come back to himself then. He reached out and wrenched open the door without looking at us. "Let's get going."

CHAPTER TWENTY-THREE

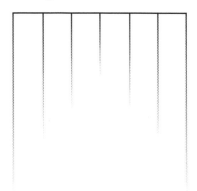

THE ABRUPT CHANGE IN Demon's demeanour was worrying even if it did end in Kit getting what she wanted. I could tell from her expression that she had expected more of a fight and, to be quite honest, so did I. The fact that he had given in so easily was not like him at all and that bothered me.

Still, it was funny as hell watching Demon stand back while Kit checked the car before he got in it. He stalked away from the car and stood in the middle of the driveway, looking everywhere but at her. His version of a temper tantrum, I thought at first. Then I realized that his eyes were scanning the area and he was standing well away from us.

Damn him, I thought. *He is making sure that if someone wants to take a shot at him, they will not miss and get one of us instead!*

I opened my mouth to call him on it but Kit, who was underneath the car (searching for bombs, I suppose) crawled out and announced the car was clear. Without a word, Demon got into the driver's seat. Kit took the front passenger seat. Abby and I squeezed into the back seat, her body pressed against mine, her hand rested on my thigh. Hell, I was not going to complain.

We drove to the Black Candle Tavern in silence. Kit kept checking behind us and warily eyeing every car that passed us. I wondered what she was going to do if someone took a shot at us while we were driving. I hadn't realized she had a handgun in her hand until I saw her slipping it into her waistband underneath her coat as we got out of the car. She was taking no chances with my brother's safety.

Kit walked around the driver's side door to open it for him, but he was already out. She frowned at him. "Next time, wait for me," she told him. "I shouldn't be standing between you and the car. I should be standing between you and the street."

Demon glanced over his shoulder. "The area is clear."

"I know that! I checked!" she snapped and stalked toward the tavern.

"She is strung tighter than a bowstring," I murmured to my brother so she wouldn't hear.

We followed her to the tavern, Demon ushering Abby and I ahead of him. Kit turned back and saw that Demon was standing out in the open again and frowned at him. "Stay between Bane and me," she told him, shortly.

Dillon, the doorman of the Black Candle, watched in amusement as Kit stopped Demon at the door to prevent him from entering Rowan's tavern before her. She opened the door and stepped inside. Dillon looked from her to Demon and opened his mouth.

Demon pointed a finger at him. "Not a word, Drakazar."

Dillon closed his mouth and smiled. Kit poked her head out and waved us in.

This time, she insisted that Demon come in first and then Abby and I followed. The minute we set foot inside the tavern, it was like magic. People started disappearing. It wasn't exactly a stampede for the door, but more than half of Rowan's customers got up and headed for the door.

Demon let a few of them pass and then he zeroed in on one customer. He caught him by the arm and without looking at him, spoke quietly. "Spread the word. If supernaturals do not want us stopping everyone we see for interrogation, they will hand Darkmoon over to us. And they had better do it sooner rather than later. Remember we can keep this up *forever*." Demon released the young man who fled.

"You guys certainly know how to clear a room," Abby murmured.

A few more people were drifting toward the door as we took stools at the bar. "I do not know about you," I said to Demon. "But I am beginning to feel rather unloved."

We warned Rowan that we were coming and though she liked us and her boyfriend was a Deadly, she wasn't exactly thrilled to have us in her place of business. "You really think that any of these guys will give up Darkmoon?" Rowan waved at her sparse clientele.

"They will once they realize that either they give her up or they will be drinking with us for the rest of their lives," Demon said loud enough for everyone in the bar to hear.

"And of course, the Enforcers are going to hang out in every supernatural bar in the area until this matter is satisfied," I added. I glanced at Demon. "I think we can easily cover it. There are not many."

I was sure that I heard some muffled groans behind us. Demon leaned on the bar and lowered his voice. "It will not be for long, Rowan."

She sighed. "All right, Fechín." She waved at a tray loaded down with beer bottles and glasses. It levitated and followed her around the side of the bar. "The least you could have done is brought Kaz with you. No offence, Bane."

"None taken," I replied.

Rowan wandered off to serve the drinks on the tray, which followed her around the tavern and hovered politely behind her while she removed the bottles and glasses for each table. As we watched, it shifted the bottles around to balance itself as the weight changed.

To my brother's credit, he kept his theories regarding Kaz and the back room to himself. "I admire your restraint," I told him.

A smile flickered over his face. Kit and Abby looked at each other and then at us, puzzled. I shook my head.

The crowd, such as it was, didn't thin out as much as I thought it would. Over the next few hours, people came in and though they hesitated when they saw us, they still came in and sat down. Most of the supernaturals in the bar had nothing to fear from us. They were just average everyday people. Many of them were human and then turned into something supernatural. Some of them were born this way. Though they could pass for humans and moved easily within the human society, they came to places like Rowan's where they could be among those who were like them and where they did not have to hide who they were or be afraid of exposure.

For the most part, they watched us with curiosity, not fear, though they did not approach us. After a few more hours and, I suspect more than a few glasses of liquid courage, some of them stopped to talk to us. No one knew much about Darkmoon or Tanith, though everyone had heard about the rogue vampires.

Demon glanced at the clock behind the bar. "It is almost four AM. In another hour or so, all the vampires will be scuttling off to bed," he remarked.

"Are we turning in for the night then?" I asked.

Before he could answer me, a tall skinny woman with pasty skin slid onto a stool next to Abby. Her black eyes stared at me through a tangle of black stringy hair. The other woman moved between Demon and Kit. She was shorter than the other woman was. She had black curly hair and the same dark fathomless eyes. Her skin was also very pale, but did not appear as washed-out as the other woman's complexion. She was dressed in a red leather halter-top, red leather skirt and thigh-high, high-heeled boots. They looked like vampires but they were actually banshees.

"Hello, Lilith." Demon greeted the smaller woman as he picked up his beer glass. He showed no surprise at seeing her but his jaw twitched when he took a sip from his drink. He was not happy that she was here.

"What are you doing here, Fechín?" she asked in a high-pitched voice. It was not a full banshee's wail but it was still grating enough.

To Demon's credit, he did not even wince. I cringed, however, and fought the urge to cover my ears. "Looking for information," Demon said calmly.

Lilith eased closer, inserting herself even more between Demon and Kit. "About the rogues?"

Demon set the glass to the bar and turned to look at her. "You have heard about them."

She flashed a smile that was surprisingly pretty. Banshees are not typically lovely creatures but Lilith is the exception to the rule, which is probably why her parents were stunned when she turned out to be a banshee and not some light, flighty fairy. "Everyone has heard about the rogues. Everyone has heard about the executions too." She stared at him thoughtfully. "Did you really put Bael Dagger on the execution list?"

"Yes."

"And he's dead?"

"He has been executed."

Lilith was staring at Demon in a kind of rapt fascination. Suddenly, she climbed his bar stool and swung her leg over his so that she was straddling his lap. She cupped his face lightly in her hands and kissed him full on the mouth, grinding herself against his groin. I darted a glance at Kit. She did not appear to like this turn of events one bit and it looked like she was thinking about grabbing a handful of Lilith's long black hair and flinging her to the floor.

Demon waited for her to draw back and then he calmly reached around her to pick up his beer again. "What was that for?" he asked.

"For executing the ogre."

Demon raised his eyebrow at her.

She smiled. "And also because I just can't seem to resist you. Odd, isn't it?"

"Very. But why are you so concerned about the death of an ogre?"

"He tried to rape my sister, Brighid." She nodded at the other banshee. "He beat her. She got away from him but he broke her nose."

I studied Brighid for any noticeable damage. Now *she* looked like a typical banshee. She was far from beautiful. Hell, she was far from plain, but at least her nose seemed straight and intact. "You healed fast," I remarked.

"It was few months ago," she told me in a true banshee's wail.

"I think my ears are bleeding," Abby whispered to me.

"Mine too," I whispered back.

"Well, I'm glad that you have healed," Demon told Brighid. Lilith was still sitting in his lap and running her hands over his chest, seeming to have forgotten her sister. "However, it was actually Kaz that executed him."

"But you were the one who put him on the list. It was not Daedalus Hellcurse. It was you." Lilith looked up from drawing figures on his chest with her fingertips. "You did every woman in Blackridge a great service. If you ever need to feed, you call me."

Demon caught Kit's eye. She was glaring at them. Demon seemed a bit disconcerted, though his tone remained cool. "Thank you for the generous offer, Lilith, but what I really need is to find Darkmoon."

Brighid hissed and Lilith's lips curled in disgust. "The stapan's mate? What do you want with her?" she demanded jealously.

"We are trying to track the sovereign who is allowing the rogue vampires to feed from the unwilling," Demon explained. "We suspect Darkmoon might be the sovereign."

"I haven't heard anything about the sovereign," Lilith told him. "But I heard that there is a new vampire in town and the rumour is that she has her eye on Hadrian's kiss."

"I have reason to believe that the new vampire is Darkmoon's sister. Her name is Tanith. She wants Hadrian's kiss, does she?"

Lilith shrugged. "That is the rumour."

"Who would know for certain?"

"That I do not know, Fechín. If I hear anything more I will let you know."

"Thank you. Do you need my cell phone number?" he asked by way of dismissing her.

Lilith smiled. "I remember the way to your place," she said softly.

Kit and Abby both looked at him and raised their eyebrows. He cleared his throat. "Oh, right."

Lilith slowly slid off his lap, making sure that her body rubbed against his. I will admit, it was a very nice body but Demon looked very uneasy. "The offer to feed still stands," she purred.

"Don't you have a boyfriend?" he asked.

She wrinkled her nose. She would have been a cute little pixie had she not been dressed like a biker chick. "I did, but we broke up."

"Why?" Kit asked.

Demon shot her a don't-go-there look, but it was too late. Lilith turned to smirk at her. "Because he wasn't Demon," she said simply.

Ignoring Kit's scowl, Lilith turned back to Demon. "Anytime, anywhere," she told him. "I don't mind a little pain with my pleasure as I'm sure you remember well."

I choked on my beer. Demon glared at me and Kit glared at him. "Thank you, Lilith," he said politely.

The two banshees left and Demon turned back to the bar, shaking his head. Abby was gaping at him. "Does that happen a lot?" she asked.

"Not to me," I assured her.

"Well, I'm glad of that," she replied with a smile.

"You appear to know her well," Kit said to Demon coolly. She did not look at him as she spoke.

He glanced at her stony expression and picked up his glass of beer, turning it in his hands. "Lilith and I are old friends."

"Lovers," Kit said flatly.

He darted another look at her. "Yes, but we are no longer together."

"It appears she didn't get the message," Kit remarked. "It is apparent that she still has feelings for you."

Demon shook his head. "Lilith isn't in love with me. She likes the idea of me."

"It is because our mother was a succubus," I said as my brother scowled at me.

Kit did not ask, but Abby did. "Yes?"

Demon was glaring at me and trying to shake his head "no" without calling attention to it. I ignored him. "You know that it is the nature of a succubus or an incubus to be alluring," I said, to Abby. She nodded. "Well, Demon has inherited some of our mother's succubus characteristics."

"You mean that he's an incubus?" Abby asked surprised.

"No! I am most certainly *not* an incubus," Demon protested.

I nodded. "Yes, to a certain extent. He does not have full incubi abilities, but some of the side effects apply to him."

"*Us*," Demon corrected. "What Bane has failed to explain is that he also has some of these abilities."

Abby grinned. "Oh, I knew that."

I could feel my face heating and glared at Demon. "I do not have incubus abilities."

"Bullshit," my pain in the ass brother remarked.

"Prove it," I challenged.

"Werewolf bar," he said.

I winced. Cherie the waitress. I had forgotten. I hoped that I had gotten rid of her phone number and that message. I would hate to have Abby find it. On the other hand, she might find some of those suggestions as intriguing as I did.

"The problem is that women seem to…become obsessed with Demon." I continued, hoping to distract her from asking about the werewolf bar. I shook my head. "And there seems to be no cure."

"That has nothing to do with being an incubus," Kit said softly. We all looked at her. She was staring at the glass of wine in front of her and now she lifted her eyes to look at my brother. "That's just Demon."

"I *told* you that Lilith was in love with the idea that I'm Wrath," he pointed out.

"That's not it and you know it!" she snapped. Then her anger seemed to fade. She added, thoughtfully, "Or do you?"

Demon and Kit were staring at each other. He looked away first.

Abby smiled at me. "So are there going to be any ex-lovers surfacing who may be obsessed with you?"

"No," I reassured her. "There are no ex-lovers of mine who are likely to come hunting me down. Women do not become obsessed with me."

Demon snorted as he lifted his beer again. "Werewolf bar," he repeated.

"Shut up," I muttered at him.

"That's a relief," Abby said.

Demon turned to Abby. "He is teasing about the incubus thing, really. There is only one daemon that has the kind of ability Bane is talking about."

"Who is it?" Abby asked.

He grinned. "Why Lust, of course! Who else?"

Abby laughed. "Now, why didn't I think of that?"

Demon drained his glass of beer. "It is getting late," he said, rising from the stool. "I'll get the car."

Kit grabbed his wrist. "No, Demon. You'll stay right where you are," she said gently. "I'll do it."

"I would rather—"

"I can drive a car, Demon. I won't wreck your precious vehicle."

"That may be," he said stiffly. "But I am perfectly capable of going to get the car. It is not that far away, Kit."

"It's far enough away that you're going to stay right here where I know you'll be safe." Though Kit was clearly in love with Demon, she was not so completely gaga over him that she would forget her job.

"Oh, for pity sake!" I settled the matter by rising quickly and snatching the keys out of her hand before they could start arguing. "Kit, stay here and defend Demon's honour in case the banshees come back. I shall go get the car."

Demon's expression changed from frustration to alarm in an instant. "Bane, no, we will come with you."

"Do not be ridiculous," I told him. "It is starting to rain. No sense in us all getting wet."

"Bane, please." He was starting to rise.

I grasped his hand, forcing him to stay put. "I will be only a minute, Demon," I reassured him gently. "Like you said it isn't that far away."

"Bane, be careful," Abby said sounding worried now too.

I kissed her. "Abby, I am indestructible, remember?"

I left the bar, waving to Dillon on my way out. I heard him say something to my brother as the door closed behind me. The rain was coming down hard and so I had to run for the vehicle. The car was parked a short distance down the street.

I was worried about Demon. He had made it seem tonight as if he did not want Abby and I dressing together because we might become involved in other activities and lose track of time, all of which was true, but I was starting to think that there was more to it than that. He was always teasing me about not driving his vehicles but this was different. It occurred to me that he was scared to let me out of his sight. I have never seen Demon this frightened before and I did not like it.

As I reached the car, I thought to myself that Demon should not have been so worried. After all, no one was out to get *me*.

"Fechín!"

Oh no. I turned, stifling a groan. "Lilith! You shouldn't be here. What are you—"

Before I could finish, she flung herself into my arms and kissed me. I stood quietly and allowed her to do it. Any second now, she would realize her mistake and let go. I only hoped that Abby didn't see us.

The thought had hardly formed when suddenly stars exploded behind my eyes and everything went black.

CHAPTER TWENTY-FOUR

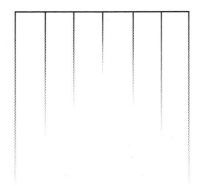

I WOKE UP CURSING. It was the second time in the last week that I had been unconscious. It was becoming an annoying habit. Something soft was brushing my face. I swatted at it only to realize that it was my hair. Someone had taken it out of the braid.

"Mistress!" someone screeched. "He's waking up! *Mistress!*"

I cracked one eye open, but the speaker was long gone before I could get my hair out of my face to get a good look at him. I tried to shake it back but my head screamed in protest. I closed my eyes again and waited for the surge of nausea to pass, but the quick glimpse I had had showed me that I was in a small room without windows.

Someone, I guessed, had hit me and knocked me out cold. They must have hit me rather hard. It is a good thing that I am immortal. Had I been human, the blow would most likely have killed me.

I tried to move but became aware that something was wrong. I opened my eyes again. Someone had shackled me to an iron cot. I was also naked. I grimaced and slowly sat up as the door opened and a woman came in.

"Ah, you are finally awake," she said.

"Darkmoon," I hissed at her.

Another woman ran into the room and stopped short at the sight of me. "Tanith." I shook my hair back. It kept falling in my face. There are some disadvantages to having hair to one's waist. I glared at them. "I take it you were the ones who took my braid out?"

Darkmoon moved to a chair. She smiled in satisfaction. "We removed your clothes as well," she told me, smugly. I gave her a look and she laughed. "Well, we needed to make *certain* that you were unarmed."

I did not reply. They had left the hair clasp sitting on the table beside me. I was still armed, but they did not know that. Yet.

"May I have my pants back?" I asked coldly.

"We've already seen all your bits." Darkmoon leered, amused by my modesty. "And very nice bits they are, Fechín. I begin to understand why my sister is so obsessed with you."

Fechín? So…they thought that I was Demon. It surprised me in a way. Tanith had made the mistake once already I thought she would be more cautious the second time, ensuring she had the right twin. However, if she had made the mistake a second time it was fine with me. If Tanith and Darkmoon figured out that I was Bane, then they would use me for bait to lure Demon to them. I struggled to clear my aching head enough to think coherently. Right now, I had no doubt that my brother was probably turning Blackridge upside down looking for me. Eventually he would find me but as long as Darkmoon and Tanith thought they already had Demon, we would have the element of surprise on our side.

Therefore, I would be Demon.

I had to do a little shapeshifting to make sure that they would see the tips of fangs in my mouth the next time that I spoke. I needed them to continue believing, for the moment, that they had my brother. It was not a major change and I did it without them seeing, but the lack of fangs would have been a dead giveaway.

I slid back on the bed and lounged against the wall. I had seen Demon do it a million times and always wondered how he could be comfortable like that. Fortunately, I found the sweet spot, a space between the wall and the bed so that the tips of my wings did not end up scrunched. Perhaps that was his secret. There was just enough chain that I was able to stretch my legs out on the bed and cross my ankles.

"It makes no difference to me." I shrugged and grinned wickedly. "As long as you don't mind your minions enjoying the show too." I smiled and waggled my fingers at the three female vampires standing in the doorway, ogling me.

"Ladies…" I purred. I think I was channelling Riot at that point, not Demon. However, it got the results I wanted.

Tanith spun around. "Don't you have something *useful* to do?" she snarled at them, jealously. Jealousy is the one of the easiest of the Deadlies to trigger in another person and I crossed my fingers, hoping that I could keep her jealous enough, long enough, to give the others something to track.

The three women fled. Darkmoon was no longer amused. She rose and glared at her sister. "Was that necessary?"

"There is no reason for them to stand there ogling Demon," Tanith said stiffly.

"But, it is fine for your sister to do it?" I demanded.

Tanith gasped, but Darkmoon hardly flinched. She recovered first. "So you know?" she asked, coolly.

"Yes."

She smiled tightly. "Did Hadrian tell you?"

"He seemed unaware that you had a sister until I told him. Even then, he tried to protect you. Hadrian deserves better than you, Darkmoon." I shook my head, carefully choosing my next words. "I never thought I would hear myself say that."

"*Hadrian*," Darkmoon snorted. She said something in a foreign language but I understood what she said and it was not very nice at all. Let me just say she thought he was lacking in ability that had nothing to do with being a stapan.

"You are very contemptuous of him," I remarked.

And angry. Very, very angry. Perfect.

Wrath is the next easiest Deadly to trigger.

Come on, Demon. Come to the buffet.

"He is an idiot!" she snapped.

"You married him." I paused and smiled wickedly. "Elissa."

Darkmoon pursed her lips. "You appear to know a lot, Fechín."

"Yes, amazing isn't it?"

"If Hadrian did not tell you, then who did?"

I smiled mysteriously. "My sources are confidential, *Elissa*."

"Do not call me that!" she hissed, baring her teeth at me.

"Do not flash fang at me!" I roared up from the bed, forgetting that I was naked and shackled.

Darkmoon forgot too. She scrambled for the door, nearly knocking over her sister in her haste to escape. I laughed and Darkmoon's face twisted in fury.

Tanith stepped between us. "Darkmoon, leave us."

Darkmoon's eyes narrowed. "I don't think that leaving you alone with him is a good idea."

Tanith looked at her coldly. "Do not argue with me! I told you that I would deal with Demon. You'll just have to trust me."

"Trust *you*?" Darkmoon gave a bark of laughter.

"Have I ever given you reason not to?" Tanith asked softly.

The question made Darkmoon hesitate. "No," she admitted finally. "But you have never had to make a decision between me and Fechín. I am not so certain that you would remain loyal under those circumstances."

"Elissa, please go. Leave me alone with him for just a few minutes. I give you my word that I will not help him escape. My desire for him will be your guarantee. I want him much more than you do."

Darkmoon scowled at her but in the end she stalked out of the room leaving me alone with Tanith. We stared at each other in silence.

Finally, Tanith began to walk toward me, cautiously. She stopped in front of me, gazing down with her eyes full of emotion. I have hated this woman since the day she betrayed my brother but at that moment, I had to admit, albeit grudgingly, that it seemed like Tanith really was desperately in love with Demon. She would do anything to have him and that made her a danger to him in my book.

She leaned down to kiss me. I let her do it, like Demon had with Lilith, and then I kissed her back lightly, hoping that some response on my part might convince her to let down her guard. "You always did have a talented mouth." Tanith smiled as she drew back.

Eww! That was more information than I wanted to know about my brother. "Is that why you kidnapped me," I replied scornfully. "For a kiss?"

"Partly." She was still smiling. The humour in her voice astonished me. "But I also needed to talk to you. Remember, we never had the chance the last time I saw you."

"Well," I said sarcastically. "Next time pick up the damned phone!"

"Demon..."

"It is a lot less painful and the other person doesn't end up with a killer headache," I persisted.

"Demon!" I stopped talking, but I noted with satisfaction that she wasn't smiling anymore. "I never meant for you to be harmed," she said softly.

"Just like you never meant to hurt me when you turned me into a vampire? You and I apparently have different ideas about what constitutes causing harm."

"Please." Tanith touched my hand. "Will you at least listen to me? Just give me a chance to explain," she begged.

"Why the hell should I?" I demanded. I would have crossed my arms, but I would have had to break the chains that held me to do it. They had clearly forgotten or perhaps they did not know that the chains would not hold me if I wanted to leave badly enough. However, I could not escape just yet. After all, I would not be able to gather any information that way, would I.

Tanith lowered her eyes to the floor and I sighed. "Very well," I said shortly. "Explain."

She sat beside me and put her hand on my leg. I resisted the urge to push it away. I was being Demon, I reminded myself. I glared at her hand until she moved it herself.

She rose and went to the table across the room. My pants lay on it, folded neatly. "Here. You can have these back." She tossed them to me. I slid them on with some difficulty. I knew better than to ask to be unshackled. This woman was not dumb. "Better?" she asked.

Pleased that my Demon act was still fooling her and relieved to be clothed again, I was disposed to be generous. "You had something to tell me," I said in a more friendly tone.

Tanith suddenly seemed nervous. She looked at the floor and fiddled with the long gold chain she wore around her neck. "I hardly know where to begin."

"Let's start with why you turned me."

She shot a puzzled look at me. "I wanted us to be together."

"We were together," I pointed out. "Then you betrayed me."

She flinched. "No, Demon, you misunderstand. I know that you were already immortal. It was not the fear of losing you that made me decide to turn you." She paused.

"So?" I prompted, raising an eyebrow.

She took a deep breath. "There is a ritual that a vampire couple can perform. It's called "raising the moon.""

"I have heard of it," I said cautiously. "It is supposed to render vampires able to walk in the daylight temporarily. I have also heard that it doesn't work. I suppose you thought that we should test the theory?"

"It is much more than that, Demon," she said seriously. "And raising the moon does work, if it is performed between the Daywalker and his mate."

Oh, shit. "You mean me."

"I have never heard of any Daywalker except you." She smiled slightly.

Except there *were* others, two of them, but I didn't want her to know that. That would be dangerous information for her to have. "You could be wrong," I suggested.

"Perhaps, but I don't think so. Most vampires have not researched the legend thoroughly enough or do not believe that raising the moon can only work with you. They think they are all able to raise the moon and somehow you have altered the legend to prevent them from acquiring this ability. I happen to believe the legend is true. After so many centuries of attempts by others to achieve what you have, you are still the only Daywalker."

Damn, this was not looking good for Demon. "But you didn't know when you first turned me that I would be the Daywalker."

"No," she admitted.

"So, you haven't really answered my question."

"When I made the decision to turn you, I was thinking of the ritual, but not for the purpose of becoming a Daywalker. It is because vampires who raise the moon together are mates."

"You did this because you wanted to be my mate? You thought that I could live the rest of eternity with a woman who would betray me?"

"I love you!" she pleaded. "I've always loved you. Who else could be your mate, Demon? Who else loves you as I do? You haven't had any other vampire lovers since me. Every other woman has been a passing fancy."

Actually, it was more as if Demon was the passing fancy of the women, but no woman wanted to be with man who would stay young and handsome forever while she grew old and haggard. He also refused to turn anyone else into a vampire, in spite of the number of women who had asked. It typically ended in the women moving on from the relationship once they realized that he was not going to make them young and beautiful forever.

Then, something Tanith said suddenly clicked. It was something about Demon not having a vampire lover after her. He had, although it was not common knowledge.

Kit.

I remembered Serkan's reaction when he found out that Demon and Kit had raised the moon. She had the permanent ability to walk in the daylight. I thought it was for the same reason that my father could, because Demon had fed Serkan his blood when Serkan was dying and Demon was the Daywalker. Tanith's story put a new spin on it, however. Kit was Demon's mate. I was certain he was aware of this particular side benefit, but I was not certain whether she was or not.

Tanith touched my cheek, recalling my attention. She leaned in, her mouth grazing my neck. "Demon."

Oh, shit. I was not going to raise the moon with Tanith. First, I was not a vampire and, secondly, I was not Demon. However, I did not want her to know that just yet.

I shifted away from her, glad that she had given my pants back to me. "Tanith," I said stiffly. "I have had a long week and very little sleep. I have been hit on the head, shot—"

"*Shot?*" Tanith gasped. "You were shot?"

Oops. "Bane was actually the one who was shot," I told her. "But the vampires in question were shooting at me."

"*Vampires* shot at you? But why?"

"Ask your sister."

Tanith gaped at me and, as it slowly sunk in, anger flared in her exotic purple eyes. She leapt to her feet and stormed out of the room, slamming the door behind her. I blew out a breath and started to tug at the chains. The door flew open again and two male vampires strode in. I released the chains.

"What is it now?" I snapped.

"Sovereign Darkmoon does not wish for you to be unguarded, Wrath," one of the men said in a hoarse voice.

I smirked. "She is a wise woman in so many ways and in others, so stupid."

They looked at each other. "We knew that to kidnap Wrath was a dangerous thing to do. We did try to warn her," the other man began. His companion elbowed him.

"And you didn't think that perhaps feeding from unwilling humans might be just as dangerous?" I asked in the smooth, dangerous tone that Demon used to intimidate. It did not fail me. Both men paled.

"Do you know what happens to supernaturals that break the rules?" I asked. "*We* happen to them. Just because I am not with them, does not mean that the Enforcers will not hunt you down like the monsters you are."

They were afraid now. "Deadlies, show no mercy," I said it as if I was giving the order to execute. I was sure the one man nearly pissed himself. Satisfied that I had made my point, I laid down on the bed with my back to them and closed my eyes. I did not sleep but a few minutes later when I heard Tanith return I decided that I would play possum.

"Get out!" She dismissed the two guards angrily. I kept my eyes closed and kept my breathing even.

"Oh, Demon. I'm so sorry," she whispered. I felt her hand on my hair. Then I heard her leave and the door lock behind her. I sat up and began to work on a plan to escape.

CHAPTER TWENTY-FIVE

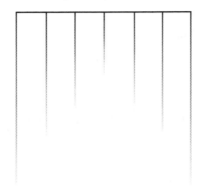

IT WAS A HUGE mistake on their part to leave me unattended. However, they rectified it quickly. I had only been alone a few minutes when Darkmoon returned with the two male guards. In those few minutes, I retrieved the hair clasp and undid it, allowing the chain to extend. It was now a lethal weapon. I could use the sharp ends to slice my enemy open or throw it so that it would wrap around the victim's throat, strangling them. I kept it concealed in my hand as Darkmoon approached.

"Stand up!" she snapped. I raised an eyebrow at her and she grimaced. "*Please* stand up. We're leaving."

I got up slowly, my mind working overtime. If we left the premises, it would delay Demon finding me. There was a greater chance that they would discover that I was not Wrath. If that happened...I didn't want to think about it. On the other hand, once outside, I might have a chance to escape. I needed more time to think. Fortunately, my head gave me a good reason to stall. It was aching still.

I sank to the bed, tucking the weapon in my waistband, and groaned. Darkmoon frowned and I was surprised to see a look of concern on her face. "What's wrong?"

"Who the hell hit me?" I asked. "He must have had hands made of cement."

"That was Tiny."

"Let me guess. Tiny is seven feet tall and four hundred pounds of pure muscle?" I said dryly.

"He is six foot nine actually," Darkmoon admitted with a slight smile. "But, he probably outweighs you by a hundred pounds or more. I believe in his fear he may have used a club of some kind."

I groaned. "He is lucky he didn't split my head open!"

Darkmoon nodded. "He did a little bit. At least, you bled a lot, but it healed up almost immediately." She looked thoughtful. "It is an advantageous power."

I glared up at her suspiciously. I did not like the way that she was looking at me. I suddenly felt like a tasty morsel displayed on a platter. Darkmoon backed away a little, smiling. "Well, we can let you rest a while longer," she said. "I will remain to watch over you."

I snorted. "If you think I'm going to sleep at all with you in the room you are crazier than I thought."

"You did earlier."

"I was *unconscious* not asleep. There is a difference," I pointed out. "Besides, I don't trust you."

"I could change that."

"Hypnosis will not work on me, Darkmoon, and that is the only way you will ever change my mind."

"I wasn't thinking of hypnosis," she told me. "I was thinking..." Her fingers trailed over my bare chest and the look in her eyes left me in no doubt of what she was thinking.

Oh, no! No freakin' way! "I thought that I was to be your sister's mate."

She smiled. "I don't think Tanith would mind if I had a small taste."

"This is beyond tacky, even for you," I said, leaning away from her.

She bent her head and her tongue flicked out, lightly touching my chest. Oh, shit. This was going to be bad. Any second now, she was going to realize that she did not have Demon at all.

To my infinite relief, the door opened and Tanith came in. She stopped in surprise when she saw her sister. Then she looked angry. "Elissa, what are you doing? I thought you were arranging to have us moved to another location."

Darkmoon scowled at her. "I have asked you not to call me by that name!"

Tanith ignored her as she approached the bed. "How are you feeling?" She directed the question to me.

"I feel like I've been trampled by an elephant. I take it his name was Tiny."

Tanith grimaced at her sister. "I told you that he was far too ham-handed for this mission. I am sorry, Demon."

"No, you're not," I told her. "*Yet.*"

She sucked in her breath and Darkmoon glared at me, coldly. "Do not threaten us, Fechín. Have you forgotten that you are at our mercy?"

"I am at your mercy for the moment," I corrected. "However, I am far from helpless, Darkmoon. You should know that. You have known me longer than your sister has."

Before she could answer, a male vampire appeared in the doorway. He was tall and pale with slicked back dark hair. He wore a long, black monk's robe. He was exactly what most humans would picture a vampire to look like. "Excuse me, Sovereign Darkmoon. The car has arrived. We are ready to go."

A tall, muscular man followed the first man into the room. He wore his brown hair in a buzz cut. His mouth hung open slightly and his brown eyes were dull giving him a distinct bovine look.

"I'll bet you are Tiny," I said to him.

The brown haired man blinked at me slowly. "Yeah," he replied.

Obviously a man of deep thought. "I have a score to settle with you," I said in the most dangerous Wrath tone I could muster.

Tiny took it for the threat that it was. He turned a sickly colour and Tanith gave me an admonishing look. "Was that necessary?"

Hell, yes, and I was already getting tired of it. I had never envied my brother his job and now I almost felt sorry for him. Scaring the shit out of people wears on you.

"Let's go," Darkmoon snapped at me. "Stand up."

I moved so quickly that it seemed as though I had suddenly appeared in front of them. Everyone jumped back and I burst into laughter. On the other hand, scaring the shit out of people also makes you feel very powerful.

Tiny and the other vampire unchained me from the bed, but kept the shackles on my wrists. Tiny was hanging on to a chain tied to my waist and standing well out of reach while his friend gingerly bound my shackles together behind my back. He quickly moved away from me when he was finished.

"You know," I began conversationally to Tanith. "This may make it hard for us to raise the moon." I lifted my hands to remind her of the shackles.

Before Tanith could respond, Darkmoon smiled thinly. "I never thought for a second that you had any intention of cooperating."

I shrugged. "Then I don't know how you intended it to work. I would have to cooperate in some way, wouldn't I? Raising the moon means she feeds from me as I feed from her."

Darkmoon laughed incredulously. "Do you think we're stupid?"

"Was that rhetorical or do you really want me to answer that?"

She scowled and continued. "Did you think we were going to give you the chance to tear her throat out?"

"How did you intend to do this then?"

Darkmoon's smile was unpleasant. "Why, the same way she did before, Fechín."

Tanith flinched and I suspected that I was going to regret asking. "What do you mean?"

"Have you forgotten?" she sneered. "We have leverage, of course."

If I could get chills, I'm sure they would have been creeping up my spine right then. "What leverage?"

"The last time it was that young woman." I must have looked blank because Darkmoon frowned. "The black haired girl with the green eyes." She glanced at her sister. "What was her name?"

Tanith gave me an apologetic look, but she didn't have to say it. I already knew. "Ansey," I heard myself gasp and I sagged weakly against the metal headboard of the bed. "Ansey."

Now it all made sense. Nothing else could have forced Demon to allow Tanith to turn him, except maybe using his little sister as a hostage. Did they have her again? If they harmed her, Demon would be the least of their worries.

Darkmoon seemed puzzled by my reaction but pleased too. She smiled. "I see your memory is coming back to you. By the way, whose blood did you take to become a vampire?"

Our father had fed Demon, but I wasn't about to tell her that. "None of your business!" I snapped. "I swear, if you laid one hand on my sister again—"

Darkmoon waved her hand. "We do not have your precious…sister, did you say?" Her eyes gleamed. "Good to know for future confrontations. However, this time we have someone else."

I felt a surge of panic, but I was trying not to show it. My first thought was they had Abby but I knew it had to be someone who was in closer proximity to me at the time of my abduction. "Lilith."

Darkmoon's smile widened. "I am so looking forward to tasting you. I think I will enjoy seeing you helpless for a change, Wrath."

"Demon, are you okay?" Tanith asked, worriedly.

The thought of Ansey's fear and Demon's fear for her was devastating. What had they done to her to force Demon into submission? I did not want to think about it. I swallowed hard, trying to keep myself from throwing up, but I leaned over and vomited anyway. I had taken far too much punishment this week and my body had had enough. I straightened again, stomach still churning angrily. "You reprehensible bitch," I whispered before I could stop myself.

Tanith stared at me for a minute and then her mouth tightened. "Your fangs are gone," she said flatly.

Oops. It appeared that I could not hold a shift while vomiting. Good to know but now I was in deep shit.

"This is *not* Demon." Tanith turned to her sister in disgust. "Your idiot flunkey has kidnapped Bane!"

"Well, how was he to know?" Darkmoon replied. "They're identical twins, Tanith! And even *you* thought he was Fechín!" Still she cast Tiny a grim look that boded ill for him.

He cringed. "The girl called him by name!"

"Apparently, *she* cannot tell them apart either!" Darkmoon snapped.

Tanith brought me a glass of water and fed it to me. She wiped my mouth gently with a paper towel. "I guess you didn't know how we managed to convince Demon to let me feed from him. I just wanted him to be my mate. I thought he wanted it too, but he was gone before we could finish the ritual—" she trailed off at the expression on my face.

"He escaped while everyone was gone for the day," I told her coldly. "You turned him and then left him *alone*. You just left him there."

"I did not expect him to wake before dusk," she told me.

"You were wise to sleep elsewhere. He would have killed you if he had found you right then."

"We did not harm your sister. I want you to know that," Tanith went on.

I snarled at her. "You think not? You used her to lure her brother." It must have been torture for Ansey to know that Tanith had turned Demon because he was trying to protect *her*. It would not matter that it was not her fault. We Hellblazers tend to believe we can save the world and then wallow in the guilt when we cannot.

I was seriously thinking about snapping the chains and killing her myself. It was with great difficulty that I restrained myself. It would be harder to escape if I broke free inside the building than if I had a clear path outside, but I promised myself that as soon as I was free, she was dead.

"Now what do we do?" Tanith sighed, tiredly. "Demon must be tearing the city apart looking for him."

"We'll send him a message to let him know that we have his brother and that if he wants him, he'll have to come and get him." Darkmoon was glaring at me, offended that I had fooled her.

Tanith rolled her eyes in disgust. "Really, Darkmoon, do you think Demon is just going to walk in here and let us capture him?"

Darkmoon's eyes raked over me, appraisingly. I did not like the way she was looking at me. I recognized that look from hanging around Riot. It was lust. As repulsive as it was, it sent out one more trail for the Deadlies to follow.

"I think he will do as we tell him now that we have a better hostage than the banshee," Darkmoon purred. "He will raise the moon with you—and behave himself—or we will turn his beloved brother into a vampire too. Maybe we'll kill the banshee just to make our point."

"Darkmoon—" Tanith began.

Her sister wasn't listening. "Think of it, Tanith. If Demon can be a Daywalker, why not Bane as well?"

I hated to admit it, but it might just work. It was conceivable that I would have the same reaction to a vampire bite that he had. However, I was not about to give them the chance to use me as a hostage. I would be long gone before they could issue their threat.

Darkmoon was staring at me, licking her lips. I gazed back at her, letting my repugnance show in my face. She smiled at me and then turned away. "Let's get going," she said to the others. "We'll call Fechín from the new house."

Tiny gave the chain around my waist a hard yank suddenly, almost pulling me off my feet. Once he realized that I was not Wrath, I ceased to scare him. "Hey," he grinned. "I have to thank you for the gift." He showed me that he had my sheath and blade on his back. "Guess you won't need it, huh?"

He was feeling very cocky. That was okay. He would learn.

I followed Tiny into the hallway. The other vampire was a little more wary of me. He stayed slightly behind me, watching every move that I made. That would make it more difficult to snap the chains unnoticed.

As soon as I stepped into the hallway, I saw that the other man was leading Lilith on a chain as well. She gazed at me with frantic eyes. "Demon—"

I shook my head.

She gave a little gasp. "They know you're not—"

I nodded.

"God and goddess," she moaned. "We're dead. No, *I'm* dead."

"No one is going to kill you," I assured her kindly. I refrained from pointing out that if she had just left Demon alone, she wouldn't be in this mess at all.

"Naw, we won't kill you. Not right away." Tiny grinned. "I wonder what banshee tastes like."

He laughed heartily when Lilith blanched and Tiny gave my chain another yank. This time, it didn't throw me off balance. I stood my ground and waited. Tiny turned when he became aware that I wasn't moving. He sneered and yanked the chain again. It didn't budge me. To my satisfaction, Tiny was starting to look a bit alarmed.

"Yank that chain again," I said darkly. "And I'll make Wrath look like a pussycat. A Deadly is still a Deadly."

He turned white. I suppose the enormity of what they had done finally sunk in. If Demon didn't kill them, the other Deadlies could and would. People forget that the rest of us are just as dangerous as he is.

"Tiny!" Tanith snapped. "That's enough!"

"Don't damage the goods, Tiny." Darkmoon smirked at me. "Wrath will be very annoyed if we break his brother."

"Bring an army, bitch," I responded calmly. "I do not break easily."

Darkmoon laughed as though I amused her. I had never pegged her as being stupid. Tiny was finally showing some smarts. He behaved himself as we began our walk down the long hallway and he did not try to yank me again. The chain was slack rather than otherwise.

We approached the steps leading to a door and I noted that the light above the door was out. "That is going to make it hard to find the steps," I remarked nodding at the dark bulb.

"The lights are off so no one sees us leaving," Darkmoon told me.

"Would it be unkind of me to say that I hope you fall and break your neck?" I asked cheerfully.

Darkmoon snarled at me. Clearly, she *did* consider it an unkind thought. "Shut up!" she snapped.

"I know it will not kill you," I continued. "I would have to take your brain, lungs, or heart to do that. But at the very least, you would hurt like hell while you heal."

"I said *shut up!*"

"Perhaps you would heal improperly," I persisted. "And end up severely deformed."

"Gag him, will you?" Darkmoon shrieked at the subordinate walking behind me.

The vampire moved around in front of me. "I have nothing to gag him with, mistress."

Before he finished the sentence, she turned and ripped one of the long sleeves off Tiny's shirt and shoved it at him. "Use this!"

"Gross," I commented. "He has been sweating in that!"

"He's a vampire!" she snapped. "We don't sweat! And shut up!"

"Yes, you do. *You* are sweating buckets. You are just a little more worried about Fechín showing up than you want to admit."

"Shut up!" Darkmoon shrieked again.

"Your sister is losing it," I remarked in an aside to Tanith.

"Be quiet, Bane," Tanith said.

"Remember how Demon said that a vampire with long black hair and purple eyes was seen in a bar with the rogue vampires?" I went on in a low voice. "Remember that he said this person looked *exactly* like you? Did it ever occur to you that perhaps she looked like you *on purpose*? Did Darkmoon know that it would lead the Deadlies right to *you*?"

Tanith's eyes darted to her sister quickly and then back to me.

"Are you sure that *you* trust *her*?" I asked softly before the vampire stuck the sleeve in my mouth and tied it off. However, I had made my point. Tanith was now watching Darkmoon with a hint of concern, if not outright suspicion.

My vampire guards had been so distracted by my argument with Darkmoon that they had failed to notice that my shackles were broken. I kept my hands in front of me, close together, the chain grasped lightly in my hands. As we started up the dark stairs, I slipped the hair clasp weapon out of my waistband quietly with my free hand, using the sound of the chain Tiny was dragging to cover any noise it might make.

The second vampire guard handed Lilith's chain to Tiny and then went to open the door. He stepped outside, glanced around, and then motioned for the two women to follow. That left Tiny alone with Lilith and me. He started up the stairs, pulling us along. Lilith stumbled forward but I remained immobile. He looked back. "Don't make this—" he growled.

Before he could finish his sentence, I lashed out with the weapon, the sharp garrotte wrapping around his neck. I jerked back quickly and Tiny's head came off with a sickening snap. It happened too fast for him to make a sound. I caught the head and the body as it fell back against me. I propped him against the wall on the stairs and put his head in his lap. Then I took my blade back. Damn, it felt good to have it back in my hands.

I turned to Lilith. She was gaping at Tiny's headless body stunned. To her credit, she had not made a sound either. She lifted her gaze to me. "You will be safe now, Lilith," I said softly and broke the chains that still held her. "Just stay here."

She nodded and I hurried up the stairs, staying just inside the door in the darkness. I peeked out cautiously. I could not see Tanith. I assumed that she was safely in the car. However, Darkmoon was still standing beside the car. The other vampire guard was standing between Darkmoon and me, watching the door. He was frowning.

"Tiny," he called out. "Hurry up!"

I did not give him a chance to come back in. I launched myself out of the door and landed on him, blade in my hand. I plunged it into his chest, through his heart. He sank to the ground, blood pouring out of his mouth, with a shocked expression on his face. I wrenched it out of him and lunged for Darkmoon. She was ready for me. She grasped my wrist as we went down, me on top of her. She was strong but I was stronger. I strained, pushing my hand downward, the blade creeping closer to her neck.

Suddenly, I heard a woman scream and something hit me hard in the back of the head. I saw stars and it stunned me long enough for Darkmoon to push me away. She scrambled away from me as I lay on my back staring up at Tanith. She stood over me with a tire iron in her hand, her face white. She dropped the tire iron. "Forgive me," she said hoarsely. "But, she's my sister. Surely, you can understand..."

"No," I said. "I don't."

The last thing I heard was the squeal of tires as the car roared off. I faded once more into darkness.

I regained consciousness a few seconds later and cursed myself for my stupidity. I should never have assumed that Tanith was in the car. Demon would never have been so foolish. I vaulted to my feet and began to run in the direction I thought the car had taken, but I knew it was of no use. I could not catch up with the fleeing car on foot.

Fly, damn it! My mind screamed. *It's faster by air!*

My exhausted body finally understood what my brain was trying to tell it. As I spread my wings, preparing to take to the air, I heard someone yelling. "Bane, Bane!"

I knew the voice and as I turned, I instantly folded my wings, forgetting Tanith, Darkmoon and everything except the man running toward me.

"Bane!" Demon almost collapsed in my arms.

I held my brother tightly. I could feel him shaking. The intensity of his fear stunned me. I had never seen Demon like this not even after Tanith turned him. I glanced over his shoulder at Kaz, standing a few feet away. He was as shocked as I was.

Demon released me and, taking a step back, all the emotion seemed to drain away. "Are you okay?" he asked me. His voice was calm but he could not hide his anxiety from me.

I nodded and looked at Kaz again for an explanation. He shook his head and shrugged. He did not know what had just happened either.

"Who took you?" Demon demanded. "Where are they? Are you hurt? What did they do to you? Did they—did they—" He was stammering, the fear back in his face.

"No, Demon," I reassured him gently. "I am unhurt. However, Tanith and Darkmoon escaped."

An incredulous expression chased away the fear. I was relieved to see it. This was more like him. "How the hell did they get away?" he demanded, the leader in him taking over.

I explained how they had taken my weapons except for the hair clasp and how I had killed Tiny with it. "Tanith hit me with that," I told them, pointing to the tire iron she had dropped. There was blood on it. I winced and touched the tender spot on the back of my head.

Demon started swearing. I knew he was upset because he was using words that I would not repeat in front of Hex for fear of her chasing me with a broom. While

Demon checked me for signs of a serious concussion, Kaz dragged the other two bodies back into the building and convinced Lilith that it was safe to come out.

She followed Kaz out of the building and into the fresh air. She breathed in deeply and then burst into tears. Kaz and I stood awkwardly by while Demon wrapped her in his arms and stroked her hair gently while she sobbed.

"And he wonders why his ex-lovers are all still crazy about him," I murmured to Kaz.

Finally, Lilith regained control and then stepped back from Demon. She gazed at him with the same sad expression I had seen on Kit's face earlier. "I love you," she said simply and then, while Demon struggled with astonishment, she kissed him deeply.

After a moment, she drew back, gave us a small smile and a wave, and disappeared into the night. Demon stood gaping after Lilith. Suddenly, he gave himself a little shake and then turned, walking back to the building.

I half expected a scathing lecture on losing the vampires and was surprised when none came.

"At least we now have evidence that Darkmoon and Tanith are involved with the rogue vampires," Kaz remarked as we watched my brother. "We can get Daedalus to give us an execution order."

"Since when does the lack of one stop us?" I asked.

"Yeah, but this makes it all aboveboard. Nice and tidy for Daedalus," Kaz joked.

Then he turned toward me, keeping his back to Demon. "What's going on with him?" he asked in a low voice jerking his head in Demon's direction.

"We will talk about it later," I whispered back.

Demon was walking back to us so Kaz dropped the subject for the moment. "Did they give you any indication of where they were going?" Demon asked me.

I shook my head. "All they said was that we were going to another hideout and that when we got there—" I broke off abruptly remembering why they kidnapped me in the first place. He needed to know because they might try for him again. However, this was not the time or the place to discuss it.

Demon stared at me, questioningly. "Yes," he prompted. "When you got there?"

I sighed, suddenly feeling weak from fatigue. As I said, it had been a long week. "I'm wiped, Demon. Let's go home. I will tell you when we get there."

CHAPTER TWENTY-SIX

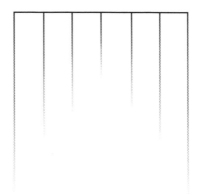

DEMON USED HIS CELL phone to call everyone home. Apparently, the whole household was out looking for me, including Hex and Toad. When we pulled in the driveway, the others were waiting in the yard.

As soon as I stepped out of the vehicle, Abby detached herself from the group and rushed into my arms. She held me tightly, not making a sound. At last, she stepped back. "I've never been so terrified in my life," she told me. "What happened?"

"Tanith and Darkmoon snatched me," I explained. "Or rather, they had Tiny do it."

"Who's Tiny?" Riot asked.

"Tiny!" Kit gasped. "They sent that lunkhead after you?"

"No," I said quietly. I turned to my brother. "Let's go inside."

I expected Demon to protest or demand an explanation right then, however he merely nodded and stood back allowing me to enter the house first. I did not like to see my brother subdued. Dev closed the front door behind us.

Demon did not speak as we entered the library. He walked over to the desk and sat down. He stared the top of the desk. When he still did not speak, the others looked at him and then at me, questioningly. I shook my head.

Finally, Riot got the ball rolling. "Okay, tell us everything."

I explained how I had gone to get the car and about Lilith calling out Demon's name. "She thought that I was you." I added, "She, um, kissed me."

"Oh?" Abby narrowed her eyes. "She did, did she?"

"While she was kissing me," I went on hastily. "Someone hit me from behind. When I came to, I discovered that they had chained me to a bed. Darkmoon and Tanith admitted to having me kidnapped, except that they thought that I was Demon. At least, they did at first."

"When did they realize that they had made a mistake?" Demon asked.

"When they told me how Tanith managed to turn you," I said pointedly.

The implications were not lost on Demon. His gaze flicked away. "I see," he said softly.

"I threw up," I went on in a matter of fact tone. "It was a dead giveaway I guess." I tried to smile. "Wrath would never have thrown up."

However, my brother's thoughts had wandered. From the look on his face, I guessed what he was thinking. I grasped his arm firmly. "Demon, do not go there. It was no more your fault than it was hers."

He took a deep breath and pulled himself back from the edge. "Keep going. What happened then?"

"They were going to use Lilith to force me—to force you—to behave."

He frowned. "But they couldn't turn me again," he pointed out. "What was the purpose?"

I was on uncertain ground here. I was unsure how much he really knew about the ritual of raising the moon. "Tanith had a strange idea," I began cautiously. "She thought that you might be willing to raise the moon with her."

Kit and Demon looked at each other and seemed puzzled. "Why did she think that?" he asked.

Okay, maybe they did not know that raising the moon meant that they were mates. Oh, boy.

"Well," I explained. "It has something to do with the meaning behind it."

An immediate change came over both Kit and Demon. He looked panicked and she seemed suspicious. I concluded that it meant that he knew and she did not. I wondered if he ever intended to tell her the truth.

Not fair, I thought. *And not my call.*

"Anyway," I went on giving him a hard look of disapproval. "When they realized that they had the wrong twin, they were going to—who the hell is that?"

A small male was sitting on the sofa. I had only just noticed him. Demon glanced his way. "Oh. Bane, meet Normie." He gestured toward the gnome. "Normie, this is my brother, Bane."

"What is he doing here?" I demanded.

"He was the one who came to tell me that you had been kidnapped," Demon explained. "He witnessed it."

Normie didn't come close to resembling any gnome I had ever met. He was taller than the average gnome was. They are typically three feet tall and Normie was just over five feet. I guessed he must have been part of something human. He had no beard or moustache, though most of the male gnomes wore them. His hair was blond, short, and spiky. He wore jeans and a black t-shirt. Most stunning of all was the number of piercings in his ears, nose, eyebrows, and lower lip. Riot had said that he was a kid, but nearly everyone is a kid to us. I thought he was exaggerating. I had still been picturing someone more Adrastos' age. Normie was about fifteen years old and apparently in his rebellious stage.

"I thought you went back to the Hills with Adrastos and your cousin," I said to him.

Normie snorted. "No way!" he sneered. "It's okay for them. I mean, they have no sense of adventure. They're, like, old, ya know? They're gonna do all the boring gnome shit like help the humans and raise a bunch of kids. Not me, man, I'm gonna *live!*"

I stared at him incredulously. He would not live long if he hung out with us. However, I had to smile. I was not the only one. Dev's face was slowly turning red as he struggled not to laugh and I had to look away quickly before I started to laugh too. I liked Normie already, but I was worried too. He was just a kid and he was going to get himself killed or at the very least, one of us would get hurt trying to keep him alive.

While Dev was busy trying to restrain himself, Demon kept a straight face. "And you want to work for us?" he asked.

Normie's eyes lit up. "Hell, yeah! I am made for this kind of shit, man! Bring on the bad guys 'cause I am ready to kick some ass!" He raised his fist in the air.

Dev was biting his lip now and making squeaky noises as he fought down the giggles. "Demon, this is a bad idea," I whispered to my brother so that Normie would not hear.

Demon made a small gesture to silence me. "I appreciate your offer of assistance, Normie," he said in a serious voice. "But, I told you that only a Deadly can be an Enforcer."

Normie's face fell. "Yeah, I know. But, I was hoping—"

"However," Demon continued. "We do have need of another liaison to assist Maia." He nodded in her direction.

Ah, there was a ray of hope. Normie lit up. "What does a liaison do?"

"Well, sometimes other supernaturals hear things and they will often give information to Maia to pass on to us," Demon explained. "Often the younger supernaturals hear more than the adults do but we have no one who can talk to them. That is where you come in."

"How?"

"You can go places that we cannot. For example, we cannot go into the high school but you can without arousing suspicion."

Normie glared at him, looking suspicious himself. "Is this a trick to get me to go to school?"

Demon shrugged. "Can you imagine what would happen if someone saw one of us hanging around the high school talking to kids?" He gestured around the room.

Normie glanced around at us and grinned suddenly. "Someone would call the cops."

"Exactly," Demon nodded. "But you can go into the school, hang out with other kids, or even go to the dances and no one would think it was weird."

"Dances?" Normie perked up. "With girls?" Just when I thought Demon had found his weak spot, he frowned. "But, what about Adrastos and Ariadne? They're not gonna want to move into Blackridge and they're, like, my guardians."

"I'll talk to them."

"But where am I supposed to live?"

"We have room here."

I think we all gasped at the same time. "What are you doing?" I hissed at Demon.

"Is it a deal?" Demon asked Normie, ignoring me.

Normie shook Demon's hand, grinning. "Hell yeah, it's a deal!"

"Maia," Demon turned to her. "Will you come with Normie and me to speak to Adrastos and Ariadne? I think they would feel safer if you were there."

Maia rose from her chair with a small, bemused smile. "Of course."

The rest of us remained behind in the library. I was not sorry. Not only was I completely exhausted, but also I needed to talk to the others privately. Abby came over and sat next to me on the sofa, snuggling in with her head on my shoulder. I put my arm around her and leaned back.

"Kaz," I began.

He was already on the same page. "I know. It was freaky."

"What was?" Dev asked looking from me to Kaz.

"Demon," I said. "I have never seen him like that." I nodded at Dev. "You said it before. He is vulnerable, subdued. He has been that way ever since Tanith turned up again. If he were just a bit edgier than usual I would not be so worried, but this is not like him."

"What happened?" Riot wanted to know.

Kaz explained how Demon had reacted when they found me. "He was beside himself," Kaz said quietly. "Up until then, he was behaving normally. You know, the strategist, just figuring out the best way to find his brother. Then as soon as we find Bane, he goes to pieces."

"*Demon?*" Onyx frowned.

"Damn," Dev added.

We fell silent. A few minutes later, the phone rang. Riot moved to answer it. He said hello and then listened for a moment. Then he held the phone out to me. "It's Serkan."

I got up and took the receiver. "Hello."

"Bane, are you all right?" Serkan demanded. "Demon said that you were kidnapped."

"Yes. I'm home and I'm fine."

"Did they hurt you? They didn't—they didn't turn you too, did they?"

I winced. He had used our real names over the phone. That was unusual for him. He must have been very worried. "No, Serkan," I assured him.

"You're not just telling me that, are you?"

"No! If I'm lying may my...hair fall out!" I almost said feathers. Wouldn't that have been a shock to anyone eavesdropping on us?

"Well—"

"I'll swear to you on Fechín's hair if it makes you feel better and if *his* hair falls out, he'll kick my ass. How is that?"

My father began to laugh. "All right," he said reluctantly. "Listen, I will be over first thing tomorrow." He paused. "Son, I'm glad you're okay."

Calling me "son" on the phone was another no-no. "Okay. Thanks," I said hastily, trying to discourage any further discussion.

At last, he said good-bye and I hung up. As I did, Maia returned.

"Well?" Dev said to her.

She shook her head and smiled. "Well, it seems that we're all now the proud parents of a fifteen year old half-gnome, half-human boy."

"Adrastos and Ariadne didn't object?"

"No. Normie is an orphan," she explained. "Ariadne's parents were raising him but then they passed away a few months ago. I think that she and Adrastos felt that a fifteen-year old boy was too much for a young, newly-wed couple to handle."

"I hope he's not too much for *us* to handle," Kaz said.

Maia looked thoughtful. "You know, I think that Demon may have underestimated Adrastos. I didn't see any fear in him at all. He trusts Demon."

"I'm not sure that I understand why Demon wanted to take on this kind of responsibility," Dev frowned.

Maia shrugged and sat on his knee. "Normie is determined to live in Blackridge. Adrastos and Ariadne can take him back to the Hills but that doesn't mean he'll stay there. If he gets lost on the streets, in a few years you could be hunting his killer. You know what happens to some of these runaway kids and Normie is a gnome. They are practically defenceless."

"Good point," I said. "If he is here then we can keep an eye on him."

Maia nodded, smiling. "I would say that was Demon's opinion." She gave Dev a kiss. "And now I have to get some papers so that Demon can show that he is Normie's legal guardian."

Maia was a paralegal and sometimes, when we needed them, she was able to get us some official looking papers. "Hey," I said worriedly. "You are not going to get into trouble for this, are you?"

"No. Believe me, Sachmet does not mind," Maia said, referring to the lawyer for whom she worked. "She will sign anything for the Deadlies. I'll call her right now."

"By the way," I said. "Where is Demon?"

"We saw Adrastos and Ariadne off at the door, then, Hex took Normie upstairs to show him to his bedroom. I think Demon was headed for the garden."

I rose from the sofa. The others stood too. I waved them back. "No. I need to speak to him alone."

They exchanged puzzled looks but they sat down again. I kissed Abby and left the library, heading through the kitchen out to the garden behind the house. As I stood in the darkened yard, I wondered why he hadn't turned on any outside lights. I wasn't even sure where he was exactly. I flicked on the floodlights and started down the steps into the backyard. He wasn't there.

Concerned, I went around the outside of the whole house, looking for him. When I could not find him, I began to panic. The vampires knew where we lived. Had they come back and snatched my brother now?

I raced back into the house to enlist the others help in finding him. I almost ran down Toad in the hallway. It did not occur to me then to wonder why he was still there after the Graces had left.

"Where is everyone?" I gasped.

"Gone to bed," he told me frowning in alarm. "What is the matter?"

"I cannot find Demon!" I gasped.

Relief covered Toad's face. "Oh. He is upstairs in his room."

I sagged against the wall and covered my eyes with my hand. I felt Toad's hand on my arm. "Are you okay, sir?"

I nodded and stood straight. I gazed down at Toad as his presence finally sunk in. "Why are you still here?" I asked at last. "Why didn't you leave with Ambrose?"

Toad made a face. "If you had the choice of following Abby or Ambrose, which would you choose?" he asked.

"Good point."

"Fechín said that I could stay as long as I pull my weight." Toad paused and looked puzzled. "What does it mean?"

"It means you need to help Hex and not leave all the hard work up to her."

"Oh." Toad looked thoughtful.

"Change your mind?"

Toad shook his head. "No. I would still rather be here working than at the Graces' house."

"Welcome to the team, Toad," I said.

"Thank you."

"I am going up stairs to talk to Demon. Good night."

"Good night, sir," Toad said softly and he walked down the hallway toward his own room.

I was soon standing in the doorway of Demon's bedroom. I did not bother to knock. I opened the door quietly. Demon was sitting on the floor, hugging his knees to his chest, his forehead resting on his knees. I moved into the room quietly, closing the door behind me, and sat cross-legged on the floor in front of him. I did not say anything at first, partly because I wanted him to sense my presence so I didn't startle him and partly because I was happy to sit quietly with him for a moment.

Finally, I spoke. "You want to tell me about the mate thing?"

He didn't lift his head. "No."

"Why?"

"You should be resting, Bane. You have had a rough week."

"And you are being evasive."

Finally, he looked up, though he stared at the wall and not me. "What happened when Tanith and Darkmoon found out that they had you instead of me?"

I frowned. "I do not understand."

"Yes, you do. Think about it. They did not say, "Oops, sorry. Wrong guy," and let you go."

"Hardly," I agreed, dryly.

He looked at me now. "So? What were they going to do with you?"

"They were going to use me as bait to trap you," I admitted. He didn't say anything. "Are you okay?"

"No," Demon answered. "They were going to use you to trap me. How can I be okay with that? This is not the first time something like this has happened."

"They told me." I paused. "Did Dad and Mom know?"

Demon shook his head. "How could I tell them that their daughter was held hostage, threatened, and nearly killed because of me? How could they ever forgive me?"

"They would not have blamed you, you know. Why did you never tell *me*?"

"For the same reason I never told Mom and Dad." Demon sighed and lowered his head to his knees again. "I do not want to talk anymore."

"Do you want me to leave?"

"No."

I shifted over to sit next to him. I put my arm around his shoulders. Demon didn't lift his head but I felt him relax at last.

CHAPTER TWENTY-SEVEN

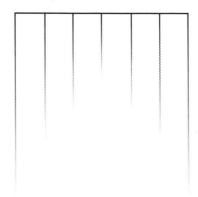

I WOKE UP ON my stomach on a cold floor and it took me a minute to remember why I was there. I sat up, confused, but when I saw my brother lying next to me, I remembered. I reached over and started to give him a shake. I drew back at the last second, deciding to let him sleep. Demon was a bit of an insomniac so any sleep he could get was important.

I went downstairs. Breakfast was calling my name. Glancing at the tall grandfather clock in the hallway, I noted that it was still very early. I knew Hex would have coffee on but that breakfast was still a half an hour away.

I was dreaming about a cup of coffee as I started toward the kitchen when the doorbell rang. I paused and Hex appeared in the doorway of the kitchen, wiping her hands on a towel. "I will answer it," I told her.

As it was daybreak, I knew that it wouldn't be vampires knocking on the door. I also knew that if they were here to hurt us, they weren't going to ring the doorbell announcing their presence. Still, I was a little nervous when I peeked through the peephole.

When I saw who was standing there, I frowned and yanked open the door. "Carys?"

She was standing on the doorstep, looking pale and wringing her hands, obviously anxious about something. She gasped and her hands flew to her chest when she heard my voice. "Oh!" Then she hesitated. "Fechín?"

"Bane," I said dryly.

She blushed. "I'm sorry. I didn't realize..." She floundered for a moment, holding onto the doorframe. She had always been able to tell us apart before and now I realized that it was because she had only been able to tell us apart by the taste of our energy. It did not make me feel any kindlier toward her to discover that she had not done it this time.

"I—may I come in?" she stammered when I did not speak right away. "It's rather awkward to explain myself while I'm standing on the porch."

I felt an arm slide around my waist and looked down startled. It was Abby. I hadn't heard her come down the stairs. Some Enforcer I was. She was half standing between Carys and me. If I had to guess, I would say that I was the one that she was trying to protect. She stared coldly at her sister. "What are you doing here?"

Carys' eyes lit up and she reached out to her sister. "Abby!"

Abby avoided her sister's embrace. "I asked you what you are doing here. I'm still waiting for an answer."

The joy in Carys' eyes dimmed. "Conrad called me. He told me what happened last night. I wanted to make sure that Bane was all right."

"He's fine," Abby said coldly.

"Yes. I—Please, may I come in? This is very important. I need to speak to Fechín."

"Good morning!" Riot came down the stairs and his expression froze when he saw Carys. "What is she doing here?" he demanded tightly.

"She wants to talk to Demon," I said as Riot eyed her with dislike. I stepped back, my arm around Abby's waist. "Let's go to the kitchen." I spotted Toad lurking on the stairs, peeking through the bars. "Toad, Demon is still asleep. Will you go and tell him that Carys is here and needs to speak with him immediately. Just be careful how you wake him."

Toad grimaced, but amazingly, he hurried upstairs without complaining.

"Just give him plenty of room to swing!" Riot called after him. "He has a mean left hook!"

There was nothing I could do except offer my arm to Carys. Riot wasn't about to do it. Her touch was hesitant as if she half expected me to rebuff her. I offered my other arm to Abby and led the two women down the hallway to the kitchen. Riot pushed open the door and held it for us.

Hex turned as we came in, smiling when she saw Abby and me, but her smile turned into a scowl when her gaze fell on Carys. The Graces' insults and cowardly abandonment of us were still fresh in her mind. "What do *you* want?" she snapped.

"I am sorry to intrude," Carys said sheepishly. She paused. "I know we owe the Deadlies an apology for our behaviour. Conrad said—"

The door opened again and Demon walked into the kitchen with Conrad. The rest of the Deadlies were with them. They stood in a line, a wall of black wings and hostility, as Demon moved toward us. "Carys," he greeted her coolly. "I understand that you have something to tell me."

She nodded and oddly, she kept her head down as if she were ashamed. "I know I don't deserve your kindness after everything that has happened. I wanted to say how sorry I am for my very rude, very uncalled-for behaviour. I didn't want to tell you what I have to tell you without saying that first. I talked to Conrad this morning and he said that I should tell you what I overheard. Please believe that if I had known what he was up to—" She took a deep breath. "It was Zane."

Demon stared at her. "What was Zane?"

She bit her lip. "He was the one who told the vampires where your house was," she said hoarsely. "And he followed you and told them that you were at Rowan's last night. I'm so sorry!" She burst into tears.

We remained silent as Abby moved toward her sister. Conrad caught her arm and when Abby looked up at him in surprise, he shook his head. She stepped back with a questioning look.

"How did you get here, Carys?" Conrad asked.

"I had Ithel drive me here. She brought me to the door and I told her to go back to the car to wait. I—I told her what happened and that I wasn't sure of our reception, but we knew that we had to tell you about Zane," she explained.

Demon glanced at Dev. "Go out to the car and ask Ithel to come in."

Dev nodded and left.

"It was very honourable of you to come here and give this information to the Deadlies," Conrad said quietly.

Carys looked amazed. "Really?" she sniffed.

"Yes." He nodded. "Now tell Demon what you told me."

Carys took a deep breath. "Zane received a phone call around two. I overheard him talking. I wasn't going to eavesdrop and then I heard him say—I heard him yelling how they had screwed up at the Deadlies' house, getting caught and that he risked his own neck by telling them where you lived."

"What did you do?"

"I went to Ithel," Carys said. "We decided that we had to come back and tell you everything. After all, we are all on the same team." She stopped and seemed awed by her own words. "I didn't realize it before."

Suddenly Toad raced into the kitchen with a look of panic on his face. "Ambrose Grace is here!" he gasped. "And—"

Ambrose stepped in behind him and kicked Toad across the room, making the poor imp yelp. "Shut up! I'll deal with you later, you miserable imp!" Ambrose roared.

We all started yelling at once. "Hey!" Kaz snapped, rushing to help Toad up. Hex ran over to him too.

"You asshole!" Onyx shouted trying to lunge around Demon to get to Ambrose.

I started after Ambrose too. He took a step back and Morgana caught my arm, a look of hatred on her face as Zane stepped into the room behind Ambrose.

We were all speechless with fury. Finally, Riot spoke. "I can't believe that you have the nerve to bring that bastard here after what he's done!" he hissed at Ambrose.

"He is my second in command," Ambrose said coolly. "He will go where I go."

There was an arrogant, untouchable smirk on Zane's face. I wanted to kill him. I took a step forward but before I could get near Zane, someone shot past me in a blur of wings and blade.

Everyone froze as Demon pinned Zane to the kitchen table, his blade at his throat. His face twisted in fury, flames flared in his eyes. His fangs flashed. "You sonofabitch, mother—" He snarled a few more curse words at him. "If you ever endanger my brother or anyone on my team again, I'll make you wish you *could* die!"

A small line of blood appeared on Zane's throat where Demon had pressed the lethally sharp blade. We all stood frozen in shock. Demon was still swearing and that was not a good sign.

Finally, I stepped forward and touched Demon's shoulder tentatively. "Let him up." Demon didn't move. Hatred blazed in his eyes. I gripped his arm tightly. "Come on, Demon. Come on. Let him go."

"I should take your head," Demon rasped.

As much as I disliked Zane, I didn't really want Demon to try to take his head. It would just make a mess and it wouldn't kill him anyway. *"Demon,"* I said with a little more force. *"Let him go!"*

I glanced around the room at the others. "Rein it in so he can regain control of himself!" I barked.

For a few seconds all I heard was the ticking of the clock and Demon's harsh breathing. Then suddenly he stepped back and yanked Zane back to his feet by the front of his shirt. Demon tossed Zane aside like a rag doll and turned on Ambrose. *"What the hell do you want here?"* he screamed. Apparently reining our own anger in did not do much toward calming Demon.

Ithel had just come in with Dev and now she clung to him for support, watching my brother with wary, frightened eyes. "Demon, easy," I said trying to keep my voice soothing, as much for Ithel as for him. I grasped Demon's arm firmly again.

Ambrose's face was so white he looked like a corpse. "I came for my sisters. B—both of them," he stammered, still trying to be belligerent but the shock of seeing Wrath up close and pissed off made it impossible. "Abby is part of my team."

"I want nothing to do with you or your team!" Abby snapped.

"Abby, this is ridiculous!" Ambrose pleaded. "You're a Grace!"

"I don't want to be a part of a team that would allow one of its members to endanger a house full of innocent people!"

Ambrose forgot that he was mere inches from Wrath. "The Deadlies are hardly innocent," he sneered.

"What about Maia?" Abby yelled before Demon could do more than hiss. "What about Hex and Toad? What about *us*, Ambrose? We were all in the house when the vampires attacked! Zane didn't give a damn about that, did he?"

"I have spoken to him about that," Ambrose said stiffly. "He understands his mistake."

"Mistake?" Abby shrieked with contempt. "I can just imagine the type of discipline you meted out to him for his *mistake!* Forget it, Ambrose. I have no interest in being a part of your team."

While Ambrose was still sputtering, Conrad stepped forward. "What about being a part of *my* team, Abby? I'm taking control of the Graces," he explained calmly.

"The hell you are!" Zane snapped. Some of his arrogance had returned but not all of it. He still seemed a bit shaken. "A Hellblazer leading the Graces? It's ludicrous."

"Shut up!" Conrad snarled, slamming Zane against the wall. "If you ever speak to me like that again, I'll show you just how much I'm like my cousins!"

"Conrad, release Zane now!" Ambrose gasped, stunned by Conrad's reaction.

"Be silent!" Conrad snapped at Ambrose who gaped, shocked by his insubordination. "You don't make the decisions for the Graces anymore. *I* do."

He turned back to Zane. "You will apologize to the Deadlies," Conrad hissed.

"The hell I—"

Conrad yanked him away from the wall only to slam him against it harder. "Do it!" he snarled looking and sounding more like Demon than ever. "Or *I* will take your head! I know it won't kill you but it will hurt like hell! I would dearly love to hurt you right now."

The resemblance to Demon was too much for Zane. He began to stammer an apology. "I—I'm sorry!"

Conrad flung him away as though he were a rag doll. Zane stumbled and caught himself against the table. His mouth hung open. Conrad turned back to address the others. "Any other objections to my assuming command?" he demanded coldly.

Constance and Ithel began to shake their heads, now watching Conrad with the same wariness that they usually reserved for my brother. Ithel was still holding onto Dev until she caught Maia's raised eyebrow and then she blushed, letting go of him.

"You can't do that! I lead the Graces! I've been doing it for centuries!" Ambrose protested.

"Yes, and we can see how effective *your* leadership has been." Conrad sneered, sending a sideways glance at Zane. While Ambrose sputtered and stammered, Conrad turned his back on him. "Well, what do you have to say about it, Abby?"

"As long as you're in charge, I'm in," Abby agreed beaming. Conrad grinned.

"But you're staying here," I interjected. She looked up at me and I added hopefully, "Right?"

"I—" She glanced at the other Deadlies.

"He'll be a pain in the ass to live with if you leave," Demon told her with a slight smile.

"He's right." Dev groaned. "You can't leave. We'll be pleading with you to come back within two hours."

"Try ten minutes!" Kaz snorted.

"Let's face it," my brother sighed and shook his head. "You won't even get out of the driveway."

I knew that they were telling Abby that they wanted her to stay, but I had to protest the way they were going about it. "*Hey!*"

"The women are grossly outnumbered around here," Maia told her. "We could use another ally."

Abby laughed and threw her hands into the air. "Okay, I'm convinced! I'll stay." She spoke to Conrad. "You can call me here any time you need me."

"But try not to need her too often," I suggested to my cousin.

Conrad laughed and nodded as though he had expected nothing less but Carys was aghast. "You—you're not coming home?"

"This is my home. Did you really think that I was going to walk away from Bane just because I said I would be a part of the team?" Abby asked quietly.

"But...we've always lived together!"

"I won't live in the same house with that bastard," Abby said, pointing at Zane. "He got Bane shot and kidnapped. Zane could have gotten you shot too, Carys, but he didn't give a damn about you or anyone else."

"But Abby, Bane is a Deadly," Ambrose protested. "He's scum."

Abby stared at him, then, she hauled off and punched him hard enough to send him reeling. He cowered for a moment and then stood up again with his hand over his nose. He took his hand away and gasped at the sight of the blood. "Abigail!"

"You know nothing about leading a team!" she snapped at him. She gestured at us. "*This* is a team. They care about each other and stand together. Maybe under Conrad's leadership we can have what the Deadlies do."

"I'll do my best, Abby." Conrad glanced back at his "team." "Go back to the Grace house and pack your things. You're moving out as of today."

"Where are we going?" Ithel asked in a small and uncertain voice.

"We're going home."

The others were stunned. "But what about the reporter?" Carys gasped.

"The house has been abandoned long enough that he should be discouraged enough to leave us alone and, as you pointed out, no one believed him anyway. I think we're pretty safe," Conrad told her.

"I can ask Rowan to cast a ward over the house just in case. It will be temporary but hopefully it will last long enough to discourage him," Kaz offered.

"Thanks, Kaz," Conrad said.

"No problem," Kaz said. "I'll call her now." He left.

"Toad," Conrad said.

Toad was cringing under a table gaping at Conrad. He crept out tentatively when Conrad called his name. "Y—yes, sir?" he stammered.

"You have a choice," Conrad told him. "Demon offered you a job here, but I would like to offer you the chance to come back home with us."

Toad stared up at him thoughtfully. "With you in charge, sir?"

Conrad nodded. Toad looked at Demon, hesitantly. Demon inclined his head slightly. "The choice is yours, Toad. We will bear you no ill will if you choose to return to your home with the others."

A big smile lit up Toad's wide face making him look like a pink football with a split down the middle. "Thank you, sir! I would like to return home."

Conrad turned back to the others. "Why are you still standing here?" he yelled. "Get your things and be back at our house in one hour!"

Toad jumped and then hid a snicker behind his hand when Ambrose and the others scurried out. However, Carys remained rooted to the spot, seemingly bewildered and fascinated at the same time.

"Come on, Carys," Conrad said gently. He held out his arm to her.

Tentatively, she reached out and let her hand slide along his arm until she could tuck her arm within his. He turned to Demon with a small smile on his face. "Thanks for everything, cousin."

"Don't thank me. Watching you put them in their places was the biggest thrill of my life!" Demon grinned.

"You need a more exciting life!" Conrad laughed. "I'm going to put my things together and head out to the house." He paused. "Come and see me any time."

We grinned. "Invite us over for dinner," I suggested wickedly. "Won't the others love that?"

"They'll be delighted even if I have to beat every one of them senseless," Conrad said fiercely.

"Good boy," I replied.

Kaz walked back into the kitchen. "Rowan is happy to ward the house for you," he said. "I'll give you a ride back to your place and we'll pick her up on the way."

"Carys will be coming with us," Conrad told him. "The others left her here. She has no way back to her parents' house."

"I have no problem driving Carys home too," Kaz said kindly.

Conrad glanced at Demon. "Is it safe to ride in a car with him?"

"Hey!" Kaz exclaimed. "Ungrateful!"

Conrad laughed. I was pleased to see my cousin's confidence was growing. I don't know what had happened to him over the last few days but I liked the change immensely.

"He is a tolerable driver," Demon assured Conrad.

"Thanks so much, Fechín," Kaz growled.

"Meet you at the front door in ten minutes, Kaz. And thanks again." Conrad led Carys out of the kitchen. Toad scurried along behind them, happily.

Kaz pointed at the door. "You've created a monster, Fechín."

"Yes." Demon smiled, pleased. "Isn't it great?"

Kaz grinned back. "Yep. But only when it's directed at Cowardice and the Idiot."

We heard a faint sound. Demon drew his cell phone out of his pants' pocket. He glanced at the display and frowned. "Excuse me," he said and stepped out of the kitchen into the hallway.

"Now that this morning's drama is over, would it be possible for me to get some help with setting the table?" Hex demanded.

While the others scattered to do Hex' bidding, I pulled Abby into my arms. "What is that smile for?" I asked.

She smiled slyly. "Did you see how sweet and gentle Conrad was with Carys? She looked completely bowled over! I was just thinking that maybe she is going to fall in love with a Hellblazer after all, just as I have. Lucky girl."

I smiled. "Yes, she is."

"I meant me," she said.

I started to lean down to kiss her and suddenly, the kitchen door flew open again. Demon came in, a grim expression on his face as he closed the cell phone. Instantly on alert, I straightened.

"What is it?" I asked.

"Daedalus," Demon said quietly as the others pressed closer. "The body of a human female was found in the park."

We were all silent. I pulled Abby against me tightly. "Does he believe this is the work of the rogues?"

"Not this time."

"Do they have a suspect?" Dev asked.

Demon gave him a curt nod and then glanced around at each of us. "Deadlies," he said in a low, dangerous voice. "Let's work."